The moment Seward was out the door, the patient raised her hand and placed it on my arm. "Aren't you going to examine me, Dr. Van Helsing?"

"Certainly that is my intention, Miss Westenra. Indeed, I believe that such is exactly what I have been doing these past several moments."

"Will you check my breathing then, and test the regularity of my heart beat?" There was a teasing note in her voice and she twisted her head against the velvet pillow, staring at me quite frankly.

"Assuredly, young miss."

"Then let me make it easier for you." And she moved lithely and in such fashion that her gown no longer covered her breasts which were well formed and free of mark or discoloration. I opened my mouth as though to protest but before I could utter a word, she caught hold of my wrist with a grip so intense and powerful I wondered if the illness had affected her mind and given her the frantic strength of the mad. She pressed the palm of my hand against a bare breast and held it firmly in place.

"Do you feel my heartbeat, Dr. Van Helsing?"

I cleared my throat somewhat uncomfortably, worried that Seward would return and find us so arranged. "Yes, my dear, it seems quite steady, quite steady indeed."

"Are you sure, Doctor?" She was teasing me, I realized, playing at seduction. "Wouldn't you like to press your ear against my bosom, listen to the very beat of my life's blood coursing through my body. My virginal body." She arched her back slightly and the movement was almost serpentine. My own pulse must have quickened and my lips were dry. Her expression was so openly carnal that it frightened me, her eyes acquiring a sharpness and depth that made me feel as though I were peering into a pair of tiny whirlpools into which I was being drawn inexorably.

Paula Sheffield is the author of:

Dark Mistress
Dark Muse (forthcoming)

DARK MISTRESS

Paula Sheffield

DARK

MISTRESS

Author's Note: The events in this narrative correspond to those chronicled in Bram Stoker's Dracula. Readers might consider reading the journal entries from both novels in parallel.

Letter from Edward Palmer to James Chatsworth, dated March 23, 1920.

My Dear James,

The parcel accompanying this letter contains the documents which we discussed the other evening at the club. As I told you at the time, I have secured them through means about which I cannot at present be too specific lest they compromise my source, but rest assured that they came to him by chance and that he is not a party to the hoax, if hoax it is. I can only repeat my stated mystification concerning both their contents and their provenance. As I see it, the possibilities are threefold. First, Bram Stoker wrote these odd documents himself, or more likely caused them to be written at his direction, as they are each in distinct hands, for purposes about which we may only speculate. Second, they are a hoax created independently which Stoker acquired in some fashion and adapted for his purposes. Last, though most outlandish of our choices, we must entertain the possibility that the authors believed themselves to be reporting the truth, perhaps as the consequence of some shared disease of the mind. In this scenario, Stoker may or may not have shared the delusion.

None of these explanations deals with the mystery of their alteration, however. If Stoker caused them to be written for some obscure purpose of his own, then surely they would not in total so clearly contradict those portions which did see print. If, on the other hand, they were the inspiration for his melodramatic novel, then Stoker appears to have taken only the kernel of the narrative from these histories, twisting it for whatever reason to a quite different purpose. Perhaps he felt that the dramatic impact would be greater in the form in which he ultimately released it to the world. Certainly the more prurient portions would never have survived the editor's hand; indeed, they may have brought the entire project to a premature conclusion had Stoker seriously tried to include them in his manuscript.

I have marked the passages that clearly vary from Stoker's account and listed them sequentially to parallel the work as published. For the most part, Stoker simply ignored those statements which did not support the published version; in a few cases, he substituted his own text for the original. Two of the journals are not even hinted at in his account and these contain a great deal of extraneous material. I have marked only the relevant portions in these cases as well, although you may want to read the balance for background. One other point of interest is that the final manuscript does not specify the year in which the chronicled events took place, however, it is implied that it was during the 1890s and some minor details have been altered to support that conclusion. The documents themselves, however, are all dated 1875. There are, additionally, no wax recordings of the text, and the portions of the story which Mina claims to have maintained in that fashion were actually written in longhand, or perhaps transcribed at a later date.

I know that you have the resources to investigate this mystery both here in England as well as on the continent. It is perhaps a foolish whim of mine that I wish to plumb the secrets of these extraordinary documents, but I have decided to indulge it. I will, of course, cover any reasonable expenses involved.

Yours in Friendship,

Neddy

Letter from James Chatsworth to Edward Palmer, dated March 27, 1920

Dear Neddy,

If I didn't know you better, I'd swear you were having me on. I've just finished a first pass through the documents and I must say they strike me as the work of a madman, or a room full of them if you will. There is, of course, no possibility that they are authentic given the rather fanciful theme, but their very existence is, as you say, most provocative.

I will certainly endeavor to confirm or disprove those details which lend themselves to such study, as I know you fasten onto things which arouse your interest like a terrier and refuse to relinquish your grip until there is no other alternative. There is no question of charging you, however. I owe you too many favors to even consider it. I have no doubt I shall be thought rather peculiar by those whom I employ on this task, but they have thought so before and doubtless will do so again.

I was sorry to hear that you and Nell have broken it off, but perhaps it is for the best. She does have a touch of the shrew in her.

When will you next be in the city? Do drop me a note well in advance this time.

Yours as always,

Jimmy

The following are the highlighted excerpts from the collected papers provided by Edward Palmer to James Chatsworth, collated to form a coherent narrative by his assistant, Arthur Peeples.

Jonathan Harker's Journal, May 3, 1875

Although the Golden Krone is, by London standards, an anachronistic and unwelcome reminder of the disparity between city and country life, I confess to finding the inn's rustic simplicity and picturesque appearance quite pleasing within its native setting. One must be prepared to forego the more luxurious perquisites of travel in this portion of the continent, which seems frozen in time a century behind the rest of the world.

The food has been extraordinarily fine at every stop, the people agreeable enough if somewhat taciturn, and my only true regret is the separation from dear Mina, to whom I must write again tonight despite my weariness. Hopefully my sleep will go undisturbed this evening, I dozed fitfully throughout the day as the train crawled its way through the countryside, and now feel distinctly out of step with the normal cycle of light and dark. I meant to include here a more detailed description of my host and his establishment, but already my enthusiasm for that task is wavering as does the flame by whose light I am writing. Perhaps tomorrow, if the condition of the road allows, I might catch up with my good intentions while we travel to the Borgo Pass. Suffice it to say that the accommodations are adequate to keep the night chill out, the linens are clean if not always freshly pressed, and although I feel somewhat cheated of what I thought might be an adventure, at least I have also been spared any true hardship.

May 4

The coach has arrived at last. The driver, inordinately pleased with himself for having shown up at all, shrugged off the innkeeper's remonstrance about his tardiness. I have left in that worthy's charge the brief letter I inscribed to Mina before retiring yesterday evening, which he promises to post for me. His good wife stood near at hand while my bags were being loaded, but made no further effort to dissuade me from continuing my journey. It is clear she attaches some supernatural significance to the date and feels considerable animosity toward my client, but I suspect this is no more than the legacy of generations of tension between the local nobility and the common people, who sometimes appear trapped less than a full step removed from feudalism.

I rested no more easily last night than the one before. Fragments of dreams still recur to me, indistinct, of little duration. Mina appeared in some of them, or rather a dark reflection of my beloved, around whom a shroud of formless dread seemed wrapped. And there were other images as well, carnal ones whose indelicate nature I will not here describe. Suffice it to say that I wakened twice, my body bathed in sweat despite the distinct chill of the night, aroused in more than one sense of the word, with a feeling of excitement that was not unmixed with fear. I have never been prone to troubled dreams in the past, but perhaps it is a byproduct of my anxiety about this posting. My employer has never entrusted me with such an important commission before now, and while I feel in my mind that I am up to the challenge, the rest of my body is not nearly so convinced. I only hope...

Damn! I have torn the page with the point of my pen and spattered ink upon my jacket. Our driver seems determined to test every irregularity in the road. I will continue this later.

May 5, at the Castle.

I am all in a sea of wonders. I doubt; I fear; I think strange things, which I dare not confess to my own soul. God keep me, if only for the sake of those dear to me! For all his generosity and manners, the Count makes me uneasy and I must constantly be on guard lest I physically shrink from the man and thus give offense. His pallid countenance is doubtless the product of generations of inbreeding among the vanishing nobility of this region, exacerbated by his reclusive existence in this sunless forest. His odd manner of speech can be explained by a lack of familiarity with the more subtle nuances of English, although he speaks it readily enough.

But there's something in those unblinking eyes that unmans me at times, and it is all I can do to abide his presence. It is as though his gaze pierced through my very flesh to examine what lies within. If the Count had not shown me the flattering letter from my employer, Mr. Hawkins, reminding me of my duty, I should have seriously considered throwing over the entire affair and fleeing into the darkness rather than spend what little remains of this night under the Count's roof.

Or perhaps not. The wolves which escorted the carriage hither seem to have congregated outside the castle walls. Their doleful crying continues even now, as though living souls were trapped inside their savage bodies, crying out for release. Such ideas might seem fanciful were I at home but in this wild and distorted landscape, there is little that seems unlikely let alone impossible.

Enough. It was nearly dawn by the time the Count showed me to my room. A night's rest will doubtless do wonders to restore my equilibrium.

May 7

Although I continue to find the Count's presence physically unsettling, I was embarrassed to read my last entry in this journal. The excitement of the journey, the peculiar appearance of the castle and its master, and the irregularity of my sleep must have briefly overcome my sensibilities. Indeed, after spending the last several hours in conversation with the man, I am convinced that he will find himself welcome in England. Behind those brooding eyes dwells an astute, inquisitive intelligence determined to conform to the expectations of his prospective hosts. His occasional lapses into prolonged introspection might be judged rude in a less self-effacing man, but I think that I read a great sadness there, perhaps the product of his isolation. Certainly neither he nor the local peasantry could ever bridge the cultural and historical chasm between their so close but so separate worlds, and as the last of his line, perhaps of his class, the Count has no one to confide in, no one with whom to share his moments of joy or sorrow. I feel a profound sympathy for the man, but no pity. He exudes an aura of self containment and honor that would make such a notion ill guided indeed.

To my immense relief, his enthusiasm for the Carfax estate was in no way diminished when I catalogued its many faults. His lineage is an ancient one and by his own admission he would feel ill at ease in more modern quarters. I recommended that the Count commission MacKay and Sons to begin a variety of repairs immediately; they have served our firm and many of our clients admirably in the past and always provide quality workmanship at an acceptable price. The roof is sound, as is the structure in general, but there are broken windows, a considerable quantity of debris, and the main staircase requires attention. I offered to draft the necessary letters for his signature, but he insisted on writing those himself.

"It is time I learned to write down your English words as well as speak them, Mr. Harker, as I will not always enjoy your able assistance in such matters, and I have otherwise little excuse to do so."

The quite palatable wine and the lateness of the hour loosened my tongue and I suggested a personal journal as a means of practicing those skills he wished to acquire. The Count seemed to find nothing presumptuous in my words and nodded solemnly. "Perhaps I will."

There is an aura about the Count that is almost palpable, composed of those rare qualities, integrity and self confidence, which are necessary prerequisites for greatness. I am convinced that whatever task the man puts his hand to will be accomplished, and that there will be virtue in that success. If it were not for the paleness of his flesh and the disconcertingly vulpine arrangement of his features, Count Dracula could no doubt aspire to even greater things. He is a man of great presence, though perhaps unattractive to conventional eyes.

My own eyes refuse to remain open any longer. Tomorrow I must write to Mina. I have been most remiss in that regard. The Count has assured me that one of his people (none of whom I have yet seen!) will post it for me in the nearest village.

May 8

The castle is a veritable prison, and I am a prisoner! I am at a loss to understand my host's actions in this regard, unless it is a consequence of that bizarre incident while I was shaving. I had half convinced myself that it was a trick of the light and angle that prevented me from seeing the Count's reflection in my glass, but now I don't know what to believe. Perhaps there was some tasteless drug mixed in with the wine that has altered my perception in some way.

When I wakened this day, the sun was already directly overhead. No one was about, though bread and cheese had been laid outside the door of my room. I made short work of these following my toilet, and fancied a walk around the grounds. It was only then that I discovered that the doors were chained securely and that shutters had been closed and locked upon every window except those too high in the castle to allow escape. I must complete my search of the ground floor and determine before darkness falls whether any possible means of egress has been left unguarded, but my efforts are constrained by the bizarre architecture of this place. Corridors and staircases frequently lead to unexpected destinations, and I have twice been lost in a maze of interconnected rooms whose arrangement makes no apparent sense. I have not yet found a way to access the windows on the north wall, if there are indeed any there at all.

Later

Now that my original alarm has left me, I am frankly of two minds about my situation. The Count has offered me no real harm or discomfit; indeed, he has been an exemplary host, even more noteworthy an accomplishment now that I know the truth about his imaginary staff, for the castle is clearly untenanted other than the two of us. He is a charming conversationalist, and his obvious pride in his ancestry is a praiseworthy quality. Despite occasional flashes of anger, his demeanor remains unthreatening and he seems to actively enjoy our conversations. At the same time, although he has undeniably taken steps to prevent my departure, I am reluctant to confront him with my knowledge of the situation. Nor have I completed the letters I had thought to write, as I am uncertain whether their privacy would be honored, or even if they would indeed be posted.

He asked after Mina today, affecting a casual air that I saw to be false. The Count does not dissemble well, it appears, but rather avoids matters upon which he cares not to be too explicit. I was resolved to limit discourse on the subject, as my feelings for Mina and hers for me are not for public scrutiny, but under his insistent questioning I fear my tongue loosened and before I reined it in once more, I had recounted almost the entire history of our relationship, from the first meeting to my proposal of marriage.

"She seems a remarkable individual, this Miss Mina of yours."

"Entirely remarkable, sir. Sometimes I fear my life is a dream from which I will someday waken to bitter disappointment."

The Count's expression changed then, a passing look I can only describe as melancholy. "As to that, we all live in our dreams, Mr. Harker, some more pleasant than others."

I could think of no appropriate response and the conversation hovered on the brink of awkwardness.

"Perhaps when I arrive in your country, I might meet the admirable Miss Mina."

"It would be my pleasure to introduce you, sir. I'm sure you would find her as charming as do I." Truthfully, I felt considerable ambivalence. For all that I respected the Count, I could not forget the ambiguity of my situation and was loathe, even theoretically, to subject Mina to any similar risk.

"I have no doubt of that fact at all, Mr. Harker."

The conversation ended shortly thereafter with first cock's crow.

May 12

What manner of man is this, or what manner of creature in the semblance of a man? I feel the dread of this horrible place overpowering me; I am in fear - in awful fear - and there is no escape for me; I am encompassed about with powers that I dare not think of even in passing. The sight of Count Dracula's inhuman departure down the exterior wall of the castle has forced me to accept what I had sought to deny, that my host is...other than human.

Now that he has the letters I wrote at his behest, have I signed my own writ of execution? Will they be followed in due course by a no doubt compassionate expression of regret about some unforeseen accident or mysterious wasting disease which claimed my life? How could I have so misjudged the man, if man he is?

Alas, Mina, I fear I shall never see you again.

May 16

I cowered in my hiding place until exhaustion and the inevitable numbing of my terror pried me away. My instincts tell me that I should run from this place, strip the memories from my mind, and never allow myself to recall my experiences within these dark, forbidding walls. What I have seen tonight should have scalded my eyes and left me sightless. Against all reason, I huddled closer into myself and watched with eyes that would not be drawn away, and listened for some hint of my own fate. My brow was moist and I knew that I was feverish as well as frightened, and that it would not even require a great shock to rob me of consciousness whether or not I willed it.

"Are we to have nothing tonight?" complained one of the pale women who had threatened me, pointing to the bag which the Count had thrown to the floor. It twitched fitfully, as though a small child were imprisoned therein, a conclusion that struck me with absolute certainty even in that last moment of awareness. I fell into the darkness convinced that my unwise decision to explore the bowels of the castle in search of an exit had instead sealed my fate.

The Journal of Vlad Tepes, Count Dracula

May 16

I inscribe this laboriously as my fingers fit these English words less readily than does my tongue. It is a necessary discipline whose suggestion I owe to my young guest. Mr. Harker is an able if rather transparently honest man. It is clear he is aware that he cannot leave without my permission, but he pretends ignorance of that fact. Perhaps it is another aspect of this famous English stoicism which I have yet to grasp.

Certainly the man is either very brave or very foolish, possibly both. I had not expected that he would find his way into the south wing, nor be so unwise as to relinquish consciousness there.

They came for him, of course. The other two might have kept their distance after my warning but Hyrkana grows more aggressive with each passage of the moon and her defiant leadership emboldens the others. Briefly she challenged me for Harker, and perhaps it would have been best had she not surrendered so quickly. I might have destroyed her then, destroyed her utterly. But more likely it would have been otherwise. They are my responsibility, after all, noblesse oblige. I created them as they are, and eventually I know that it will fall upon me to destroy them as I have destroyed the others of my get. At times I tell myself it is no mercy to withhold my hand. Their prison is even more closely circumscribed than my own. My judgment was impaired when I brought them across, thinking somehow to create the companions I could not find among my former kind. Instead I succeeded only in increasing an already unbearable burden. But to end them? Would such a deed truly be an act of charity, or an attempt to expiate my own guilt? And so I remain, indecisive, and imprison them lest they multiply my evil and spread it forth.

Of all those whom I have created in my distorted image, only Josef has proven himself reliable. He remains loyal in his new life just as he did before, following my orders without question or reserve. I told myself I was rewarding a faithful servant when I brought him over, for he lay on his deathbed after devoting his life to my service. Some of my family blood must run through his veins, for he could almost be my older brother, and looking into his face is as close as I shall ever come to seeing my own reflection. In retrospect, I fear that it was simply another act of self indulgence. It was convenient to have him around, and I so dislike inconvenience. It was perhaps the habits of a lifetime that spared him the chaotic madness that usually follows the change. And now he is off to deal with Herr Leutner and make the other arrangements I require, and I confess to missing his calming presence within these decaying walls.

Had I returned a moment later, Mr. Harker might have presented quite a different problem than he does already. Fortunately I found suitable prey close by this evening, a blessing not likely to be repeated, and returned earlier than usual. The metallic scent of his blood was in the air and I hastened quickly to forestall them.

Harker was already so thoroughly under Hyrkana's influence that he may well dismiss this all as a dream when he next wakens. That would be best, I think. She is far stronger than the others, and more brazen. Elizabet and Natalia still cling to memories of their old lives, but Hyrkana has embraced the new, believing herself free of the shackles of mortality. I remember my own feelings after the change, years during which I felt eternal and invulnerable, above the petty laws or fears of mortals, sufficient unto myself for all that was necessary. Youthful foolishness dies slowly even among the unimaginably old. Hyrkana will learn the truth one day, if I allow her sufficient time.

She was crouched over his supine body as I entered, naked, her heavy breasts brushing against his chest as she prepared to feed. I had not seen her so for a long time, and for a moment, I was lost in memory. She had come to me in the field behind her father's croft, removing her clothing as she walked. Her breasts were full and warm and I imagined at the time that I felt a stirring of the old lust. Perhaps I did, but more likely it was an illusion born of wishing. The old passions persist, but in shadowy form, pale in color and with little texture. In any case, that greater lust swept through me as she pressed her flesh against my chest and intertwined her arms with mine. I could feel the blood coursing through her veins, the beat of her heart hypnotic, the engine of life. She brushed her hips against me, still ignorant of the real nature of our tryst, or perhaps knowing but not caring, and when at last I could refrain no longer and bent to her throat, she surrendered herself without even that momentary resistance I had come to expect from my victims.

But that had been times and lifetimes ago. Her affection for me, if it was genuine even at the start, did not survive the change. She wakened a nearly mindless thing, driven by unconscious instincts, governed by no restraint. Left to her own devices, she would have been discovered and destroyed quickly, for she acted impulsively. For a time I thought she had become one of those occasional mad things whose minds are forever disarranged by the change, and who must be ended quickly for their own sakes. But I had sheltered her, hunted and provided for her, hoping that the craven dependence would pass quickly and that some of the old personality would emerge. And emerge it did, though ever so slowly, and to my very great sorrow, ever so selectively. Her virtues seemed not to have survived to the slightest degree, and only her baser desires reasserted themselves. She had ever been a willful girl, but now she tolerated no restraint upon her behavior not imposed by force. I could not trust her to hunt as I did; she would have betrayed us both by preying upon the villagers as I once had but will no more.

Perhaps I could be forgiven Hyrkana. She was not the first I had brought over, but those others had been meant as tools, used as such until I had no further need of them, then disposed of as one might put to death a draft animal no longer capable of pulling the plough. I had meant her to be more than that, and even while I knew that I had failed, I conspired against my own better judgment again with Elizabet, hoping her mild spirit would shape the change. Too mild, as it happened, for almost nothing of her personality survived; a century after the change she was still incapable of speech, and shivered uncontrollably when I tried to reach her. Natalia was my last great sin. Her strong spirit survived but it had curdled during the transition. I had misjudged her self-absorption as strength of character, and afterward, when she began those first small self mutilations, watching avidly as the cold flesh reconstituted itself, I was so sickened that I finally admitted to myself the truth. I could not judge them for their actions when it was I who was the greatest sinner, for had I not created them all, and was I not therefore guilty of all their sins as well as my own?

But Hyrkana's rebellions have always been easily quelled before. This day, for the first time, she openly opposed my will, lunging for Harker's throat, her fingers clawed, eyes flashing, her chest shaking with what should have been breath but which was in fact only rage.

Almost, I ended it there. I closed my fingers around Hyrkana's neck and lifted her up, struggling to control my wrath. I could have torn the head from her body and impaled both in the courtyard to wait for the cleansing light of day to finish what should have been consummated years before. Strength comes with the passage of time, but not even I could survive a prolonged exposure to the scourging sunlight, although the day is no longer completely forbidden me. Had she fought rather than submitted, I might well have done so. But she must have sensed that this was not the time to challenge me, not yet, for she let the tension drain from her muscles and her face relaxed into its usual grotesque sexuality. Still I was tempted for a moment, seeing in her my own weakness, which perhaps I might destroy by proxy. Abruptly aware of my own duplicity of thought, I tossed her aside instead.

"How dare you touch him, any of you?" I roared. "How dare you cast eyes on him when I had forbidden it? Beware how you meddle with him, or you'll have to deal with me."

Natalia taunted me briefly with eyes averted, teasing rather than a challenge, but I had no patience for it, not for any of them and gestured toward the bag I'd dropped in the doorway.

Mercifully Harker lost consciousness before they tore out the young lamb's throat and momentarily quenched their interminable thirst with its life's blood, snapping at each other as they fought over the last few drops. They were more animal than human then and I felt a fresh rush of despair. Unable to watch further, I turned to the prostrate Harker and lifted him up. I carried him back to his room, arranged things as best I could to convince him it was all a dark fantasy of his own creation. But given what he already knows or suspects, I have little hope of success.

It is at best a short term solution. Mr. Harker's presence here poses a dilemma. The possibility of coincidence is too absurdly remote for serious contemplation. Somehow I have been anticipated, though I thought my inquiries sufficiently circumspect to escape detection. The young man has a remarkable memory for detail, useful in his profession I imagine, and was able to provide a chronology of events as seen from his point of view, accurate to the day in most instances.

Less than a month after I first employed Hawkins to pursue certain investigations for me, Harker was introduced to Mina Murray through the agency of a mutual friend. Their subsequent courtship seems to have proceeded rapidly though rather ethereally. I imagine he interprets her restraint as virtue and has no hint of her true nature. As their engagement became official, Harker emerged rapidly from among a handful of clerks to become Hawkins' protégé, subsequently delegated to represent the firm on my behalf. That they were both set upon this course without their knowledge, I have no doubt. Harker, for all his good nature, has few depths in which to conceal secrets.

Evidently my plans have been transparent, though to what degree the veils have been pierced remains to be seen. I knew that I had not been forgotten, but it had seemed that I would be allowed to remain undisturbed so long as I cowered in my castle. Undisturbed but not, it would appear, unwatched. It would probably be safest to dispose of Harker, unpleasant though that prospect might be, but it might be better to pretend ignorance for the moment. The game has grown more complex. Time is limited, however; if I am to act, it must be soon.

May 18

No solution has yet offered itself. I have decided to coerce Harker into writing more letters to counterfeit his departure. It will probably fool only those who do not matter, but it might at least raise doubts among those who do. I am determined to see this matter through and if I must sacrifice Harker in the process, then so be it. Many a soul has entered these hills never to emerge again. One more will cause no great surprise. Another sin added to my already heavy load could not tip the balance any further.

May 28

Harker proves continually troublesome. Today he attempted to bribe one of my Szgany into posting two letters for him, one to his employer, the other to Miss Murray. The latter was encrypted, a fact I find particularly ominous. Have I underestimated him? Has he been an active opponent rather than the innocent pawn I believed? Whatever the truth of the matter, I must consider him an enemy. This makes my course of action simpler, though no less unpleasant. Still, I will put off the ultimate act for as long as is practical. I have not taken a human life in living memory, and had hoped never to do so again. Perhaps he will yet be reprieved.

But if I am to spare his life, even briefly, I must take further precautions. Once beyond this immediate vicinity, Harker might well escape my grasp. He is resourceful and spirited, speaks enough German to make himself understood, and his appearance is comely and inspires sympathy. The possibility exists, however remote, that he may yet win free of the castle.

Tonight I will remove his papers, identification, currency and anything else which might prove of assistance. He will miss them, of course, and know that I am responsible, but the pleasantness between us is now mutually understood to be a mask concealing a darker face.

June 24

I have made significant progress. The boxes of earth are ready for shipment and I have arranged for the provisioning of my...wards...during my absence. Josef will return soon, but I cannot trust him to deal with them unassisted, and the villagers will not tolerate his presence or treat with him, although they take my gold readily enough when proffered by the Szgany in my stead.

An old enemy provided the answer. Najina is quite mad, still believes me responsible for the disappearance of her daughter. I suspect her wastrel husband, whose unnatural interest in the young children of his neighbors might have turned to material closer to hand, but he is dead now, stabbed in a tavern brawl two years past, and will never yield up the truth. Najina was left a widow of not inconsiderable means after she sold his tin shop to the Rackozy brothers, but her mind has been unbalanced by her losses.

She prostrated herself at my doorstep, accusing me of having made off with the child, just as she does on every anniversary of that sad event. And as always I waited patiently for the fit to pass.

But this time when she recovered her composure and turned to leave, I moved to bar the way. God forgive me for taking advantage of a madwoman but my need was great. I offered the return of her daughter.

"At what price?" Her eyes moved restlessly, never fastening on my face. I believe that she knows the fault lies elsewhere and is afraid to see the truth in my eyes. If this illusion brings her some comfort, I am glad for her sake.

"Six months service. Each day, you will bring or cause to be brought to my doorstep food and drink for three men. One of the Szgany will take it in charge. And every fifteenth day, you are to tether a goat or lamb in the small garden beside the south wing of the castle. It shall be brought no later than dusk, and you will not linger after."

"And you will return to me then my daughter?"

"I will relinquish any restraints I might hold upon her." An easy promise, since I have no power over the truly dead.

And so it was done. Two of the Szgany will watch over Harker as well as I, better during the daylight, and the sacrificial animals should...must keep the others satisfied. When Josef returns, he can oversee such other arrangements as may be necessary. Najina will be cruelly disappointed as she always is, but she can hate me no more than she does already. And I can think of no better alternative.

June 29

With but two days remaining before my departure, my plans have gone awry. It was Hyrkana's doing, although I believe it is only a matter of time before Natalia and perhaps even Elizabet grow similarly rebellious. Truly they are as damned as am I.

I discovered their disobedience as I was sealing a letter to Herr Leutner. They are forbidden all but the south wing, which I abandoned to them long since, but suddenly I felt their presence above and behind me, in the castle proper. They were after Harker, of course. The smell of his blood is like an invisible tether.

My anger was a glowing ember as I confronted them in the hallway close by Harker's room. I was finally ready to move against my nemesis, and now must needs deal with my own indiscretions. Each of these - Natalia, Elizabet, Hyrkana, and several more - I had caused to be as they were. In years past, I had searched out and destroyed all the others of my making, all except Josef and these three whom I imprisoned and suborned to my will out of pity, or self flagellation, or perhaps to remind myself of the depths to which my soul had descended.

I knew in that moment outside Harker's room that they would have to go the way of the others quickly, that otherwise it would be simply a matter of time until they were capable of escaping my governance. They must be destroyed, yes, but not this day. When I return from England, if I return, I shall deal with them. A promise to the God I have never believed in if He chooses to smile upon my solitary crusade. It is a small cowardice on my part to dissemble in such manner, I suppose, but there are many ways in which I am not the man I once was.

Furiously, I ordered them away from Harker's door, ignoring their reproachful looks. "Your time is not yet come."

Once more Hyrkana thrust herself forward. "If not now, when?"

"Tomorrow," I lied. "After I have gone from this place you may do with him as you will."

I will have to make other arrangements for my guest. He will no longer be safe here following my departure.

June 30

Mr. Harker has shown his true colors at last, thereby simplifying matters. Somehow he managed to gain access to the passageway from my room to the secret chamber behind the dungeon where I normally sleep throughout the fearful day. Clearly I underestimated his intelligence, or perhaps he possessed all along a small store of hidden knowledge provided by the will which has sent him to me.

I spent the hours of darkness preparing for the long journey that lies ahead. The prospect of an ocean voyage is not a pleasant one. From a living soul, I could take sufficient nourishment to last at least ten days, but I am sworn to take no further lives in this fashion. Instead, I have learned to subsist on small quantities of blood, taken frequently, which I acquire from livestock in the surrounding villages, oxen and horses by preference, since they are best able to spare what I need. This solution is clearly problematic while I am in transit so through Herr Leutner I have arranged for the passage of a dozen thoroughbred mares on the same ship. If I am cautious, all should go well.

I will not be able to feed fully even so, lest the crew notice evidence of my predation. These carefully restrained feedings deplete my vitality, however, a disadvantage I must overcome if I am to succeed in England. So I slaughtered a bullock and drained the corpse, gorging myself as I have not done in over a century. The blood was like liquid fire in my veins, a tidal wave of strength and rejuvenation that stirred old, best forgotten feelings. Human blood would have been far more efficacious, but that resource is denied me. My appearance must have altered dramatically, although that is something I will never be able to ascertain except through the reports of others. It has been many years since I have indulged myself in this fashion, and I fear my image has reflected this deprivation.

I felt strong enough to face even the light of day, for which I have this past century acquired some considerable tolerance, but I must ration such excursions as they sap my power and increase my unnatural thirsts. As is my custom, I made a last circuit of the castle just before wolfsong, then descended quickly to my resting place.

The blood sang its way through my veins even as I lay on the brink of that rest which is no rest. Conflicting urges strove for dominance, most particularly an exuberant self confidence which I would have to bring to heel lest I over reach myself. And certain baser urges stirred, urges I had thought long since expunged. Human blood would have been much more invigorating, of course, but like opium it would be difficult to find future satisfaction in the blood of livestock if I tasted even the slightest drop of that forbidden nectar. It had taken a long time and much discomfort to wean myself.

It was this internal struggle for self mastery which saved me from even greater inconvenience. Harker somehow penetrated to my resting chamber and, ill prepared though he was for the encounter, took in hand a shovel which I can only assume he planned to fashion into a stake. There can be no doubt that he knows my true nature now, but fortunately his will is malleable. Even in my dormant state I was able to deflect his purpose and drive him from my presence, although he retained enough presence of mind to strike out at me before departing.

So be it. I will abide by my original plans and depart tomorrow. Harker must make his own future. If he can avoid Hyrkana and the others until my return, I will set him free. He would be master of his own fate in that instance and no longer a danger to me. If Hyrkana and the others claim him for their own and he survives, he must simply be destroyed along with them, for I have again today resolved that once my great enemy has been destroyed, I will eradicate this last evidence of my great sin, and follow them into eternal rest at last.

Enheduanna's Journal

May 30

Ur. Lagash. Gudea. Bagdad. Susa. Jerusalem. Antioch. Tarsus. Carthage. Rome. Paris. And now Whitby. Each different in its way, but all the same to eyes that see with a wide enough perspective. Generations of memories crowd one another within my head. If it were not for the journals I have kept through the centuries, I would have lost my own beginnings by now. Already, the earliest volumes seem like the story of some stranger and it becomes more difficult to remember the old tongues. Perhaps I should transcribe them before the markings become no more than gibberish even to their author.

I am, or was, Enheduanna, daughter of King Sargon of Akkad, Sargon the Bloody to his enemies, although that which he shed was spilled wastefully on the field of battle. Since then I have worn many names and personalities, each a guise to be discarded like out of fashion clothing. I am or at least was Marta of Antioch, Mary of Bethlehem, Tarika of Alexandria, Marie D'Artaud of Paris, Baroness Wilhelmina Bloch of Baden, and now Mina Murray, lately of London. As a child I was sickened by the sun, which raised blisters on my flesh and left me weak and raving, but with the passage of time I learned to tolerate the light, briefly at first, gradually for longer periods, until now I can move freely so long as I avoid long periods in direct view of the sun. I was a sickly child even then, with no strength in my arms and legs. If my father had not been who he was, I would have been cast out to perish lest I pass on my infirmity. But he doted on me, nursed me with his own hand at times, even when my own mother refused.

I was a strapling girl before I discovered the key to my own strength. Children were fed on overcooked scraps after a feast and for twelve years the only meat I was given was stringy and bloodless. It took an act of defiance to reveal the truth. My father had invited a rival king, a sometimes friend and sometimes enemy, to discuss another shift in alliances, and a pair of bullocks had been slaughtered in his honor. I was drawn as always by the tantalizing odors from the kitchen, where the carcass was being prepared, but this time the temptation was irresistible. I waited and watched for an opportunity and when it came, a few seconds only, I raced into the room, wrenched a strip of raw flesh free, and made my escape. No alarm was raised and I concealed my treasure under my shawl until I reached the small room where I slept. There I felt a moment of sudden despair, for I could think of no means of cooking the meat without being discovered.

Necessity and instinct overcame my ignorance. The smell of the blood was irresistible, and I bit into the cool flesh. It was as though I had placed hot embers in my mouth, although the glorious pain of that first blooding was more pleasurable than not. I could feel the strength flowing into my body as it had never done before in my life. It would be some time yet before my mind realized the truth, but my body truly awoke for the first time. It felt strange and I was both exhilarated and frightened. In a kind of daze, I went out through the hall into the courtyard with some unfocused plan to find my father and ask him what this all meant, and when I found myself outside in the full light of day, I flinched instinctively, even though the familiar sting of its touch was absent for the very first time.

I think even then I suspected something of the truth of my nature, because I reconsidered my intentions. I never told my father, never told anyone, but thenceforth I began to systematically steal bloody scraps from the kitchen, entrails and other parts normally thrown to the dogs, sucking what little blood remained in them. The dogs had always hated me, but now they had good reason for I deprived them of what they felt was their due. And I grew stronger and more confident from that day forward, and my father expressed himself as pleased, although I caught him from time to time watching me with that same wary glance that became commonplace in the eyes of my playmates and nurses and even the castle guards. They avoided me when they could, but my father ordered otherwise and we eventually reached an uneasy truce. They left me to my own devices and I reported that they were treating me well. And so it was that I first learned to play the part of another person entirely, living my real life in secret, play acting for the benefit of those with the power to harm me. But my father despaired of finding me a husband and finally appointed me high priestess, where he believed I would be profitably and conveniently preoccupied.

Mina Murray is a new role into which I have most recently thrown myself, one which requires careful crafting. Among the wealthy of any culture, a certain reclusiveness and peculiarity of character is permitted, even expected. Gold buys acceptance, privacy, and the power to indulge even the most bizarre behavior. There is no difficulty misleading those who so openly invite a masquerade, who no longer seem capable of discerning the difference between what is real and what they pretend is real. They are so enwrapped in the minutiae of their fleeting existence that their minds are closed to the possibility that things might not be as they seem. The Age of Reason, as Dr. Seward calls it, seems to me the Age of Self Deception.

Mina Murray is a role in which I can relax and allow others to manage the routines of society while I have leisure to prepare for what is to come. Mina, as I have created her, is a simple soul possessing adequate though unremarkable resources, unsophisticated but with friends who hold keys to the doors of society. Suspended between two worlds, she provides access to both. I sculpted her personality and circumstances carefully. John and Martha Murray are recently moved away from London to Netherby, subsisting on his government pension, a reticent couple with narrow horizons whose empty minds held more than enough room to house false memories of the child I am supposed to have been. I had originally thought to abide with them for a few years, but the rural life numbed my brain after a short time and I was forced to range ever farther for my prey lest my presence among the citizenry of Netherby be suspected.

Lucy Westenra presented herself by accident, a casual encounter on a shopping trip, a shallow mind home to no thought not placed there by others. Almost I acted precipitately then, but I have learned more than ordinary patience in my dealings. If I was to successfully interject myself into this child's life, I must first know the geography of her world. Her father proved equally pliable, a remote man of no particular intelligence and limited outlook. He wished the best for his daughter because it was appropriate he do so rather than because of any paternal attachment, and had taken so little interest in her childhood that the introduction of an imaginary childhood friend required not even the slightest application of the glamour. His unexpected death shortly after I first visited Whitby was greeted with the same degree of emotion that might have been expected had a favored neighbor relocated to Paris.

Mrs. Westenra was a different matter, a strong minded woman whose life was so wrapped up in that of her only child that she resisted all but the most powerful suggestions. I regret that my persistent use of the glamour somewhat scrambled the woman's wits, not that her transient life is of any concern to me, but rather because I detest clumsiness, most particularly on my own part.

In any case, having laid down the pattern, all that is necessary now is that I fulfill the role I have scripted for myself. To that purpose I have molded my new identity with as fine a degree of craftsmanship as I can manage, leaving no detail to chance, even keeping a false journal through which means I hope to make Mina as real as needs be, to myself as well as others. Little enough effort the latter takes, in truth; it's a rare mind that doesn't openly invite misapprehension.

And so I might have continued without incident had not my one time friend and now committed enemy stirred from the ashes of his last defeat, thinking to challenge me again. In times past, I might have wakened with fury to this impertinence, but now I find myself welcoming the diversion. I have spun a wide web, into the outermost strands of which he has already stumbled more than once.

It would have been simple enough to mislead him, send him on a false trail to the New World perhaps, but where's the game in that? And it is always better to know where your foe is than where he is not. To that purpose I have expended considerable effort and resources in assisting him to find me, not the least of which is young Mr. Harker, my promised husband, who excels at such things. And Herr Leutner, who owes me an old debt which he will now have the opportunity to repay.

I have had another letter from Lucy imploring me to visit her in Whitby. Since this suits my purpose, I shall accede to her wishes, although the news of her engagement to Arthur Holmwood complicates things. She has been impatient to surrender her maidenhood of late, but given the brevity of mortal lives, I am not particularly surprised. Holmwood indeed may prove interesting, or perhaps I might find amusement with one of the other suitors, this Dr. Seward she finds so admirable that she quotes him extensively in her otherwise banal letters, or even the American, Morris, who sounds an interesting sort.

They might serve as useful playing pieces in the game to come.

August 1, Whitby

I fear Jonathan has come to a bad end, since I have heard nothing which might not be counterfeit from him this past month and nothing of substance for even longer. I had expected as much from the outset; my hope was that his innocence would adequately mask the fact that he was my unwitting instrument. Perhaps Vlad has grown more clever or just more suspicious than in the past, or mayhap his attack of soft heartedness has finally passed and Jonathan was ready prey. He was in any case expendable. I will have to provide a convincing display of grief when the inevitable news arrives, possibly accepting comfort from one or another of Lucy's castoffs.

Herr Leutner has sent word that he has successfully conducted my business on the continent. I expect to fail there; sometimes a sacrificial pawn encourages one's opponent to indiscretion. If he believes me grown careless and clumsy, he may be encouraged to move hastily in turn. At the least I will cause him some inconvenience.

August 2

I had feared that Whitby's rusticity would afford me some disadvantages. Fortunately, it is a larger community than I had expected, and moreover contains an establishment ideally suited to my purposes. Lucy had mentioned Dr. Seward's sanatorium in one of her letters, but I had not until now realized the potential value of such an institution for the satisfaction of certain needs of my own. True, I must be discrete lest I arouse undesirable suspicion or fear, but in a madhouse, even if my visits are witnessed by those incarcerated there, no one would give credit to the ravings of lunatics.

Mrs. Westenra caused me some unease yesterday evening. I felt her watching me all through dinner and recognized the puzzlement in her eyes. The false memories lie uneasily in her mind and she cannot resist pushing at them, trying to read what truth might lie underneath. Twice she started to ask me a question, twice shook her head and insisted she'd lost whatever thought she had been about to express. It was not until sometime later that I had the opportunity to speak to her in private and reinforce the superimposition of my history upon her recollections. She disappeared to her room shortly thereafter, declaring herself in the throes of a migraine.

I have yet to meet Lucy's fiancé, or her castoffs for that matter, although I have glimpsed Seward twice during my nocturnal visits to his asylum, and feel as though I have known him for some time thanks to the endless prattling in Lucy's letters. There will be sufficient time to cultivate his friendship before I will have need of it; if I have learned nothing else over the span of my existence I have learned patience.

As is my custom I have taken certain precautions to protect the secrets of my existence. I have called Lucy from her room in the night and commanded her to walk in the gardens, a trait which her mother and the older servants now "remember" as having afflicted her periodically since early childhood. In fact, Mr. Westenra apparently experienced similar somnambulistic episodes in his youth, a happy coincidence that lends credibility to the story. From close at hand, no one could possibly mistake the vivacious Lucy for her demure friend, but my occasional nightly excursions are more likely to be noticed from a distance if at all.

I entertained an unexpected visitor in my room this evening. It would seem that Lucy is even more impressionable than I had already surmised, for she walked in her sleep without my intervention this time, drawn to me as a moth to a flame. She came in from the balcony which our two rooms share, barefoot, her nightgown twisted immodestly about her body.

Even after all this time, existence holds its surprises for me. My first impulse was to send her back to her room and be about my own business, for I had decided to sup this evening, and not from among the lunatics this time but a fresh life, a child from one of the squatter's huts or from the small fishing village just up the coast from Whitby. Someone whose life I could safely steal. I would be taking somewhat of a chance, but I doubted that a single disappearance would excite that much attention considering the clear danger presented by the cliffs and the precarious walks that wound across their faces.

Almost I sent the compulsion, might have done so had it not been for a memory from earlier that same day.

We had been walking in the gardens while lunch was prepared, Lucy prattling on about her wedding plans and how joyously happy she would be once she and Arthur were wed.

"It all sounds quite marvelous, Lucy."

"Yes, it does, doesn't it." She sounded less than certain of a sudden. "Oh, Mina, put down that parasol and come sit beside me."

I was reluctant to do so, for the sun was particularly fierce that forenoon and I had not fed for several days. But one end of the bench lay in the shade of a towering lilac, and I begged her to allow me to sit there for the sake of my overly sensitive skin.

"You sound troubled, Lucy. Do you regret your decision to marry Arthur?"

"No, of course not. But by doing so, I have rejected Jack and Quincey and ruined their lives, perhaps forever."

Her vanity was amusing on most occasions but the sun had made me cross and intolerant. "I'm certain they will recover in time, Lucy. Love wounds but the wound is rarely fatal. And both have pledged themselves your friends for life. I should think you'd be very happy."

"Well, I am," she protested, stamping her foot for emphasis. "But it won't be the same at all, you know. We will grow apart directly as Arthur and I grow together." Her eyes suddenly widened. "And the two of us as well, Mina. Can we ever again be such good friends once I am Mrs. Arthur Holmwood? Surely loyalty to my husband must transcend our friendship."

"Transcend but not displace, Lucy. I will always be your friend, always ready to come if you need me."

"Yes, I suppose you will." She spoke more to herself than to me, and with such clear confidence that her own concerns must be paramount that I experienced a rush of rage more intense than I had felt in nearly two centuries. I turned away lest some hint of that emotion show itself in my face, although Lucy remained so self absorbed she might not have noticed had I sprouted horns and wings and flown about the garden for the next few seconds.

And then one of the maids called us in to dine and the moment was safely past.

I remembered it, however, in the darkness and called Lucy to my side.

In the land and time of my birth, she would likely have been more than once a mother by now, if she hadn't been drowned in infancy as a hopeless weakling. Here, in this time and place, she remained a child pretending to be a woman, planning her marriage the way she had once placed miniature furniture in her doll house. A child, but a spoiled, self centered, even cruel one.

"Disrobe," I commanded.

She made no move to comply but the fixed glaze of her eyes flickered uncertainly. I rose from my seat and called again upon the glamour's compulsion, repeating my order without speaking, and this time her hands came up quickly, unfastened the bindings of her clothing, which fell soundlessly to a puddle around her ankles. The dancing in her eyes was ever more animated, and it was not fear but excitement. It has been my experience that the more enamored a people are of cosseting their sexuality with restrictive "moralities", the more avidly they seek excuses to set them aside. Lucy might not be conscious of what she was doing at this moment, but the true person inside was clamoring for release.

I hated her, I realized in that moment, a discovery that gave me pause. Even after all these centuries, I still have much to learn about my own motivations. I had long since thought myself past all but the most transient of angers. The sight of that flawless white body, bathed regularly in scented lotions, wrapped only by the softest and most elegant fabrics lest a coarse thread irritate her fine skin, freed by her late father's wealth from all physical travail, governed by a mind whose deepest thought was to choose which male should take over her father's lapsed stewardship and pamper her into her dotage...well, I confess it fanned the embers of an old fire to flame anew. Who was this thoughtless child to have full freedom of the day while I must lurk in its shadows? How did it come about that this frail, finite creature could live her thin life openly while I must conceal my own nature behind the costumes of my various identities?

I approached her, warring within myself, almost surrendering to the need that burned within my veins. Lucy Westenra came perilously close to ending her vacuous existence in that moment, saved only by the sound of a servant snuffing the lamps in the upper hall, a momentary distraction that deflected my rage. Or at least some of it.

Lucy's death would remove my reason for visiting Whitby, and cast my plans into disarray. Poor Vlad would find himself misdirected, which would also work to my disadvantage. Forced to search me out, he would enjoy sufficient time to replenish his strength after the long sea voyage. No, although I promised myself this child-woman's life, I would not take it this night.

But I would exact a small punishment nonetheless.

She moaned as I caught hold of her breasts, but made no move to withdraw, not even so much as would require the employment of my will. I dared not draw blood even inadvertently, but I handled her flesh quite roughly, knowing she would waken in painful perplexity in the morning and be forced to wear unfashionably modest clothing or perhaps an obscuring scarf to cover the bruising. To my surprise, even when I finally relented there was no hint of fear in her posture. Truly, there is a wanton spirit lying buried within my companion; perhaps I have briefly set free the woman who lies dormant in this child.

She is gone back to her room now where she will no doubt experience enigmatic dreams which she will not understand, and will choose not to recall. I confess to having derived a strange pleasure in her humiliation, though not a candle's breath to what I will feel when I draw her life into my own body. Whatever hint I ever had of the old urges of the flesh withered within me while the cities of Sumer still littered the desert, but their ghosts linger yet, flickering at the limits of my awareness, receding instantly when I reach out to grasp them. Long experience has taught me that reclaiming the past is beyond even my powers. This body I wear will forever be that of the half child I once was, for it has never fully changed as did those of my early companions. My figure remains much like that of a boy. I have had children of a sort, but they are not born of my body and it is I who do the suckling. Nor have I ever fallen prey to the moon's blood calling. The stuff of life is too precious to be spent so profligately. I confess to some curiosity about the transformation granted to those such as Lucy, but no regret. I have received in its place a far more precious gift, for I shall live to see the deaths of all those around me, and the deaths of their children for generations to come.

Still, I believe I will suggest to Mrs. Westenra that Lucy and I share a bedroom for the next few nights. I will express my concern that Lucy might hurt herself during one of her somnambulistic episodes, and that it would be wise if I were near at hand to restrain her. If I must content myself with the shade of human desires, then I will embrace what is offered me and not deny myself the crumb where I cannot have the loaf. I am not above the pleasures of petty cruelty; where there is pleasure, nothing is petty after all, and there are other vulnerable portions of her body which even Lucy Westenra would not dare display to others.

August 7

My agent reports that he has not enjoyed full success, an intelligence which affords me neither surprise nor dismay. Vlad was always rebellious in thought if not in action, even in those early days of transformation when most remain bereft of directed self will. It was a feature of his that I admired, the reason I spared him rather than cast him down as I periodically do all those whom I have made, lest any might one day rise to challenge me as he does now. Foolishly, of course. I walked the Earth thousands of years before he was born in his mortal form, while he is still trapped in the shadow of his own grave, unable to sustain his strength without resting from time to time in a box of his native soil. I much prefer a featherbed. This weakness of his seriously impedes his mobility. He would have been far wiser to bide his time until he was no longer bound in this way, but patience was never one of Vlad's attributes. He rushes to his own doom.

I have reflected upon those last few lines for some time now because it caused me to think back to when relations between the two of us were happier. Sad to say I can no longer remember the exact moment when I first laid eyes on young Vlad Tepes, although it must have been 1445 or thereabouts. He was a bold, brash, but not particularly handsome young man in those days, just casting childhood aside and beginning to let emerge the man he would soon become. Vlad was a prisoner then, held hostage by the Ottomans for the good behavior of his father, who was charged with the protection of the passes through Transylvania. He and his younger brother, Radu, were treated well, and they both acted like honored guests rather than the prisoners they actually were, but Radu's antics were merely tolerated where his older brother was respected by all, and feared by some. He had even then the ability to focus so completely upon the accomplishment of a single task that everything else in the world seemed to recede. I was visiting the court under a Turkish name, I forget the details now, and was initially drawn to young Radu, who was extremely comely even then. I had recently destroyed all of those whom I had made, a precaution I had adopted since very early in my life, and was interested in finding a new companion rather than simply another bit of prey. But Radu was, I realized, much too young.

I considered Vlad then, but the conditions of his imprisonment added a layer of complexity that dissuaded me, although not until I had marked him in my mind. Even unfinished as he was, Vlad had fascinating qualities, a contradictory nature that warred within itself. I might have played at seduction, but despite the maturity of his body and the sobriety of his nature, he was strangely childlike when it came to women. He played at being attracted by them, but the falsity was obvious to senses as sophisticated as mine.

I left after only a brief visit, drawn by the inviting battlefields that surrounded me. Some of my get have insisted on hunting, delighting in the kill, but most are like myself in that they are content to accept the largesse of circumstance. I followed one army or another for the next two or three years, visiting the dying after each battle, hastening them on their way, or adding a casualty of my own during periods of prolonged inactivity. Turkish and Christian blood taste much the same and I have no politics. For a time I abandoned the thought of bringing anyone new over as conditions were too unsettled. Disorientation and occasional madness afflict the newly reborn, and it is easier to deal with that transition under more predictable circumstances. There was no hurry, after all. The passage of time was not, for me, a matter of concern.

Eventually I ended up in Nicopolis, where I ingratiated myself with the Turkish Pasha. Not long after arriving I learned that young Vlad had escaped his captors and returned to Wallachia. The Pasha was pliable and the Turks were amenable to my suggestion, through him, that Vlad be proclaimed Prince of Wallachia in his father's stead, since old Dracul and his oldest son Mircea had been executed by agents of their old enemy, Jon Hunyadi.

I planned to visit this young Prince and see what kind of man he had finally become, but my position in Nicopolis was a pleasant change after years of temporary encampments and I luxuriated too long. Barely two months had passed when word came that Vlad had been driven from his home by Vladislaw's forces. Rumor said that he had gone to Adrianople, but I had only begun to think about searching for him there when contrary stories placed him in various other cities. I learned much later that he had in fact originally escaped to Adrianople, but that he had almost immediately continued his flight into Moldavia, where he had distant family.

I find it pleasant to recall these long forgotten events, as though I were rummaging through wardrobes of memory. During my long existence, I have met few people whose company I valued and none as much as Vlad. Our present animosity makes me regretful, and reminds me that even now I am not completely free of those human emotions with which I was presumably born. Where and when this started I know, but the greater question is why did this chasm open between us? Because chasm it is, and so wide that neither of us can lay a bridge across even if we were so inclined. The answer is somewhere in my memories, no doubt, and I will persist with the hunt later. But for now, I must complete my account of more recent events.

A storm was imminent and it required little effort to redirect its energies, although it erupted with rather more ferocity than even I had expected. I have from time to time during the past several days expressed a general interest in the activities of the port of Whitby in order to conceal my specific desire to acquire intelligence of Vlad's arrival.

"If I can be in any small way of assistance to Jonathan in his business, it will be worth the time devoted to such tedious matters," I explained to Lucy, who turned her head in a poor attempt to conceal an utter lack of interest. I smiled within myself, having just obtained Mrs. Westenra's enthusiastic consent to the temporary change in our sleeping arrangements. Lucy never mentioned her earlier bruises, although I had noted with great satisfaction that her movements were stiff and unnatural that following morning.

I will chronicle further imaginary nocturnal excursions in my false Mina Harker diary to lend credence to my accounts of Lucy's continued restlessness. And perhaps I shall mention her occasional clumsiness of late, which has resulted in a number of unhealthy looking bruises.

August 8

He has arrived, and quite dramatically. I suspected so even before a servant brought the news of a ship run aground by the storm. Lucy is insistent that we examine the wreck with our own eyes, so I was not even called upon to find an excuse to do so.

Vlad remains impetuous, approaching my screen of pawns with his unprotected king. I had hoped he would make a better match of this but once more I seem likely to be disappointed.

The Journal of Vlad Tepes

August 9

With the wreck of the *Demeter*, my plans have been cast into considerable confusion, although I have reached refuge ashore in good order, having purloined one of my prepared boxes of earth to the basement of Carfax Abbey right from under the noses of those laboring among the wreckage. I carried away as well this journal, which I have not had the opportunity or will to add to since the day we departed Varna. I had not thought to continue it, in fact, and have raised my hand to do so now only because I feel great trepidation about my endeavors here. My enemy has been awaiting me, clearly, and I have escaped her recent attack only through considerable effort allied with happenstance.

Clearly the outcome of the coming struggle is not preordained in my favor. If I fail, perhaps by recording the history of my efforts, I may provide the means by which some other warrior might carry on. So I will keep it as current as time and circumstance permit.

Know then that the *Demeter* departed Varna as planned on July 6, taking advantage of a quiet sea and a favorable wind. I lay concealed in the hold in one of the fifty and one boxes of "experimental earth" which were consigned for delivery to Whitby, there to be taken in hand by a contractor I had engaged for that purpose and subsequently delivered to a variety of sites which I had, with Harker's unknowing assistance, determined upon. I have of late discovered that these rejuvenating slumbers are not absolutely essential, but I find that I waken refreshed and restored from the glorious oblivion they hold. I was resigned to an uneventful voyage, hoping to steal out of my resting place every fifth night to replenish my failing reserves with the noble blood of the thoroughbreds whom I had purchased for that purpose.

On the night of July 7 I rose for just that purpose, moving quietly and swiftly in the darkened passageways, avoiding the less than alert gaze of the watch while doing so. To my puzzlement and dismay, there was no trace to be found of the livestock. Through mischance or fraud, my orders had been disobeyed and I found myself stranded far from shore with no source of sustenance other than the crew, whose life's blood I had forsworn.

If circumstances permit, I shall one day pay a visit to Herr Leutner for clarification of this matter. Frankly, I suspect a petty treason at my expense. My nemesis was ever skillful at suborning those weaker of will, myself included, I regret to admit.

I returned to the hold to consider my options. Fortunately, the bullock's blood would sustain me for some time to come, but even if I could survive the complete voyage without being driven to the state of bloodlust which at one time seized me with relentless regularity, I would arrive so depleted in strength that I would be no match for my opponent, if indeed any amount of preparation could be sufficient for that purpose. I resolved to deal with those difficulties as they arose and settled into the welcoming cool earth while discomforting questions clamored for answers.

Six more cycles of day and night passed before the urge became too great to resist. Once again I waited until the small hours of the morning before coming forth, expecting to find all but the watch asleep. There was a murmuring from the crew's quarters, however, from which I gleaned the information that one of their number, a Russian named Petrovsky, had mysteriously disappeared during his watch. I thought little of this intelligence at the time, as it is not uncommon for a sailor to be lost at sea, and circumspectly catalogued the resources available to me.

The *Demeter* was a sound ship, but elderly of its kind, and both the forward and aft holds swarmed with rats. Their blood was thin and unsatisfying, but their numbers were such that they sufficed for my purposes. I took a dozen plus six of them that night, and the ship's cat as well, so that their number would not be further diminished.

On July 22, I wakened so ravenous that I slaughtered a score of the vermin in short order, unwisely creating such a commotion that two of the crew came down to investigate. I disposed of the corpses through a porthole before sheltering in the darkness, undiscovered as they quickly found an excuse to retreat back abovedecks. From their chatter I learned that a second of their number had disappeared, a fact that seemed to me an unlikely coincidence indeed.

I gorged myself twice more during the next ten days without leaving the hold, but on August the Second I determined to investigate two circumstances. First, the depletion of the rats was proceeding far too rapidly to be explained by any combination of normal attrition and my own predation. Second, the ship was strangely silent on those occasions when I was up and about, almost as though abandoned and cast adrift.

The Captain was asleep in his quarters, though he turned restlessly beneath the blanket and even in repose his features were drawn and haggard. Another man whom I later learned to be the mate stood duty at the wheel, while the observation point aloft was unmanned. A third crewmember, whom I had once heard addressed as Abramov, lay motionless in the otherwise empty crew quarters amidships.

I was sorely beset to understand what malady afflicted the *Demeter* and resolved to remain at large until an explanation offered itself. After some effort, I cast overboard the depleted corpses of a dozen plus one of the surviving rats, but I was unable to discover the presence of any others of their brethren. Perhaps because of my depleted energy, I was careless and let myself be seen briefly by the mate as I exited from the forward hold. Immediately I retreated to the recesses of the ship hoping he would dismiss the sight as a waking dream.

Alas, such was not to be the case. The following night I was wakened by his efforts to pry open the box adjacent to my own. I thought to remain silent until the disturbance subsided, but the mate next put his lever to the very box in which I rested, speaking in a low voice to an audience visible only to himself about devils and monsters and such. I bestirred myself, hoping to use the glamour to bring some semblance of peace to his troubled mind, but he prised open the lid and caught sight of me straightaway, dropped the lever and rushed from the hold so quickly that I, in my weakened state, could simply follow behind. He then threw himself over the rail with a cry of horror, declaring that no devil would steal his life even if he must take it himself.

The Captain and the remaining crewmember were attracted by this shouting. The former immediately ran to the unattended wheel, cursing loudly in Rumanian. It was the second man, Abramov, who drew all my attention.

How had I missed his scent before, I wondered, and knew immediately the answer. He was not as I, but he was one of *her* unfinished creatures as well, tainted but not yet transformed, a thrall subject to her will, serving her purposes, enslaved by the call of the blood. He yet lived, but already his fate was sealed. I had no doubt that this was the source of the *Demeter*'s curse, the agent by whose hands her crew had perished.

Even as I hesitated, his eyes moved to impale me and his lips curled in a smile that held neither gladness nor welcome. With a cry, he rushed across the deck, intent upon striking down the Captain before I could prevent the murder. That worthy, warned perhaps by some hidden sense, turned to confront his attacker, raising one hand to ward off the onrushing creature. Abramov sank his teeth into the man's wrist, was sucking from it greedily even as I reached their struggling forms and wrenched him away.

The sight of so much spilled blood was too great. Had I remained there, I might have slain the Captain myself. Instead I caught up Abramov's body and carried it off to the hold where I gorged myself even though the blood held the sour tinge of her presence. And so it was that my fast came to an end, for the life I took then was still mortal, though barely. The taste of it banished all conscious rational thought from my mind and I did not recover myself until his pale, drained body was already noticeably cool.

After I had regained enough presence of mind to consider my circumstances, I tossed Abramov's body overboard from a place of concealment. I had made certain that he would not rise again. Then I surreptitiously proceeded forward, where I discovered the Captain still at the wheel. I thought to approach him, but doubted I could do so without throwing his mind into such disarray that all reason might flee forever. Instead I retreated below deck to consider.

On August 4, I resolved to reveal myself to the Captain. He had remained at his post since Abramov's death except for brief excursions below for food and water. As much as I admired his steadfastness, he could not hope to bring the *Demeter* safely to port by his own resources. With my assistance, it might just be possible, although I confess that seamanship is one of the few areas of human knowledge to which I have devoted almost no attention during my long span. The sea poses obvious difficulties for one such as I.

Nevertheless, I acted that very evening, showing myself to the Captain but keeping a safe distance away. His terror was tempered by exhaustion but it still burned fiercely in his eyes and he trembled violently from the moment he first saw me. Alas, I had hoped to spare him more hardship, but as I approached, I felt in his blood the faint aroma of her taint. Abramov's bite had been sufficient to doom the man. It was simply a matter of time until his body's life fled, though thankfully it would not play host to the foul engine of animation that allows my kind to walk the Earth.

"You have nothing to fear from me," I sought to reassure him. "The agent of your distress was Abramov, who shall trouble us no further."

"I know ye for what ye are," he replied feebly. "Devil, thou shalt not have me." So saying, he removed from within his clothing a Christian cross, thinking to repel me with its supposed power against evil.

I was struck with great sympathy for the man, who found the courage to stand against what he must consider the very personification of evil. If it had been within my power to flee the ship that moment and trouble him no more, I would have done so, but I was restrained not only by the physical barrier of the surrounding waters, but also by the knowledge that he was doomed no matter what I did.

The Captain made no effort to flee as I moved closer. Indeed, he could not have done so. Even if his weakened condition, brought on by exposure and loss of blood as well as the shock of his situation, would have permitted, he had somehow managed to lash his wrist to the wheel, so that it could not turn without his knowledge.

As I sought to comfort him, he fell into a series of retching coughs and dropped the cross he held as the deck gave a mighty heave that almost threw me from my feet. I caught the chain just before it eluded my grasp.

"This may comfort you, my friend," I said softly. "And perhaps with faith it will draw out the poison in your wound." And so saying, I wrapped the chain as gently as I could around the wounded wrist and pressed the cross itself against the ragged tears left by Abramov's foul attack. Had he held the cross himself, I could not have touched it, for it would have focused the power of his faith into a shield which my kind cannot penetrate. But once out of his grasp, it was as harmless to me as to any mortal.

I brought food and water before retreating to my resting place, but it was to no avail for when I rose the following night, the Captain was cold and stiff in his self imposed bonds. After satisfying myself that all life was truly extinct, I returned to my lair, adding yet another entry to the ledger of my enemy's evil deeds.

On August the Seventh a great storm arose, with such turbulence that I feared the *Demeter* would break up. The thought of passing through eternity as a starving creature imprisoned beneath the sea was, I confess, even more imperative a concern than my plans for retribution. Whether it was simple mischance or the hand of Enheduanna, I could not tell. I have some small influence with the weather myself, but the raising of such a storm was as far beyond me as it would be beyond that of mortal man. She, on the other hand, had the advantage of an existence countless centuries longer than my own. Her tolerance of the sun was considerable even in those long past days when I walked the earth as a normal man, and the passage of time has no doubt strengthened if not added to her powers. It would not surprise me to learn she had developed other abilities as yet denied to me. Even when we first met, more than four centuries ago now, she could call up the thunder through force of will, a power still denied me.

By good fortune, the ship missed the rocks I espied through the driving rain and came ashore in relatively good shape, although even to my unpracticed eye it was clear she would never sail again. The impact threw my boxes from one end of the hold to the other, but they were sturdily built and girded with iron and all but one withstood the violence successfully. I remained aboard long enough to reassure myself of this, and thereby found myself in danger of discovery. Would-be rescuers and curiosity seekers were already flocking toward the derelict, and while I might pass scrutiny in the darkness, my presence there aboard a ship crewed by a single corpse would require explanations I was not prepared to supply. I therefore assumed the form of a wolf despite the discomfort such a transformation brings and fled into the darkness, eluding a few desultory efforts to capture me.

I returned just before dawn to secure one of the boxes and transport it to my new home. Most of my strength had been depleted, and the following night I was reduced to preying on the rats of Carfax Abbey, just as I had previously done aboard the *Demeter*. These were fatter and more satisfying, however, and the night following I encountered and, I confess, ruthlessly slaughtered a mastiff for the sake of its blood. That is what courses through my veins now, in fact, providing the strength with which I record this history of my recent experiences.

I am less confident of my plans than before, but unwilling to abandon them without better reason. I will, however, be more circumspect in future, and take pains not to rush into a situation which may be more complicated than it might first appear.

Enheduanna's Secret Journal

August 10

I made a foolish mistake yesterday evening, a careless lapse which I must not repeat. Fortunately, it has gone unremarked. I stole a child from a tumbledown fishing hut just north of Whitby, calling her outside as she lay sleeping on a straw filled mat. She was a plain child of twelve years or so, but healthy and full of life. The call of her blood was loud and glorious and I had waited so long that it was as if a rush of sustaining fire coursed through my body when I first tapped into her veins, a sensation that I wanted to prolong for as long as possible.

To that aim, I resisted the impulse to finish quickly and instead carried her back to Whitby, stopping every few minutes to sup lightly, just enough to suppress my need and to keep her quiescent. Finally, on the lookout point above the coast where Lucy and I often sit in the shade of a convenient tree, I finished my repast, regretting its brevity but rejoicing in the renewed energy it had brought. I ensured that the child would not rise again and threw the body far out over the rocks so the tide would take it, and had just turned back toward Hillingham when I realized I was not alone.

Old Man Swales had been sitting back in the shadows, sleeping perhaps, but wide awake now. He raised his arm and pointed vaguely in my direction with a shaking hand, and action preceded thought as I advanced upon him and broke his neck with a single blow. I emptied his pockets and left him seated there, fearing that two disappearances in a single night might provoke unwanted alarm, hoping that he would be thought to have died at the hand of some transient thief. As it happened, the foolish man who purports to administer medicine in Whitby concluded Swales had fallen back against the bench in his sleep, thereby causing the injury to his neck. I am at a loss to understand how this charlatan persuades anyone of his competence, but in this case at least he has proven to be my unwitting ally.

Today, Lucy and I attended his funeral. It was a tedious affair, but it would not have been in character for Mina not to have gone given her previous friendliness toward the man, and the somber clothing required for such an occasion provided adequate protection from the sun, which had emerged brightly from the passing storm clouds.

All went well until that lecherous sailor Digby took a seat adjacent to us. He has an eye for the ladies, and clearly his aspirations are higher than his station. But a cat may look at the queen, so they say, and his sidelong glances at Lucy at least diverted his attention from me. Would that the same was true of his dog, a haggard mongrel to whom Lucy has been kind at times in the past, though the miserable cur will naturally not approach me under any circumstances. Oddly enough, such beasts always tolerated Vlad, even after he became my creature, but they cannot abide my presence. Digby was impatient today and tried first cajolery, then a commanding voice, and finally brute force to compel obedience, but the animal simply whined and snarled and barked until he finally abandoned the effort and left us with a barely polite word.

After walking along the cliffs for a time, we returned to Hillingham only to discover that Mrs. Westenra had invited that pompous curate to take supper with us again. He has been a guest several times recently even though Lucy and her mother are at best irregular churchgoers. Lucy herself barely tolerates the man's insipid conversation and I don't think Mrs. Westenra actually cares for him either. It may be that she is unconsciously seeking some weapon to use in defense of her mind and has fastened upon him in some form of instinctive groping in the dark. If so, it is a poor tool to which she had put her hand. He might cause me some difficulty if he was intelligent and perceptive, but he's a dull, worldly man self deluded into believing himself pious. Nevertheless, I pretended fatigue in order to retire early and escape his company, and have avenged myself by ordering beglamored Lucy to stand on her toes in the corner of our room while I ran my hands over the secret parts of her body. Tomorrow morning, she will find it difficult to stand, let alone walk along the cliffs, and since she will remember nothing of the cause of her pain, it will make her mind uneasy as well. Her father, after all, died of an undiagnosed illness after several months of petty physical complaints. Her imagination will add flavor to her punishment.

She stands there even now, balanced on her toes, her nude body illuminated in the faint moonlight. I mean to keep her there while I finish writing this entry, although I must allow her sufficient sleep to avoid alarming her mother in the morning.

Vlad continues to be much in my thoughts, the Vlad of today who is my enemy, and the Vlad of yesterday, who was – if not my lover – at least the closest approximation I have ever known.

The Journal of Vlad Tepes

August 10

I have not dreamed since that long ago day when I ceased to be what I was and became what I now am and forever will be, at least until I cease altogether. I once asked Enheduanna if she also ceased to live within her mind while her body slept away the days, but she did not answer me directly, and it may be that she never really understood what I was asking. I sometimes pity her, for she has never known mortal life at all and never shall. As much as we grew alike for a time, we were also forever different. She was born as she now is, unchanging and unfeeling. As a child, she only pretended to sleep, lying awake in her blankets wondering at the strange vacancy she felt in the minds of those around her. Never sleeping, she had never dreamed, and knew of it only as one might hear of some strange animal on another continent. She disliked speaking of it.

I no longer dream. I lay quiet like the dead thing that I am, all thoughts vanished from my mind. Sometimes while I am active and aware, thoughts creep into my consciousness, memories but often altered, showing me possibilities that might have come to pass if I had chosen another course. The experience is as close to dreaming as I can approach, or perhaps they are waking nightmares, since they only underscore the terrible consequences of the road I have chosen to follow. These malformed memories hover in the corners of my mind, bedeviling me when I least expect them, and it has occurred to me on more than one occasion that I might lay them to at least a semblance of rest by writing them down, imprisoning them within the pages of this journal. And it may be also that by recalling the past, I can bring to mind some fatal weakness in my enemy which she may have been less careful to conceal when we worked for a common cause than now that we have become foes. If nothing else, it will fill the idle hours of daylight at the edges of darkness when I am awake but must be cautious of the sun.

I first laid eyes on Enheduanna in the summer of 1447. I know the year well, because it was later that same year that John Hunyadi slew my father and my older brother Mircea by treachery. My younger brother Radu and I were held hostage by the Ottomans for my father's good behavior in defending the passes through Transylvania. Our imprisonment was not harsh; we had the freedom of the castle and occasionally beyond, were well fed, clothed, and tutored, and might easily have been mistaken for honored guests. Radu was content enough, but I was angry, and not just with our captors. I felt betrayed and abandoned by my father, and when news arrived of his death, I felt as much satisfaction as grief. That must sound cold and unfeeling today, but those were very different times, and family bonds were honored out of pride and honor rather than honest affection.

Radu was docile, as I have said, but I delighted in making life uncomfortable for everyone around me, particularly the guards who were ordered to ensure that we remained within our proscribed limits. At first I played simple, childish pranks on them, safe from reprisal because of my noble blood. As I grew older, and more bitter, my jibes became sharper, and more than one of our guards received injuries at my instigation. On one occasion, I was set upon by a newly assigned man who was recovering both from a wound sustained in battle and a petty humiliation I had instigated. Although Hugo was half again my size, I deprived him of his weapon and beat him senseless, after which his fellows treated me with more respect, though even less liking. Following my father's death, our imprisonment continued more through habit than for political purpose, but our status diminished. Our allowances were reduced and became irregular, we were greeted with pointed coolness, and the guards were less likely to look the other way when we broke the rules, as I so often did. The situation grew intolerable for me, and so I began to plot my escape.

Looking back through the many years that have passed since then, I realize that my situation could have been far worse. I suffered no more than petty cruelties, and received no better than petty kindnesses, but I was far better off than most of my countrymen, caught between warring factions, ruled by avaricious and incompetent leaders. But at the time, it seemed to me a great injustice that my freedom was denied me, and I chafed at the insubstantial bindings and fought back in the only way that I could think of – disobedience, ingratitude, rudeness, and contempt.

My younger self was not an admirable person, but not so bad as history has made me. I had spent some part of my small allowance bribing the guards to bring me caged birds from the marketplace where I was rarely allowed to venture myself. They were pretty things, but I confess that it was not so much their gentle appearance or their sweet singing that appealed to me so much as it was their ability to soothe my ego. They were my captives, subject entirely to my will, and that meant that I was not entirely without power. Shortly after the incident with Hugo, I returned to my quarters to find that each and every one of my captives had been mercilessly slain, spitted on sharpened sticks. A few were still alive when I found them, and I broke their necks quickly as an act of mercy. It was Hugo, of course, or someone acting on his behalf, but word quickly spread that I had done the foul deed myself. I had made too many enemies, and no friends at all to speak up for me, so the falsehood became another part of my personal history. It did not help that I would not trouble myself to deny it.

I had seen women of various classes and different races in the past, but Enheduanna made an immediate impression, even though I saw her only briefly that first time. I did not even learn her name until after she had departed. We were practicing swordsmanship in the courtyard when I happened to look up and saw her watching from a balcony, short and so slender I might have thought her a boy had she not let her long hair down to cover her shoulders with an ebony curtain. My first reaction was disinterest; I preferred more buxom wenches. But that night she came to me in my dreams and I woke more than once drenched in sweat and with an aching between my thighs that eased slowly and reluctantly.

I inquired about her, but the guards were taciturn or ill informed or both, and all I learned was her name and that she was from some distant land thought to lie beyond Egypt. She had arrived with only a single servant, but was treated as though she were a queen in her homeland. Twice more I saw her during her visit, but on neither occasion did we exchange words, although our eyes met briefly one evening when we passed one another in the Great Hall. Her gaze was direct and steady and I felt strangely discomforted, so much so that the brazen greeting I was preparing died stillborn on my lips and I even nodded politely as she passed.

The following day I learned that she had left that morning for Nicopolis, and felt a sense of loss deeper than that on the day my father abandoned me to Turkish custody. I vowed to free myself from bondage and follow her, but the opportunity to do so did not come for many months, and by then her image had faded to a shadow in my mind. I fled to Adrianople, but my enemies pursued and I was forced to escape under cover of darkness, eventually finding friendlier faces in Moldavia, where King Bogdan offered me his protection and the friendship of his son, Stefan. There I was indeed an honored guest, but before many weeks had passed I found that my life had slipped back into the old pattern, that even though I was a free man, I was also very much like a prisoner once again, dependent on the largesse of my host, limited in my ability to travel, my comings and goings closely watched. Kings and princes have their privileges, but they are also enslaved by the necessities of their position. They cannot trust even their closest associates and must ever be on the watch for treachery, deceit, or even simple foolhardiness.

Deliverance came from an unexpected quarter. The Pasha of Nicopolis sent an envoy bearing word of his support for my succession to my father's title. We had never met and I was suspicious of his motives, but shortly thereafter I was formally proclaimed the Prince of Wallachia and returned to my homeland, which I had not seen for the past six years. It would be some time yet before I learned of Enheduanna's involvement in my sudden change of circumstances. Alas, my accession lasted only for a short time. I had barely begun my reign when I was driven from Wallachia by the armies of King Vladislav. I returned to Moldavia disheartened and full of pent up fury, my future more uncertain than ever, and there it was that I found Enheduanna again, and there it was that she claimed me for her own.

Stefan and his father greeted me warmly and proffered their support, but I knew that no matter how well meant their intentions, they lacked the means to enforce their will. Stefan cheered me somewhat by entering into a pact with me whereby we would support each other when the time came that either of us commanded sufficient forces to act, but the prospects for neither of us were bright in the immediate future, and I was faced with another period of virtual imprisonment. I could not sleep and prowled the castle late at night, and that's where we truly met for the first time.

My mind has become so crowded with memories over the years that some have been forced over the precipice into oblivion, but the events of that night are as clear to me now as the moments just past. I begin to understand at last why Enheduanna was so determined to set down her thoughts and actions on paper, so that she might recall them at some future date, although the truth is that I would be better off without most of the dark memories that lurk in the corners of my skull. That long ago night had started clear and crisp, the moon full and bright, but as I walked the battlements, ghostly galleons of cloud had sailed across the sky in ever increasing numbers, obscuring first the stars and then the moon herself. It was damp and chill and the guards were huddled in what sheltered recesses they could find, but my anger and frustration were like a furnace and I climbed to the castle's highest vantage point and looked down over the foreign countryside.

The weather began to roughen more quickly, a sharp edged

wind rose, and thunder rumbled like distant cannon. It will rain soon, I thought, but I made no move toward shelter. I had been driven from my homeland, but I vowed not to be driven from that place, not on that night.

"The darkness does not frighten you?" The voice was so gentle, so controlled, and so unexpected that I thought at first that some bodiless spirit was addressing me. I think perhaps I felt a touch of fear, but it was quickly whelmed by my smoldering rage.

A flash of white caught my attention and I turned to see a slender young woman, her body almost completely wrapped in billowing white silk, standing just an arm's length away from me. Her garment could not possibly have protected her from the bitter cold and I immediately thought that some ghostly apparition had addressed me rather than a solid body.

"I am recently arrived here and we have not been introduced. I am the Lady Mara and you, I imagine, must be the Prince of Wallachia."

"Prince in name only," I admitted ill naturedly, hoping to conceal my relief that it was after all flesh and blood I was addressing. Had I known then the nature of that flesh, and particularly that blood, I might have thrown myself from the parapet immediately. But perhaps not. I was of that age when life seems interminable and destiny a goal to be sought rather than a trap to be avoided.

"So it is with me also," she said quietly, moving so close that I could almost feel her presence even when I looked away. "My estates have been trampled underfoot until only barren fields remain in their stead." The Lady Mara, whom I would later know as Enheduanna, stood at my shoulder, sharing my view of the shrouded land below.

"You should take shelter, my lady. The night grows violent." Even as I spoke, a fork of lightning split the clouds.

She laughed and tossed her head slightly, so that the folds of gauzy material covering her hair fell back. "I am not afraid of the darkness or the thunder, Prince of Wallachia."

"Don't call me that!" I clenched my fists and something throbbed behind my eyes. "I should not bear the name until it is deserved," I added more moderately.

"What shall I call you then?"

"My name is Vlad Tepes."

"And mine is Mara, to those I call my friends. Would you care to be one of that small number, Vlad Tepes?"

"I have no friends." Which was all but true. Stefan was the only one I thought of in that fashion, and he was out of my mind at that moment. I had been with young women before. It was considered an essential part of my education while I was a hostage, and there had been others during my brief reign in Wallachia, though never the same more than once.

"Then perhaps I might become your first." I thought I felt her touch upon my arm and turned, but she was facing away, out toward the distant mountains. The darkness had not abated in the slightest and most of the torches had been blown out, but I could see her clearly, as though she generated some internal light of her own.

Thunder rumbled again, closer this time. "You should go inside, Lady Mara. The storm will break at any moment." But I did not wish her to go.

"It will hold off until I release it," she said, turning to glance in my direction. I thought her merely teasing, but even then she had the power to influence the weather. She may have summoned the storm in the first place. She leaned forward onto the stonework and averted her face again. The wind caught at her clothing, pressing it tight against her body for a moment, and I saw that her figure was slim and unwomanly and I was disappointed. Her self confidence seemed out of place in what I thought now to be just a half grown girl.

The wind became much more violent of a sudden and I staggered before it. Such small pieces of debris as littered the upper levels of the castle went dancing up into the night and somewhere an unseen guard cursed. I placed a hand against a battlement to steady myself, marveling at the way she stood her ground. The thunder and lightning was all around us now and I could hear a rhythmic thrumming in the distance that must have been rain. Not a drop fell on the castle, however. I had a sense that marvelous events were happening, and then she turned to me and I saw something in her face, or perhaps just in the eyes, that captivated me so completely that the strangeness of what was happening around me seemed inconsequential.

After four centuries, I can suppress the will of a single person for a time, but she had walked the Earth for more than ten times as long by then and she had mastered the glamour, the power to modify the thoughts and memories of others. It is her strongest weapon and it was only after I became powerful enough to resist that I was able to be truly free of her. But that night, I had no knowledge of that, no hint that such a thing might be possible outside of the legends of my people, legends which I had dismissed as children's stories with no power to frighten those who had put aside childish things.

Even now I cannot bring to mind exactly what happened next. I recall only that I was suddenly struck dumb by desire and that I would have forever renounced my claim to Wallachia, to my noble name, to whatever fortune might be due me, all that and more just to enfold her in my arms and make her my own for an evening, an hour, as little as a moment. It was the glamour, I know now, but I think more than that, for I had already felt the force of her personality and had been drawn to it. Perhaps I saw something of myself in her, for both of us stood apart from the rest of the world. It had long seemed to me that life was a great game played in an enormous room, a game from which I was always excluded. But I stood at the window, peeking in and wishing to take part, while she played carelessly in the dooryard, disengaged and uninterested.

I retain a handful of images of those next few moments within my mind, but how much was real and how much illusion I shall never know. Her clothing billowed up like a white shroud and hid the darkness and the storm and I felt lost within this space of her making, safe and calm but excited and expectant all at the same time. Her face was close to mine, and it seemed both familiar and unfamiliar. I could not drop my eyes, even when I felt her hands on my body and then she leaned forward, her lips light against the side of my neck, and I experienced a moment of such exquisite intensity that I knew my life would never be the same again.

And of course, it was not.

She took my will but did not bring me across that first night. Instead she met me each evening, sometimes in the battlements, sometimes in an unused part of the castle, sometimes in the grounds outside. We rarely spoke, not even to arrange our assignations, whose time and place I somehow knew without being told. We were never once disturbed, and I lived each day in anticipation of embracing her once again. Stefan noticed my languor and distraction, of course, but seemed to believe that it was a fugue brought on by my recent reversals and present low prospects.

On the seventh and last night, we met outside the gates and found our way to the densest part of the nearby forest, and there for the last time I touched her as a completely mortal man. Bogdan's retainers found me in the morning, pale and disoriented, with a wound on my throat and a smear of blood down my shirt and breeches. I retained enough wit to make up a plausible story, an attack by a boar whom I had driven off, but only after receiving a small wound of my own. I had fallen directly afterwards, I told them, striking my head and rendering myself senseless, and had only regained my wits a few minutes before they found me. They seemed less than satisfied, but dared not question the word of their master's guest.

I still lived, but already my skin reddened easily in the sunlight and I could no longer tolerate the smell of garlic, which unfortunately was a common condiment in Bogdan's kitchen. Symbols of the church did not repel me unless they were worn as personal adornments or held in the hands of the truly faithful, but I found it impossible to remain long in the presence of a true believer so equipped. Although I did not grasp the significance at the time, it amuses me in retrospect to realize that I was never troubled by Bogdan's favorite priest, whose faith was apparently as shallow as his penchant for prolonged sermonizing was deep. My new idiosyncrasies were tolerated, and a story began to circulate that I had renounced my faith in response to my ill fortune. I little cared what was said about me so did not stir myself to contradict this tale, which held at least an element of truth.

The Lady Mara remained in the castle for some considerable time longer, but our relationship had altered. I had always been her servant, ever since that first night on the castle wall, but the distance between us had somehow been magnified now. Where before she had beckoned, now she commanded. She instructed me in the ways of my kind, half human, half what I am now, and promised that I would join her completely when the time was right. I had become her thrall, and my will was no longer my own.

"We will be together for all eternity," she had lied, knowing full well that she intended to destroy me as she had all who had followed this dark path before me, laying each to their final rest, or rather their ultimate damnation, before any could rise to challenge her own power. So she had lived through centuries without number, and so she intends to continue even now. And only I have survived long enough to disturb her plan.

I begged her not to make me wait, to bring me over immediately so that I could stand at her side, but she laughed at my impetuosity and told me I was being foolish and short sighted. "What use would you be to me now, a landless young lord with no wealth, no prospects, and little wisdom? I charge you to find your destiny first, draw power and hold it tightly, prove yourself worthy of the honor I have bestowed upon you. Then we shall know what you are made of and can fashion you into something greater."

"I can accomplish all that and more," I insisted, "if you will remain at my side. If you abandon me, I am nothing. I will rot in exile while my enemies laugh at me."

"No. You will hone yourself into a dagger for my hand. You will triumph over your enemies and grasp the privilege that power brings. You will provide a refuge where I may stop for a time when I choose, and where I will not need to conceal what I truly am. You will serve me as I wish, and when I am satisfied, I will grant you my greatest gift and we shall be together and watch the lives of lesser beings come and go like mayflies."

And then she was gone, departing without fanfare or notice, and for the first few days I was without purpose, and during those same nights I was without hope as well. The shadows would fall across me wherever I was and I would turn, waiting for her to emerge from the darkness for yet another tryst, but she was never there and each disappointment drove another dagger into my flesh. The wounds refused to heal, but neither did they fester. I began to take interest in the world again, much to the delight of Stefan who professed himself worried about me, and my renewed determination to better my own situation pleased his father as well. My brooding was interpreted as a sign of growing maturity and my new idiosyncrasies and my more ruthless nature were generally regarded as creditable. Those were far different times, in some ways.

I began to plan how I should one day be worthy of her favor once more. She had become the goal of all my endeavors, and the meaning of my existence.

Enheduanna's Secret Journal

August 11

I am very disappointed with myself. Perhaps I am not yet as completely in control of my powers as I have believed, or perhaps it is simply that these many pale years without the stimulation of a genuine challenge have left me careless, lazy, and over confident. I must remember father's words, as valid now as they were so long ago that our people are barely a memory today, and a distorted one at that. "If you would govern others," he told my brothers, "you must first learn to govern yourselves." Sage advice which they did not heed. They were all three destroyed by their own vices, one assassinated by a political rival, one killed by a jealous husband, the last taken by too much drink. Our father would have never believed it possible that frail Enheduanna would prove the strongest of all of his children. But I am straying from the point, avoiding the moment in which I must formally acknowledge my failure.

I had hoped to learn something further of Vlad's intentions and quickly. He survived the shipwreck, of course. I don't require physical evidence to apprehend that, and in fact I would have been greatly surprised if he had not. It is probable that he realizes now that his arrival has come as no surprise. Not that it matters, since we both know what purpose has brought him to this upstart island nation. I tasted more than just his blood when he became my thrall, back when he was still a worldly prince with pretensions of greatness and ambitions narrowly channeled by his obsessions. I also touched his spirit and know him as he may never know himself. Vlad could never confront two problems at the same time, and his sometimes precipitous violence was often designed to dispose of an annoying distraction that prevented him from concentrating on what he considered more important issues. The changes I wrought upon him and his subsequent independence do not even now seem to have affected that basic flaw in his personality.

I still remember that night when I first tasted his life, a moment so distinct that it illuminated the days surrounding it, distinguishing them from the weeks and months that had gone before and those that followed thereafter, months when I took the life I needed to sustain my own existence, but only as a matter of survival, the act accompanied by neither joy nor fear. I am not completely without human emotion, and I have experienced loneliness at times during the long centuries, a longing assuaged only to a degree by those I have made into creatures like myself. They have been a poor substitute. Some were driven hopelessly insane by the process of change, and all were mentally deficient in one way or another, regaining their full faculties only after varying periods of time. Perhaps all would have done so had I the leisure and patience to wait, but why mend a broken tool when a serviceable one lies near at hand? It was only those who recovered most of their self control and intelligence who were capable of providing the company I desired. Unfortunately, with that restoration came increased independence of spirit, and sooner or later it became necessary for my own safety that they be destroyed before they could acquire enough power to rival my own. In all those thousands of years, only Vlad severed the bonds between us of his own volition.

That first night, I made Vlad subject to my will but only as a thrall. He was of more use to me alive, at least for a few years. If he could regain the title and privileges to which he was entitled by virtue of his bloodline, he could provide a welcome and comfortable refuge for me. I was beginning to acquire a taste for luxury and splendor, if only because they provided a contrast to the killing fields and abattoirs which always provided easy prey. There was always an increased risk that I might betray myself in close quarters, however, so it was reassuring to have a powerful patron. Even if Vlad failed and remained an outcast, he would grow in experience and maturity with the passage of time, and would become a more valuable and interesting companion when I claimed him completely and drew his life into myself. Even at that early date, I sensed something different about my young admirer. His will was powerful; he was obedient, sometimes fawning, but restive and demanding until I exerted my authority. He responded to my wishes but never lost sight of his own desires. I saw in him a kindred spirit, not my masculine counterpart exactly, but a faint echo of myself. Perhaps if I had claimed him completely while he was still a youth, things might have turned out differently, but I deferred that act until a later time and by then Vlad had become a different person. The die was forever cast and even I cannot change the past. Now we are enemies and can never go back to what we were, or what we might have been. It is one of my few regrets, and at least he has gifted me with that novelty.

Vlad has almost certainly gone to ground within Carfax Abbey, as I had anticipated. The alternatives which Jonathan carried to him were carefully selected to make its choice inevitable. I walked past the grounds today, confident that he would not detect my presence with his weaker though no doubt equally alert senses. Although I feel certain that he was hidden inside, I was unable to confirm that fact. When last we met, he betrayed his cause in ignorance. I could feel him in the air long before he appeared in the flesh, and I was prepared for his attack. I have never known him to repeat a mistake, and am neither surprised nor disappointed by this new revelation of his growing sureness.

In a contest of wills or wits, I believe myself more than capable of dealing with Vlad, but in a purely physical confrontation, he may possess resources that surpass my own. Vlad's abilities have surprised me in the past and I shall not underestimate him again. I have survived as long as I have in part because I avoid unnecessary risks, and I shall not stray from that path now.

He must be destroyed, because his determination to destroy me is now his primary obsession, and he will not rest until he has succeeded or failed completely and finally. Love and hatred are much more akin to one another than most mortals would like to admit, and love turned to hatred is a powerful emotion indeed. I think Vlad truly loved me once, or at least believed that he did, but he has grown to hate himself, and blames me for what he has become. One of us must cease to be, and I have no desire to leave this world just yet. It is to this purpose that I must direct all my efforts now, and it is time to bring capital pieces into the game, so that they may strike past my screen of pawns.

But first I must arrange the sacrifice of another of those lesser players.

At the stroke of midnight this evening, Lucy became more completely my own. Our little games have begun to bore me. She has so easily become mine that there is no sense of triumph in the accomplishment. Her willingness to passively accept humiliation robs the act of much of its pleasure, and of late even in her waking hours she grows ever more dependent upon me, such that it is becoming increasingly difficult to take in hand certain matters of business which won't bear accompaniment or close scrutiny. She still prattles on about Holmwood, but for the past few days it seems to have become a litany rather than a peroration. The darkness within her has been stirred by my attentions, awakening a facet of Lucy that neither she, nor frankly I, ever suspected. A woman, perhaps, slumbers within the child.

The last few nights, we have shared the same bed. Lucy moves uneasily in her sleep, draws herself close to me and clutches her limbs around my body, as though seeking even what feeble warmth I am able to provide. At times she speaks as though I were her beloved Arthur, a situation which amused me at first, and if I didn't know better I would be tempted to believe sweet little Lucy had already sacrificed her maidenhood on the altar of passion. If I had thought to corrupt her mind as well as her body, I would have faced a great disappointment. The ease with which I overcome her will is at least partly because she seeks the freedom offered by abandoning herself to me.

Tonight I felt her hands creep around my body as I feigned sleep, moving up from my hips across the flesh of my ribs until they clutched me tightly below the breasts and I felt just the faintest hint of human passion, a stirring lost to me since Sumer was a thriving nation and I its proudest priestess. Then as now, it was only a teasing; the capacity for physical passion remains beyond my reach, and at times I fear it, for I suspect that it is a reflection of mortality. I turned within the circle of her arms and by light of the moon that flowed in through our window I saw that she was awake and not enwrapped in a dream, but even then she made no move to relinquish her grip.

"You're so cold, Mina," she whispered. I am sure she thought her face amply shielded by the darkness, but that is no veil to my eyes and I saw the way her tongue moved over her lips. The beating of her heart was like cannon fire and the heat spreading from her loins was an open hearth. She could not have known how close she was to death at that moment, at least not with her conscious mind.

"I am warmed by your presence," I replied softly. "Your blood runs hotter than mine, Lucy, and ever has."

"Do you love me, Mina? Do you truly?" Her voice was husky, laden with secret meaning. She moved slightly so that one of her breasts pushed against my own.

"Truly I do, Lucy," I lied, and knew in that moment what role she was to fill in my service. I smiled to reassure her and pressed close against her body, my knee nudging her thigh until she raised one leg and set it half across mine.

"Will you kiss me then, Mina?" It was her child's voice, but with a deeper, older undertone.

"Yes, of course I will." She closed her eyes as I raised my head from the pillow, but it wasn't her lips I meant to touch. Her body went stiff against me as I bit into the river of life that flowed through her veins, her nipples hard, her thighs gripping me with surprising strength. Almost I lost myself in the rush of feeling that comes with a really satisfying kill but I still had need of this slip of a girl and I had already unwisely given in to impulse once recently. I supped deeply but drew back when I sensed the faltering of her spirit.

I left her weak and confused but still alive. My restraint took its toll, however, and I felt restless, incomplete, and finally swept out into the night to further assuage my hunger elsewhere. She will recall nothing in the morning except dream images too personal to speak of even to me, her closest friend. Her lack of vigor must pass as illness. It is time for dearest Lucy to enter her final decline. I have decided that it must be accomplished before she is wed. The presence of Holmwood, in her life if not her bed, must make that eventuality more difficult and I have no time at present for complications other than those I contrive for my own reasons.

August 12

The memories come back to me more vividly now. When I left Vlad at Bogdan's castle many years ago, I feared that he might destroy himself with grief rather than live on to serve me, although I had high hopes for him even then. Without the benefit of my restraining hand, those I choose as living servants are unsettled in their minds, the extent of that disruption dependent upon their individual natures. Nor was it always possible for me to predict the outcome. Sometimes the strongest souls proved to be the most brittle, and they might snap at the smallest provocation like untested trees that refused to bend before the wind. On the other hand, I have taken others of a mild or self effacing nature, expecting little, only to find that they are so accustomed to adapting themselves to the wishes of those around them that they make the transition to being my servant with barely an outward sign of upset. These latter are slow to challenge me, but usually more dangerous because they are often able to conceal their innermost thoughts even from me and more than once I have uncovered secretive and well advanced plans to secure their independence at my expense. I have learned to watch the quiet ones most carefully.

Independent spirits like Vlad are less adept at hiding their secrets. I knew from the outset when Vlad began to desire his old freedom, and I tolerated his growing unrest only because I thought it possible that I had finally found another spirit who might sit at my side throughout eternity. In the end, I learned an old lesson, that mercy is only seen as a virtue by the weak, that the strong know better.

I recall now very little of Vlad's history during the two years following our trysting, although there is no doubt a record of some sort in my older diaries. He and his cousin Steven had been as close as is possible among their class, and their friendship survived after a fashion, although for Vlad it was now almost certainly a matter of political expediency rather than comradeship. Steven was, I seem to remember, more than slightly cloddish, not nearly the tactician that his father was, and a poor judge of men. He may well have believed Vlad to be his steadfast friend despite obvious evidence to the contrary.

For my part, I remained for a time among the Turks, altering my identity more than once, following the tide of battle and visiting the dying fields after darkness fell. Not once during those years was I forced to hunt my prey; I merely harvested what had already fallen from the vine.

Despite the easy existence I enjoyed in the wild, I grew tired of the countryside and took myself to Pesht or Giurgui or Genoa to sample the new luxuries that mortals contrive to distract them from their perpetual fear of death, and it was in the last of these that I heard of Bogdan's assassination. Steven was reportedly in hiding, but there was no word of Vlad, although I had no fear that he would have perished defending his patron. There was room in his mind for only one loyalty, and he would have declined to involve himself in merely mortal affairs so that he could continue to wait in my service. If I ever asked Vlad about that time, I have forgotten it, but when I finally discovered his whereabouts, even I was caught by surprise, and his resourcefulness pleased me.

I hear Lucy's voice approaching. She has asked me to help her choose her wedding gown and I could find no plausible way to decline the honor.

The Journal of Vlad Tepes

August 12

The past is very much with me of late, and my thoughts do not always seem entirely my own. Ever since reaching this tepid shore, I have had a growing sense of another presence scratching at the corners of my mind. It is she, of course. Our old affinity has dulled over the years and I cannot read her thoughts, and hope that my own are opaque to her as well, but the link is still there in some form. I am a part of her as she is a part of me, and we are drawn to the same memories, our past together, the days of my bondage to her will, and my reawakening to myself.

I am not entirely free of her even now that I am intent upon her destruction. The deep need to serve her which she planted in my heart and soul so many years ago has burned down to an ember, but the ember will not extinguish and perhaps will continue to glow for as long as I walk the Earth. It will not divert me from the course I have chosen to follow, but it may deny me any satisfaction from the deed.

When she abandoned me, or so I believed, in the palace at Suceava, I thought that I would die of grief. Steven believed me distraught at the loss of my birthright and pressed me to enter into a sacred vow that we would aid one another at the first opportunity if either of us were to ascend to a position of authority, but I insisted that it be a vow of shed blood rather than one sworn on the reliquary as he proposed, for by then the touch of any such holy object held by a true believer had become acutely painful. She had left me alive to suit her own purposes, but her taint was already in my blood. I shunned the day whenever possible, disturbed the workers in Bogdan's kitchens by demanding that my meat still bleed when it was served me, and I no longer attended religious services, claiming to prefer a quieter communion. Bogdan was troubled by this last, but Steven convinced him that it was a transient willfulness of which I would eventually repent.

Although Steven still called himself my friend, he had become like all the others around me, shadows and puppets, things of no concern or toys to be manipulated for my amusement or benefit. I took to hunting, alone when possible so that I could devour unobserved that part of my prey which satisfied my secret hunger. At night, I took myself to the battlements, for I no longer needed more than a short period of sleep, yet never felt weary. The soldiers shunned me more than ever, some of them openly frightened when I appeared. I learned to merge with the shadows and walk unseen among them, listening to their trivial conversations and petty complaints. Bogdan was a fair enough ruler for that time, but he was subject to fits of temper, and lacked sufficient intelligence to perceive let alone cope with the intrigues and treacheries that swirled around him.

I learned of the plot against my patron several nights before the blow fell and might have warned him, but I had already decided that I could reap no further benefit where I was. It was time to abandon Suceava and promote my fortunes elsewhere. They came for him in the darkness, and his own soldiers opened the gates and absented themselves for those necessary few moments. Bogdan perished, quite horribly in fact, at the hands of his enemies. Steven was spared, which would advance my cause later, but I had no reason to suspect that at the time and did not raise my hand to help him. Nothing was important except service to she whom I served even in absentia.

I slipped out of the castle that very night and never looked back. My destination was clear. Hunyadi had murdered my father and brother, and my earlier self would have been appalled at my decision to ally myself with him, but it was new kind of blood tie that commanded me now. I traveled incognito, posing as a gypsy tinker after murdering a lone traveler and confiscating his property. It took weeks to reach Transylvania. I was unused to traveling alone and took the wrong track more than once, and I was thoughtless about the horse that pulled my cart until it collapsed one day and nearly died. I almost slaughtered it as it lay there and might have done so, slaking my bloodlust at the poor animal's expense, but another party of travelers came by and offered their assistance, which I accepted with as much grace as I could muster.

More cautiously, I continued my journey and finally reached my destination. I was reluctant to announce myself, for Hunyadi had no reason to love my family and good reason to fear my intentions. Although I had considered the matter at considerable length during my travels, no good solution had suggested itself, and I wasted several days mending weapons and household items before impatience led me to the solution.

Some cautious inquiries told me which room in the keep was Hunyadi's sleeping chamber. I waited until much of the night was past before climbing over the outer wall and slipping through an open window to enter. There were guards about, but those who weren't sleeping were almost equally unobservant. Three played dice in a filthy hallway and another was trysting with a scullery maid on the great table in the dining hall.

With the shadows wrapped around me, I moved from room to room without raising the alarm, although truthfully I could have walked the same path openly with similar results. The door to his chamber was closed but not secured, and I opened it stealthily, stealing inside. A candle was guttering in one corner of the room, but by its fading, flickering light I could see that my quarry was not alone, and that he was awake and aware of my presence. He could not have recognized me, for we had met only once and very briefly several years earlier, but even a dull witted man knows to take alarm when his bedchamber is invaded.

He reared up in bed and lunged for the sword that hung from the wall. His companion, a wisp of a girl, tumbled back in my direction. I caught her by the hair and pulled her from the bed, then threw her against the wall with such force that she fell silently and never moved again. My feet left the floor as I leaped forward, crashing down onto his legs and pinning him in place, his questing hand just short of his sword hilt. My own dagger was at his throat and he wisely ceased struggling and settled back, watching me with eyes that moved quickly and constantly, searching for advantage.

"Who are you and what do you want?"

His eyes changed when I told him my name, and for the first time I saw a man accept his death. But I surprised him when I answered the second half of his question.

"What I want is to bury the past and see to my own future." I withdrew the dagger from his throat, but I didn't return it to my belt, not just yet. I wanted his undivided attention for a while longer. "You know that I have just cause to kill you where you lie."

He nodded, but remained silent.

"And you know that I could do so this in an instant, leave the same way I entered, and no one would know the name of your killer or the reason for your death."

He nodded again.

I waited a few seconds until I was sure that he had considered the implications, then reversed the dagger in my hand and handed it to him, hilt first. "Take this then as proof that I harbor no ill feelings toward you and wish only to end the conflict between our two families. Then perhaps we may strike a bargain to our mutual advantage."

It may sound foolish for me to have taken such a chance, but it was not so. I could have taken the dagger from him again without risk at any time. The greater danger was that he might call out for assistance. Hunyadi accepted the dagger silently, and we faced each other for an uncertain time, each of us caught up by our separate thoughts. I began to fear that my gambit had failed, but at last his eyes softened, his lips moved in what was just the faintest suggestion of a smile, and his hand fell to his side, although he did not relinquish his grip on my dagger.

"You're a bolder man than your father was." He paused. "And a wiser one as well." And I knew that I had won.

Enheduanna's Secret Journal

August 13

He dares! I should have expected as much, but it still comes as a shock. Vlad has come to Hillingham, fluttering around the windows of our bedroom in the shape of a bat. Almost I struck then, throwing open the sash to confront him, but caution prevented me from doing so. Why would he be so bold unless he had reason to believe himself safe from me? I must give this some thought before I act too precipitously.

Lucy seemed to sense his presence even before I, which is equally distressing. As I feared, he has learned to mask himself from me, at least to a degree. Lucy had been restless in bed, so much so that I sent her back to her own, but I could tell by the sound of her breathing and heartbeat that she did not truly sleep even then. I dismissed my own uneasiness at first, but then Lucy was up, crossing to the window, and it was as though a thousand trumpets were suddenly sounding in my head.

"Get away from there!" I commanded with both voice and mind.

"But Mina, it's so hot and stuffy in here. Surely the night breeze..."

"Get back to your bed!" She obeyed this time, eyes glazing as the glamour took effect, and it was I who swept aside the curtain and stared out into the darkness with eyes that saw what would be invisible to mere humans. Even in his altered shape I recognized him, for those of our kind can always see a shadow of the true face lying behind the illusion. He hovered just out of reach, unable to enter Hillingham without invitation, a proscription that strikes all of my get, although I have never been thus hindered, perhaps because I alone of my kind have never passed from life to death. It is one of the mysteries I have never solved.

This was a direct challenge, designed to provoke me to hasty action. There was a time when I might have responded immediately, blind rage driving me to destroy my enemy, confident that my power was so much greater than theirs that the outcome was beyond doubt. I was older now, and wiser, and I know that Vlad is the greatest enemy I have ever faced; it will take more than simple provocation to push me onto an unwise path. And unwise it would have been. Weakened though he must be after the voyage from Varna, Vlad's power is a force to be reckoned with; he has found his own path to knowledge since last we met, and may have traveled roads I have overlooked. Perhaps I have underestimated the magnitude of the game we play. He is not some churlish innocent to quail at the first application of the glamour; rather, unlike any other creature who has ever walked the Earth, Vlad has achieved a degree of self mastery that rivals my own. For the first time in centuries I felt the prickle of an old, unpleasant emotion. I felt fear. It was so unexpected that the shock of it, paradoxically, restored my calm.

The confrontation lasted only a few seconds before he flew off, back toward Carfax Abbey, having accomplished little of substance for his effort. King's gambit rebuffed. I was shaken by the encounter, however, and it was some time before I could think clearly. His insolence in the past had alternately amused and frustrated me, but it has become something I can no longer tolerate. I will feel no further regret about what must come.

August 14

I heard no more certain news of Vlad for some time after Bogdan's death, although a Turkish officer told me that he was rumored to have joined Hunyadi, a report which was later confirmed by several prisoners. His exact location was unknown and I was in no position at the time to inquire further. In a careless moment, I had been surprised by a party of cavalry while supping on one of their fallen comrades. I had escaped easily but their persistent searching during the days that followed convinced me that it was time to leave the battlefields for a while. I went to Constantinople, originally only as an intermediate point, but the chaos in the city in the months preceding its eventual surrender to the Turks was ideal for my purposes. Refugees swelled the streets and the city officials were overwhelmed. Parties became separated and could not find one another, and I had no difficulty picking off the occasional stray, usually children, whenever the need arose. The bodies could be tossed into one or another of the open communal graves with impunity.

I suborned one of the city's wealthier citizens, an elderly Greek widower named Theides who was easily manipulated and by nature reclusive. I promised him immortality in return for his loyalty, and he obediently dismissed most of his servants. The glamour was available to me by then, but it was a weak, uncertain power still and I dared not rely on its effect in my absence. He introduced me to Emperor Palaeologus on one occasion, whom I at first thought might be an even more useful tool, but the Emperor's life was too public for such secrets as I kept.

Word arrived reconfirming the earlier rumor about Vlad and fixing his location. His apparent reconciliation with Hunyadi favorably impressed me, because it proved that he had retained his wits at the very least. I thought about visiting Transylvania to see for myself what had become of the slender youth I had known before, but then I heard that he had departed from Sighisoara without naming his destination, and it was in any case such a comfortable existence in Constantinople that I was loathe to interrupt it. I had plenty of time, after all, to satisfy my curiosity about him.

I tarried too long in Constantinople, as it turned out. The inevitable fall of the city had been obvious to those willing to face the truth, but much of the population mistakenly believed that the city was impregnable even when the Turkish troops were running through the streets and burning the outlying buildings. The ensuing chaos might have seemed ideal for me but eventually the random killing became so widespread, the violence so all encompassing, that I was twice accosted in a single evening. A horseman nearly decapitated me with his sword, from which wound not even I could recover, and a short time later I was stabbed in the back by a looter while I crouched over a dying woman, preparing to slake my thirst. The wound was painful if not serious, and I forced the man to consume his own manhood before tearing out his throat.

Once the rush of rage had passed, I recognized my continuing peril, however, and made haste to abandon the city, leaving behind a handful of possessions I had hoped to take with me. I destroyed Theides as a precaution, even though I had not turned him, then stole out of the city under cover of darkness. I was uncertain of the Turkish troop emplacements, but turned eastward, thinking that Trebizond would perhaps be far enough from the battle lines to provide a safe haven.

It had now been five years since Vlad had been bonded to my service. Never before had I allowed one under my influence to remain independent for so long. Most I destroyed when their usefulness was exhausted, a few I brought across into a new existence. The latter could not be relied upon too readily. A few were driven mad and had to be destroyed immediately, others retained enough of their wits to function at my direction, though even these could be trusted only for so long as they remained subservient. Sooner or later, they all began to chafe under my hand and sooner or later I was forced to destroy them all before they could challenge me openly.

All except Vlad. Vlad was my weakness. He appealed to

whatever vestigial humanity I retain. I wished to see the man that might emerge from the boy I knew, and so I put off the day of reckoning three times, once when I allowed him to pursue his destiny in the Balkans, once when I knew that he had turned against me, and at last when he sought to destroy me in Trieste.

But I shall not spare him again.

August 15

I am careful not to drink too deeply from Lucy's veins, and I have let her taste my own blood. She is thereby fated to join my get unless I choose to release her, but for the moment it is better that she not attract unwelcome attention. She complains that brightness hurts her eyes and shuns the direct sunlight, which provides a welcome excuse for my own preferences in the matter. Her flesh has lost some color as well, but this attracts little attention and is even looked upon favorably by some. Arthur is still detained at home by Lord Godalming's illness and Mrs. Westenra's health has also taken a decided turn for the worse. The doctor has instructed her to remain in bed and drink spiced tea hourly.

I am of two minds today. I must take no chances, but rather find means to strengthen my position. That requires time and opportunity. I will feed without any unnecessary restraint until my power is at its peak, a task I cannot readily accomplish in Whitby. A large number of disappearances or unexplained deaths in such a circumscribed area would have repercussions that must be at least awkward. Vlad will be even more greatly discommoded, particularly if he still persists in his childish disinclination to take human prey. I must find an excuse to remove myself from Whitby for a time. This requires thought.

The Journal of Vlad Tepes

August 18

Now that I have started this account, I feel compelled to complete it. Some record should exist to explain my past, and my present actions. It is not meant to be a justification of what I have done and I doubt such could be accomplished no matter how skillfully I turned the phrases. During those years in which I was in thrall to my mistress, I remained alive and human, and the capacity for the terrible acts which I committed must have resided within me before I ever met her. She shares my guilt, for she gave those dark parts of my soul free reign, but the fault is primarily my own. I was weak when I should have been strong, cruel when I should have been compassionate, deceitful when I should have been honest, and pliable when I should have been intransigent. I went to her willingly on the battlements that first night. She had no need to use the glamour on me. And for that I am eternally shamed.

I detested Hunyadi, but I was careful to conceal it from him and although he might have suspected my insincerity from time to time, it was not due to any disloyal act on my part. I played the faithful servant, flattered him but not to excess, and most of all I learned. He taught me military tactics, with particular emphasis on fighting against the Turk, who has his own peculiar weaknesses in battle. He also taught me the finer points of court politics, although there I was a less cooperative student. The constant dance of state, the petty intrigues, the application of a hint of pressure here, a tease of concession there, confounded and irritated me then as it does to this day.

"Politics is just another field of battle," he told me. "You must lure your opponent out, lull him into lowering his defenses, strike only when the battle is already yours. The weapons may be different but the objectives are much the same."

I saw the tactical value, but lacked the patience to put what I learned into practice. "The most important facet of strength is strength itself," I argued. "Crush your enemy with overwhelming force. Refuse to parley unless it is to accept surrender. If your enemy fears you, he will respect you." Hunyadi would just shake his head, chuckle, and insist that I was too young to understand.

Years had come and gone since I had last seen my dark mistress. I was a grown man now, despite Hunyadi's jest, not the uncertain and angry young stripling she had known. But my determination to serve her had not diminished in the slightest, and my impatience to do so, to become worthy of her company, made me restless and ill at ease. I lived now in Sibiu, near the border of Wallachia, which I intended would someday be mine to rule as my father had ruled it. Then, surely, I would have proven my worth.

Hunyadi had set me over Fagaras and Almas, but they were a poor substitute for the homeland to which I was, by right of birth, the presumptive heir.

Three years after the fall of Constantinople, I was finally given permission to act. Hunyadi was off to Belgrade with the bulk of our army, but I still commanded enough to grapple with the Danesti forces, many of whom had been drawn off to participate in the battle for Hungary. We fell upon them quickly, catching them largely by surprise. They were mostly peasants and the landless, impressed to fill the ranks left vacant by the seasoned warriors who had marched to Belgrade, and we slaughtered them almost at will whenever we encountered them. Word came that my patron, Hunyadi, had succumbed to illness rather than the sword of his enemies, but I would not have had time to mourn him even had I been so inclined. Wallachia was mine, and it was time for a reckoning with those who had cast their lot with the usurper. The roads and fields bore new crops, human figures impaled on sharpened posts, a fate which seemed to me the most horrid of all possible. It was inspired by the deaths of those many small birds I had once owned while languishing in a velvet lined prison. They had unjustly named me the impaler then but now I earned that title with bloody deeds of my own.

My cousin Steven was enjoying similar success against his father's old enemies and a fresh crop of new ones he had made for himself, and he was acknowledged as the ruler of Moldavia only a few months after I reclaimed Wallachia. We were both thereby freed from our old vow of mutual support, a vow which I would only have honored if I had believed it served her purposes. In such ways did she unman me, or perhaps I should say that in such ways did I allow her to steal away the last vestiges of my honor, such as it may have been.

With my position restored, I set about applying the principles that I had learned from Hunyadi and, in some cases, despite him. How much of what followed was a part of my character all along I will never know, nor does it matter at this late date. I ruled through fear and terror just as Enheduanna ruled my heart through fear and terror. Yes, I feared her. I fear her even now. But in those early days it was entwined inextricably with what I convinced myself was love, and I thought that through some contagion of magic the people might come to love me even as they feared me. Just as my love evolved to hatred and then determination to rid the world of a terrible scourge, so eventually did theirs. But I am ahead of myself.

For four years, I held Wallachia in my fist, an island of stability in a world that was increasingly torn between the Turks and Christendom. Ostensibly I served the latter, but I slaughtered the enemy not through love of Christ but for love of the butchery itself. The images of shafts of wood penetrating mortal flesh that haunted my dreams became reality as I sacrificed the enemy, along with a good number of my countrymen. Each spasm of violence whetted my appetite for more and I began to look for excuses to exact reprisals against my own people, and eventually continued even without the formality of an excuse.

During the fourth year of my reign, I received a message from her.

Enheduanna's Secret Diary

August 19

Jonathan, my Jonathan, it was a stroke of genius, or perhaps just luck, when I chose you. As they have done countless times in the past, my instincts have anticipated my needs. I have had a letter from the continent today, from Jonathan, though by another hand. Vlad's squeamishness allowed him to survive, although by report his mind is sorely troubled and his body weakened to the brink of death.

I have announced my intention of going to him, to help nurse him back to health sufficient to allow his return to England. In the remote countryside where he has taken shelter, I should certainly find ample prey to suit me and we will be gone from there by the time any general alarm may arise.

And there is another purpose to my journey as well. Lucy is faltering more quickly than I had expected, betraying an inner weakness that I should perhaps have recognized but did not. There is no turning back for her now even were I to allow it, and I would not be surprised if she perished even without my further involvement. Mrs. Westenra is also failing and is not expected to last out the summer. I fear that the usefulness of this family has been exhausted, and I confess that I will not be sorry to seek other company. Lucy's vapid nature offends my sensibilities even when it suits my purposes, and her mother's strong will requires constant attention to prevent her from seeing the truth.

While Lucy's imminent death is not in itself a matter of serious consequence, it does cause me some inconvenience as her departure will deprive me of an excuse to remain at Whitby. Even should my fiancé choose to recover here rather than in London, it would be inappropriate for a single woman in this culture to remain nearby unchaperoned. I have therefore decided that Jonathan and I shall become husband and wife while still on the continent and return to London as soon as he is physically able. I have certain business to conclude there, and Whitby is not so distant that I cannot of a night travel clandestinely to obtain certain intelligence of Vlad's activities. In due course, we may openly return, as I think it will disquiet Vlad sorely to discover that Jonathan has escaped from whatever imprisonment was fashioned for him. He was always proud of his ability to foresee future problems and set plans against them, and he was cast down and critical of himself whenever his careful plotting failed. Every doubt I can cast upon Vlad's sense of his own mastery will serve as a silent ally in the struggle to come.

Tonight I took another precaution. It is necessary that a pair of loyal eyes remain alert to Vlad's endeavors, even should Lucy perish. To this end I have exerted influence over one of Dr. Seward's patients, a wretch named Renfield, through whose infirmity I hope to remain cognizant of what transpires here even if Lucy should expire prematurely. He is a brilliant madman whose mania is ideal for my purposes, and I have promised him much in return for his service. My grip will be uncertain at so great a distance as I dare not taste his blood prematurely. Vlad would surely feel my influence in the madman and that would destroy his effectiveness. Renfield's grasp of reality is frail in any case, and I am minded not to impair his intelligence by further dividing his loyalties. He will require all his wits and energy to escape the asylum with the regularity required, and to return unobserved.

I dare not trust him entirely. The twisted minds of the insane are difficult to hold to a straight course. In the throes of a brain fever, he might reveal evidence of my interference. Seward would not likely lend any credence to such ramblings now, but as events unfold he may become credulous enough to admit possibilities to which his mind is currently closed. I have therefore concealed my true identity from Renfield, speaking to him from the shadows, my voice altered to the low tones of a man by means of the glamour. If he should choose to spill his soul, he will unwittingly perjure himself in so doing.

These precautions seem adequate to the circumstances, but I find my thoughts straying to Carfax Abbey even so.

The Journal of Vlad Tepes

August 20

I broke off writing this account because I knew that what I must set down next is in all likelihood the greatest of all my sins. No, that is not true. It was the sin I committed on the largest scale. During the time when my heart beat and I breathed the air as a mortal man, I was responsible for many deaths. Countless thousands. Death and cruelty were my constant companions. But during the fourth year of my reign, I surpassed myself.

It all started when a party of my soldiers returned to the castle with a prisoner who claimed to be bearing a message for me. I had not heard from Steven in some time but he would have sent a more formal delegation, so I was prepared to dismiss the man unheard until I was told that he had insisted the message had been entrusted to him by a "great lady".

I scarce allowed myself to hope, but I had him brought before me. He had committed the message to memory, he insisted, and was under strict instructions that it was for my own ears and none other. The man was small of stature and had been disarmed and I felt no fear for my person, so I sent my courtiers and guards away, then ordered the man to speak.

"The lady told me to say the following to you, Prince of Wallachia, and to bear back to her your reply, if any." He then recited words that would have meant little to anyone who might have listened in, but which held great import for me. "The days since we met beneath the storm have been long, but they near their end at last. I will be with you before the summer has flown to see what you have made of yourself. All that we have been to one another before is as nothing compared to what we shall be when reunited."

I cannot adequately describe my reaction. In her presence, I had experienced a form of ecstasy which is beyond anything human, though it was mixed with a terrible dread. I shivered at even the pale echo of that sensation which thrilled my body when I heard those simple words. Elation and the deepest anguish were intertwined beyond my ability to distinguish one from the other. My emotions may have been uncertain, but my response was assured.

"Return to your mistress and say that her servant waits to be commanded. All that I have shall be hers, and more if she should so wish it." I summoned my guards and instructed them to feed the messenger and provide him shelter for the night, and to escort him on his way on the morrow with a purse of gold coins to speed him on his way.

I have never slept easy and that night I rested not at all. When I could no longer stand to pace up and down in my chambers, I climbed to the highest point in the castle and stared out toward the east, knowing instinctively, or at least believing so, that she was somewhere in that direction. I stood for hours, as if I could somehow see her spark no matter how distant if I was only patient enough. It must have rained sometime during the darkness, because I was soaked to the skin when I descended in the morning, but I never noticed it, and my servants were too used to my idiosyncrasies to make any comment.

The next several days were an agony of anticipation. I alternated between moments when my frustration goaded me to one cruelty after another, and others when the thought of seeing her again produced such joy that I ordered the dungeons emptied and gold coins strewn through the neighboring villages. As the days fell before the scythe of time, I became anxious. Would I prove worthy of her? Would she be disappointed in what I, her servant, had made of my life? Was there some preparation I should make prior to her arrival? She would not want a great fanfare, preferring to remain in the shadows, but would I fail some arcane test if I was unable to anticipate her desires?

Less than ten days remained before the end of the summer when stories reached me of a witch burned in Sibiu. It was said that the witch coveted the souls of young children whom she stole from among the peasants and sacrificed to some malevolent god. She was run to ground by an angry mob and stoned mercilessly, her broken body then thrown on a pile of rubbish and burned beyond recognition. I knew that Sibiu was on the road she was likely to follow and I felt a terrible sense of loss that quickly gave way to an anger beyond anything I had previously experienced. I ordered my army to assemble and marched against Sibiu, and though there was uneasiness among my soldiers when they were ordered to deal with the residents there even more harshly than the rough justice we had meted out to the Turks, I told my generals that there was a pervasive, evil heresy in the city that had to be rooted out. They believed me, or at least pretended so, and the slaughter commenced.

We killed thousands of them and I might have ordered my men to continue until the entire population had perished if she had not come to me in the inn where I slept, slipping past my guards and entering to find me sitting on my bed, unable to sleep. It was not she who had perished, but some other poor wretch of a woman. Even then I should have realized that. When she dies, I will know it instantly, and would have known it then. The supposed witch was one of her making though, a woman who had accompanied her on her travels as maidservant and whom she had brought completely over.

"I sent her to hunt for me but she was rash and took a child from a watchful mother."

I remember little of that night. We left the inn, of that much I am certain. We passed through the forest under a sky filled with stars. She expressed surprise at my ferocity, but no displeasure, although she chided me for wasting so much blood. Enheduanna could be cruel at times, but she felt none of my heat. She killed from necessity rather than pleasure, without remorse but also without deriving any satisfaction from the act itself. My excesses were tolerated among men, she told me, but once I became a monster like herself, I would need to be more circumspect, if not more merciful.

"Those who slaughter each other by the tens of thousands in a single battle would recoil in horror to learn that I take a few score each year."

Although I commanded twenty thousand men I was totally powerless in her presence. I did as she bade, felt shame when she chided me, and great pleasure when she expressed her satisfaction in my accomplishments. I would have died for her without hesitation, and killed for her with zest. It shames me now, even knowing that her hold on me could not be resisted, no matter how noble my soul.

Enheduanna's Secret Journal

August 20

I have long given over wondering through what agency I received the gift of eternity. Even as a child playing in my father's tent, I knew that I was not like the others my age, and as the days passed, I watched with some early alarm certain changes that transformed the bodies of my playmates but which never touched my own. If there was some event or charm that affected me, it happened while I was too young to recognize it, but I doubt that this was the case. I was ever separate from them, even my own brothers and sisters who avoided my company and rarely attempted to torment me as they did each other. Even my mother shunned my company and commanded her attendants to watch over me, which they did reluctantly and carelessly. Toward the end of her life, she pronounced me cursed and would not tolerate my company at all. Only my father continued his devotion to me, valuing me as if I had been one of his sons.

He told me once that he approved that I did not laugh. I felt amusement at times, but it would be years after he died before I learned to mimic my fellows and pretend to a feckless abandonment of composure. Neither do I weep except by artifice, nor dream. That last is my one sometimes regret, for through that device these mortals who surround me seem able to escape into a world I can never touch. My sleep is an instant cessation, as abrupt and distinct as the blow of an axe. My body tires but my mind remains lucid until the instant in which I surrender consciousness, and it is restored to me in the same condition when I waken. It is a minor regret, and I sometimes wonder what images would fill my head if I did in fact dream. Tonight, I believe I would recall pleasanter times, when Vlad was at my side, my devoted slave.

It undoubtedly pains him to remember how he waited upon me so diligently when I joined him in Wallachia. With some the passage of time loosens the bond of blood, but with others it burns brighter with each passing day. When I came to him in Sibiu, he was delirious with joy, offered himself to me so completely that I might have surrendered to impulse and brought him across that very night. His soldiers had left so many pouring out their life's blood in the streets and shops and homes of that city that I was well fed and he was of more use to me then as he was than as he would later be.

His castle was not as grand as I had anticipated. I had visited once during the early years of his father's reign and had thought it a finer place. My sojourn in Constantinople no doubt colored my view of it now, but there was evidence as well of a growing decay. Those in thrall to me evince little concern for their own condition, and years of turmoil and neglect had taken their toll. Several rooms were closed and unused, the staff was poorly trained and surly, and the general condition of the furnishings appalling. I expressed my displeasure and Vlad hastened to correct matters, impressing the population of an entire village into service cleaning, refurbishing, and repairing. They worked through the night so assiduously that I doubt any but myself was able to sleep through the sounds of their industry, and within two days I was willing to pronounce the results satisfactory. Vlad would have dismissed the small army of laborers immediately and without a word of thanks, but I suggested that he reward them with a feast, which was presently done. A lesson I learned at my father's knee was to rule through fear and respect, but never to make an unnecessary enemy.

I kept my own chamber, insisting that we maintain the illusion of propriety, promising to come to Vlad after the castle fell silent at night. He was, after all, married, a bondage imposed upon him by court politics and public expectation. His wife rarely left that portion of the keep set aside for her use and I was barely aware of her presence. If I ever learned her name, I have long since forgotten it. I kept that promised assignation from time to time, but more often I used the glamour – which I was finally beginning to master – to lay the illusion of my presence in his thoughts. I had not yet learned the damage that often results from repeated tampering with mortal memories, but luckily Vlad was of strong mind and displayed none of the troubled doubts and confusion which affects those with weaker wills.

I hunted discretely during my stay, ranging far outside the castle walls. Sometimes I found a shepherd nodding over his flock, sometimes I stole through a window and took a child. I was circumspect and varied my hunting ground, but inevitably stories began to circulate, and once I was espied from a distance because rumors of a dark lady prowling the forest reached my ears. I knew then that it was time to move on. There was no immediate danger, but I have never felt dishonor in being overly cautious. Having made my decision, I considered bringing Vlad across the divide between us so that he could continue to serve me, but upon consideration I decided that he might best fill my needs as he was, preserving a safe haven should I need one. Had I known how soon he would be ousted from his position, and for how long he would be beyond my reach, I might have chosen otherwise, but at the time his forces seemed likely to hold against the Turks.

That last night I took just enough from Vlad to strengthen our bond since I had earlier happened upon a party of refugees passing not far from the keep. A young girl of their party was sent to gather fallen wood for a fire, and it was she who fell instead. After disguising the kill so that it would appear the work of Turkish marauders, I returned for one last tryst before leaving for the west. Vlad must have sensed something of my intentions; the link between us was strong even then. He clutched me more tightly than was his wont and implored me to remain with him forever. I responded that we would be ever together even when we were apart, and he saw through my duplicity and threatened to destroy himself if I should ever leave.

"You shall not!" I answered with both my voice and the glamour. "You will hold yourself in readiness for my return. You may be master of your people but you will never master me!"

Chastened, he abased himself and continued to insist upon his loyalty until I tired of his craven behavior and cast him into the uneasy rest that passed with him for sleep. I left the castle moments later, expecting to return when it suited me, but never imagining that such a great time would pass before that event came to pass. Vlad was always confident of his ability to hold back the Turk, but within the year they were moving freely in the forests within sight of the guards on the battlements and many of the lower passes were completely within their grasp.

Vlad was driven into exile, threw himself upon the mercies of Mathias, a self righteous monster whom I had met while his father still lived and from whom I felt an instinctive and violent animosity so intense that I wondered if in some fashion he suspected something of my true nature. I did not flee from his presence in panic, but I removed myself at the first opportunity. Had I known what he intended, I might have warned Vlad not to seek succor there, but when word reached me, it was already done and Vlad was banished to the dungeon, a ruder imprisonment than that of his youth. The survivors of Sibiu had their revenge after all, though they undoubtedly hoped for more.

And there he remained for twelve long years. More than once I thought I might fly to his aid, but I had grown fond of my luxuries and preferred travel in a fine coach to my earlier furtive journeys. Mathias would not have welcomed me no matter how fine my appearance, and the constant ebb and flow of the conflict with the Turk added further difficulties. Nor does time mean as much to me as it does for mortals. Twelve years was but a blink of the eye to me while to Vlad, languishing in his cell, it must have felt like a succession of eternities.

Enough of this for now. I must be off.

The Journal of Vlad Tepes

August 21

I have issued my challenge. This elaborate dance of move and countermove suits me not at all. I am stronger now than I was before and whether my fate is to succeed or fail seems almost irrelevant now. I was ever one for the direct approach, and that has not changed with the passage of years any more than it did with the passage of my humanity. But Enheduanna is a spider who weaves intricate webs wherever she goes, and if I am to defeat her, I must keep my wits about me.

Last night I ventured out into the country and felled an ox, which has helped restore me to nearly full vigor. I dismembered the body and tore it open as wild dogs might have done, and in that form allowed myself to be seen on two occasions so that a false trail would be laid.

Otherwise things proceed as well as could be expected. The fifty remaining boxes of earth have been retrieved from the *Demeter* at my direction and delivered to Carfax in preparation for their dispersion according to my plan. The damaged one I shall send to be repaired.

Enheduanna is rumored to have departed from Whitby yesterday evening. I cannot believe that she would so readily abandon the field of battle, and tonight's discovery confirms my skepticism. It was just midnight when I sensed the presence of another intelligence nearby, and came upon an escaped madman lurking in the abbey grounds. His mind is quick but pliable and it was a simple matter to intrude there and discover his purpose.

For this first time, she has underestimated me, or else she plays a subtler game, one far beyond my grasp. This poor soul has been set as my watchdog, though his mind is fractured and unreliable. At first I thought another force had joined the fray, as the image I found in those convoluted recesses was like unto myself rather than her human form, but her touch was unmistakable despite the rudely constructed mask with which she concealed herself from Renfield. This worked to my advantage, however, as it required only the slightest of efforts to superimpose myself upon the image. He now believes himself my guardian and will be easy to manipulate so that he observes and passes on only that which I care to have known.

August 24

This enforced idleness does not sit well with me. It reminds me of an even less pleasant time, a time when my past sins caught up with me and I suffered a punishment even worse than the one wished upon me by my enemies, for they had no way of knowing how strongly I was bonded to another, and the agonies I experienced in her absence.

Enheduanna had left without explanation, but I was not completely ignorant of her intentions. The insubstantial ties that bound us one to the other held me subject to her will but they also gave me insight into her mood. Foolishly I hoped to sway her by demonstrating even greater devotion. I wrapped her in my arms and held her against my chest, feeling the way her heart beat ever so slowly, one beat to every score of mine, which now beats not at all. I relished the feel of her cool flesh against me, the way her long hair swept across my skin almost as though it had a life of its own. I had always favored buxom lasses until I met her, but now her slender, boyish form seemed to be the ultimate in female beauty. I would have measured every other woman I met against her if there had been any room in my mind or heart to even consider them.

Although I guessed her intentions, when I woke that morning and found her gone, I raged through the castle as I had never done before. I am shamed by my memories of that day and those that immediately followed. I slew many for no good reason, and drove my servants and attendants from the castle so that I could walk its too empty corridors alone, tolerating their return only after days had passed. The pale wraith who called herself my wife locked herself in her chamber, wise enough to avoid me, although her forbearance was not enough to save her at the last.

During the following weeks, I was a wreck of a man, alternating between deep depressions and senseless rages. I neglected to supervise the patrols and many of my best men left in search of more amenable masters. When word came that the Turks had grown bold and were massing a force with which to overwhelm those who remained, I ignored the threat until it was too late, and finally was forced to flee in ignominy. My wife became hysterical, berated me for my thoughtlessness, beat upon my chest with her fists and named me less than a man. In a fury, I raised her up in my arms, climbed to the parapet and sent her plummeting to her death. Perhaps I performed a small mercy in doing so. I left within the hour, taking only a small party of retainers in my train. Mathias and I had never been friends, but neither were we enemies, and my reconciliation with his father had not seemed to displease him, so I hastened to his keep to request asylum.

Alas, justice dealt harshly with me. Certain letters had come into his possession, forged I am sure by those who hated me because of the terrible misplaced vengeance I had leveled against Sibiu. I cannot blame those long dead plotters now, but when Mathias confronted me with them, I shouted at him with such ferocity that he might well have thought me mad. And mad I was. Madness consumed me, her madness, a foul taint within my blood that clouded my judgment and walled off my soul. I think perhaps I offered violence to my host, because I was overwhelmed forcefully and carried off to his dungeons, where I spent the first few days very near a death that would have been a merciful release. Had I not been made one of her thralls, my livelihood strengthened by her corrupt vitality, I should probably have perished there and then, but I recovered, albeit slowly. At length I became uncharacteristically circumspect and cooperative, believing that my incarceration was only a temporary expedient, but when day after endless day passed with no change in my situation, no visit or even a message from my jailer, I became restive again, angrily belaboring anyone who ventured within sound of my voice, but secretly grieving for my lost love.

The days were like years, the weeks like eternities, the years, well, the years passed inevitably. My situation improved, but only because I debased myself even further than I had already. Mathias had a sister, Esther, who suffered a cleft lip and a lazy eye. Her existence was barely acknowledged by her brother, who kept her in pampered seclusion within the castle, whose secrets she came to know better than even her lord. She wandered through underground passages known only to her, one of which led to the Tower which had become my new home. The first time she came to my cell, I drove her off with curses and threats, and for some time after that I merely ignored her, too caught up with my own problems to trouble myself with someone who could be of no apparent use to me or my cause. Sometimes she spoke to me, tentatively at first, then with more confidence. I think she might have been somewhat simple in her mind, but she had a sweet, transparent nature, and I decided to make her my tool on the chance that someday she might prove useful.

And so it was that I pretended to warm to her, replying occasionally when she asked a question, with gentle encouragements when I recognized that she was responding. I had long since lost track of the passage of time, but it must have been in the fourth or fifth year of my incarceration that I began to woo her, gently, carefully, for she was fragile of spirit. She did not visit me frequently, perhaps once a fortnight, and sometimes she stayed for only a moment, although at other times she sat in the murky darkness for what must have been hours. Sometimes as well she brought me parcels of food, after which I would thank her profusely and praise her character and courage, even though food had lost all taste for me and I discerned no difference between the finest delicacy and the stale bread and gritty gruel that was my standard fare.

She would not come within arm's length for a very long time, but I forced myself to modulate my voice and suppressed my anger and grief when she was present, complimenting her in subtle ways because she was too crafty to believe me if I had pronounced her beautiful. I spoke of her bravery and the purity of her spirit, seducing her with modest speech and subtle hints until she came to trust me. At first she stood at the far wall opposite my cell, then relaxed enough to bring a rude stool with her and sit just beyond my reach. It required years to entice her closer and by then, unknown to me although it worked to my advantage, she had already begun to speak to her brother, Mathias, imploring him to ameliorate some of the more onerous aspects of my imprisonment. I was allowed more time outside my cell, although closely supervised, the quality of my food improved, and the guards began to treat me with as much respect as was possible under the circumstances.

I had not seen Mathias for so long that I did not at first recognize him that first day he came to see me. By then I had been moved to a larger cell, though I was still confined to the Tower, and my furniture was somewhat less crude though far from luxurious. He did not enter, and at first did not speak, and I saw nothing to be gained from initiating a conversation. It was his voice that identified him and I stood up slowly, even gave him a slight bow, measuring my response carefully. It would not do to grovel, nor to be excessively brazen. I decided to maintain my dignity but to show no disrespect, and allowed him to set the tone. He inquired about my health, which was of course quite excellent. I have not suffered from even the slightest illness since my first night in Enheduanna's company. I described my accommodations as spare but adequate, made no complaint about the demeanor of my guards, and wryly thanked him for his hospitality.

For his part, Mathias seemed uncertain of his ground and hesitant in his speech. He left abruptly, but two days later I was brought fresh clothing and allowed to walk in the courtyard during the afternoon. More than a month passed before I saw him again, but Esther came more frequently than ever. We exchanged words of mutual admiration and she allowed me to hold her hand, although a guard always stood nearby, no doubt a spy for Mathias as well as the protector of his sister. The possibility that I might be free again began to gnaw at me and it became increasingly difficult to rein in my temper, but I knew that Esther was my only real chance of regaining my liberty so I forced upon myself a harsh discipline that stood me in good stead then as well as later.

When I expressed my wish to make her my wife, she fled in a panic and so many days passed before she returned that I feared I had acted too precipitously, but even as I hovered on the brink of despair, she returned, blushing, eyes downcast, and told me that she hoped to satisfy the desires I had expressed. Mathias returned the following day, and he questioned me quite closely, revealing his knowledge that those documents which had indicted me were likely false. He never apologized and insisted that the pressures of politics made it difficult for him to reverse the sentence he had pronounced upon me, then asked about my intentions toward his sister. He was skeptical, and with good reason, but I insisted that I had learned some small wisdom during my confinement, that I was more interested in Esther's soul than in the flawed container of flesh in which it resided. I don't know if he believed my words, but he wanted to believe, for he truly loved his unfortunate sister.

More time passed. Esther visited with increasing frequency, but would not speak of her brother. A priest began to appear from time to time, exhorting me to renounce Orthodoxy in favor of the local flavor of religion. My first impulse was to drive him away with foul language, but I restrained my temper. The Church meant nothing to me anymore; I worshipped only a single being and she walked the Earth in physical form. Too quick a conversion would be suspect, so I pretended to listen to the priest's arguments, softening my own views over a period of time. I professed uncertainty and confusion at last, and the next day Mathias visited me again.

His proposal was straightforward. I was to marry Esther and treat her with honor. My previous marriage was declared irrelevant after I insisted that it had never been consummated, which was true, and that my wife was a suicide and therefore barred from Heaven, which was false. I would renounce my faith and embrace that of my wife and brother in law. In return, I would be freed and domiciled with my new wife in Pest, beyond the Danube, distant enough not to embarrass my benefactor, close enough that he could maintain a close watch over my activities, particularly my treatment of Esther. I was barely able to conceal my impatience, expressed my gratitude, displayed a newfound humility, and agreed to all of his terms. I would have accepted far worse for I felt no obligation to hold to my oath.

More time passed and I feared that nothing would come from all my careful playacting after all, but then things began to happen, and very quickly. I was moved from my cell to lodging in the main castle. My hair was trimmed, I was assigned personal servants, and provided with a wardrobe suitable for my rank. My movement was relatively unrestricted, but two guards accompanied me at all times. Guards also stood outside our bedroom the night that Esther and I were married, and not just to protect our privacy, and a score of them accompanied us to our new home, ostensibly under my authority although I knew from the outset that their primary allegiance was to Mathias. I had only moved from a small prison to a much larger one, but now the options for escape were much greater.

Renfield has been placed into harsher confinement. Apparently the conflicts caused by my intervention have unsettled his fragile sanity even further and he raged throughout the day, causing great consternation and considerable upset. I was at pains to soothe him with promises tailored to his own peculiar requirements and hope that his improved condition will return things to normal. I regret the necessity to use such a sad tool and perhaps that guilt is why I think so much of long dead Esther lately. She may not be the gravest of my long list of sins, but she is nevertheless one of those which pains me the most.

I have visited the house once again, keeping to the shadows to avoid human eyes, although I have no doubt that if my one time mistress resides within, she can feel my presence. The link between us has attenuated with the passage of time, but it has never broken.

August 25

There is no question that she has quitted Hillingham, although her influence still clings to that sad home. From conversations I have overheard in the town, it is clear that the woman of the house is on her deathbed, and there are rumors that the daughter is in ill health as well. One or both of these are likely her creatures. I cannot believe she would relinquish a victim once taken without very good reason, so the only possible good I can do there would be to release whosoever she has afflicted into the true death.

Because of their confinement, I have been unable to arrange a chance encounter. If I can find the means to obtain an invitation to their home, I could confirm the true state of affairs in the blink of an eye. The custom of introducing oneself to one's neighbors remains, but I am as yet reluctant to advertise my presence here in Whitby as the arrival of a foreign gentleman of some wealth and mysterious habits would certainly invite a degree of notoriety which would hamper my activities unacceptably. Still, it may be my only recourse.

August 25

It is the younger, the daughter, I am certain. Tonight I prowled the grounds of Hillingham while there was yet activity within the house. Again and again I saw her face pressed to the glass, peering out into the darkness as though she sensed something imperceptible to the others within, as indeed was the case. My proximity doubtless disturbs her in much the same fashion as does that of her unnatural mistress.

A young man arrived at the house today, presumably this Holmwood of whom I have heard mention. There was considerable activity shortly after his arrival, a servant was sent hastily into the town, and no great period of time passed before another man appeared, a physician judging by the bag he carried. From this I surmise that either the senior Westenra's condition has worsened, or the younger's ill health has alarmed her promised husband.

They can do her no good, of course, and only harm in prolonging her final days. I would spare them all the inevitable pain that must accompany what will follow, but that is a power denied me. The best that I can hope to accomplish is that by some means I might gain access to the poor young woman long enough to do what is required to end her pain and preserve her soul.

The Notebooks of Abraham Van Helsing

September 3

I have arrived at Whitby shortly before noon this day in response to an urgent wire from Seward. He claimed to have encountered a unique disease affecting the blood of a local woman. I would ordinarily have disregarded any such statement as I am lately overwhelmed with requests for consultation, but Seward was always extraordinarily level headed and, if anything, prone to understate a situation. His wire was worded in such explicit and melodramatic terms that my curiosity was sufficiently piqued to draw me out to this spiritless countryside.

Seward met my train and conveyed me by hired carriage to my lodgings, waiting in obvious impatience while I arranged for the installation of my belongings and settled terms with the landlord. From there we proceeded to a large house set among topiaries and floral gardens on the west side of the town proper, where we were greeted with enthusiasm by several servants, and a degree of ambivalence by a young man identified as the patient's betrothed.

Nevertheless, we continued in good order to the lady's chambers. There I discovered a delightfully attractive young woman with elfin features and a well developed body, who was alternately tearfully self absorbed and almost frantically good humored. She was wrapped in a frilly nightgown that enclosed her body like a cocoon, except when she contrived to provide a brief glimpse of what lay within, a tendency which I initially dismissed as artless mischance but subsequently judged to be a deliberate waywardness.

There was no fever; if anything, she was to the touch a bit cool, her skin dry despite the oppressive heat of the early afternoon. The fashionable English shun the sun, but even so there was a marked pallor considering the time of year. Other than during brief periods of frantic animation, the young lady seemed listless and distracted.

"Some rare form of anemia perhaps?" suggested Seward.

"Perhaps," I allowed. I examined the eyes, which seemed mildly unfocused and slightly reddened, the pupils narrow.

"Do you think you can help her?" There was a quite unprofessional emotional undertone in Seward's words that indicated his involvement transcended purely clinical interest. It was a distraction I preferred to avoid just now.

"Could you arrange for fresh bed clothing for this room, Jack? It has been my experience that some patients benefit from such changes." True, but I was more interested in occupying him elsewhere for the moment.

"Certainly. I'll get one of the maids to take care of it immediately."

The moment Seward was out the door, the patient raised her hand and placed it on my arm. "Aren't you going to examine me, Dr. Van Helsing?"

"Certainly that is my intention, Miss Westenra. Indeed, I believe that such is exactly what I have been doing these past several moments."

"Will you check my breathing then, and test the regularity of my heart beat?" There was a teasing note in her voice and she twisted her head against the velvet pillow, staring at me quite frankly.

"Assuredly, young miss."

"Then let me make it easier for you." And she moved lithely and in such fashion that her gown no longer covered her breasts which were well formed and free of mark or discoloration. I opened my mouth as though to protest but before I could utter a word, she caught hold of my wrist with a grip so intense and powerful I wondered if the illness had affected her mind and given her the frantic strength of the mad. She pressed the palm of my hand against a bare breast and held it firmly in place.

"Do you feel my heartbeat, Dr. Van Helsing?"

I cleared my throat somewhat uncomfortably, worried that Seward would return and find us so arranged. "Yes, my dear, it seems quite steady, quite steady indeed."

"Are you sure, Doctor?" She was teasing me, I realized, playing at seduction. "Wouldn't you like to press your ear against my bosom, listen to the very beat of my life's blood coursing through my body. My virginal body." She arched her back slightly and the movement was almost serpentine. My own pulse must have quickened and my lips were dry. Her expression was so openly carnal that it frightened me, her eyes acquiring a sharpness and depth that made me feel as though I were peering into a pair of tiny whirlpools into which I was being drawn inexorably.

Of a sudden, I felt a rush of panic and wrenched my hand free, just in time as it happened, for Seward opened the door that very second. The young lady somehow managed to shift her body in such fashion that it was once again modestly covered, although there was a lingering hot excitement in her eyes that I found unnerving.

"The maid will be here presently," he informed me, and then stood at my side as I completed my examination with hands that shook despite my best efforts to hold them steady, finding nothing more remarkable than what appeared to be two small insect bites on the side of the young woman's throat. The marks were neither tender nor inflamed, and seem unlikely to be related to my new patient's malady. Miss Westenra made no further inappropriate remark or action, but there was a spark in her eyes that was most disquieting, and her lips curled into a secretive smile that came and went furtively so that only I chanced to see it.

Later, over sherry, Seward attempted to force me to commit to an opinion.

"That would be premature at the moment," I retorted with some heat. "I have written a diet regimen to which she must be strictly held. During the day, she may frequent the grounds so long as she is accompanied, but at night her room must be closed tightly to prevent the intrusion of unhealthy night airs. I must stress that the red meat must not be cooked beyond the point where it remains pink in the center. Blood makes blood and that is what she is most lacking. I may have more to say when I have had time to consult my books."

"Must you leave in the morning, sir?" He seemed most dismayed at the thought, and I recognized once again that his interest was not strictly that of a doctor for his patient. "My affection of Miss Lucy is more than just that a physician owes his patient."

"Yes, I must. I would, however, hope to return shortly to observe Miss Westenra's progress. It is a most interesting case, but I see nothing that would suggest an urgent intervention."

But I confess here that it was the warmth of the young lady's breast that occupied my thoughts. The coals of my fire may have cooled with the passage of time but there remains an ember that even now glows hotly if secretly. And there was as well the frightened child I had sensed crouched behind those seductive eyes. There is something wrong here, something more than simple illness. I recalled a story I had been told as a child, but quickly put it out of my mind. This was the age of science, not superstition.

The Journal of Vlad Tepes

September 4

Alas, I have decided to discard Renfield. His fevers of the mind are too all consuming; he is a tool that constantly turns within the user's grip. The man is devilled enough by his own inner tortures. I cannot bring myself to add to the load. His invitation has gained me access to the asylum which may or may not prove useful, but he proves too unreliable for further employment. He will be of no value to Enheduanna even so, as I am forewarned of him.

I feel whole again and prepared for her best efforts, though I have still failed to gain access to the Westenra house. Neither is there any definitive word regarding Enheduanna's anticipated return to Whitby. It is unthinkable that she would flee with so little reason and I can only believe that she means to mislead me into an impulsive act. If so, she will find that I have acquired a certain amount of caution since our last encounter, though I am churning with the desire to confront her.

I have set down a part of my story in these pages, and now I feel a compulsion to continue. I would like to say that it soothes my soul to confess in this fashion but the truth is that my misdeeds burn even more brightly in my thoughts when I put words to them, and though that brings fresh pain, it is from that agony of spirit that I may draw the strength I need to finally confront the one who brought me so low and perhaps, in doing so, I will balance in some small measure the scale I have tilted so far toward evil.

Although Mathias had set me free to move about without serious hindrance for the first time in years, I chafed at the tenuous bonds that still held me, and my growing irritation could not be concealed from Esther, who retreated into herself and kept out of my way, although I think she loved me still, or at least believed herself in love. Not once did she respond in kind to my outbursts of temper even when they were clearly unjustified, and judging by Mathias' continued restraint and support, she refrained from complaining to him or in the presence of his no doubt attentive spies.

Only once did my smoldering rage break free during those months in Pest, when I surprised a drunken officer who wandered into the grounds and had the ill fortune to pass my guards without being noticed, perhaps because they were more interested in preventing my departure than barring uninvited visitors. When I found him in the gardens, he seemed the embodiment of everything that kept me apart from my mistress and I fell upon him with my fists, beating him senseless, then retrieved one of the gardener's tools and used it to sever his head from his body. The guards came running and witnessed the final stage of my assault, and despite my admonition to hold their tongues, distorted versions of events had spread through the city by nightfall. Happily the officer had an unsavory reputation and was known to have stolen goods in the past and it was assumed that this had been his purpose again and that I was justified in having killed him, although the ferocity of my assault raised more than one eyebrow.

Mathias must have grown satisfied with my treatment of Esther, or perhaps resigned to the impossibility of watching over her forever, because he conveyed to me his willingness to lift his remaining restrictions over my movement. I was not sorry to leave Pest, which had never welcomed me, and decided that we would move to Sibiu, where I would live openly among those same people who stolen twelve years of my life. They would not dare move against me while Mathias was on the throne and I was wed to his sister. It was the kind of irony that appealed to me and I acted upon my decision quickly.

Barely had we settled in when Crimea fell to the Turks and Mathias was forced to go to war. He made use of my talents then, for he gave me an army, promising to restore my title in Wallachia if I served him well. At last I was able to vent my rage openly as we rode to war, and while the poor forces available to me were not sufficient to win decisively, they comported themselves well enough that Mathias pronounced himself satisfied with my service. When the tide of battle receded once more, he made good on his word, setting me over Wallachia with Esther at my side.

And it was only then, when I was returned to my own castle, that Enheduanna reappeared, coming out of the darkness and without warning.

I had thought to find some sense of freedom, if not peace, by returning to Sibiu, but that was not to be. It had been still another prison. Many of the local residents fawned upon me and pretended not to remember the havoc I had wreaked on their city years before, but I could sense the thoughts that lay behind the smiles, and they were not pleasant. I ventured into the city regularly to show that I was not afraid, but never without my guards and even then there were shouted insults and occasionally objects thrown from windows or from within anonymous crowds.

Mathias had set a precondition to our departure from Pest. He wished to see physical proof that this marriage, unlike my first, had been consummated, hoping thereby to prevent me from disavowing Esther at some future date. I found the physical act repellent, not because of Esther's ill formed features, but because no human woman had stirred my interest since that first assignation with Enheduanna. Nor has any since, even though I am no longer under her power. But while I derived no joy from the act, neither was it an onerous prospect. I thought of it as a necessary task and dutifully visited my wife's bed chamber until she pronounced herself with child. Mihnea was born to her in Sibiu and she devoted all of her energies to his welfare. The infant itself was of no further interest to me.

Mathias declared himself pleased by my service and by fathering his nephew, and he had restored my title in Wallachia. I found a very different country there, however, beset by Turks and marauders with no allegiance, bandits and rogues preying on the peasants. The garrisoned soldiers at my disposal were an undisciplined, slovenly lot and I had just begun to beat them into some sort of order the night she returned.

I still slept poorly and was given to restlessly walking the parapets in the darkness, as if I could somehow see her approaching from afar. She found me there, appearing out of the shadows as if from the mist, and I never did learn how she had entered the keep, although the guards had not impressed me with their efficiency. She stood silently at first, just a hint of a smile on her face, and I was unable to move. She had not changed at all since our last meeting. I had imagined this reunion so many times in the past that I thought it might be some trick my mind was playing upon my eyes, that if I reached out, if I even spoke, the sound of my voice might disturb the image before me and leave me alone as before.

"You are still a man of power, Vlad Tepes. I had feared otherwise."

The sound of her voice thrilled me and I began to believe. "I have waited for your coming for a very long time, my mistress."

She sighed and shrugged her shoulders. "These are unsettled times and I have not always been free to do as I wished. But I did not forget you."

"Nor I you." I wanted to throw myself upon her, catch her up in my arms, but I still half believed this to be an illusion that would vanish if I acted hastily. "Am I still your servant?"

She laughed lightly and told an untruth. "You are and always will be."

"Then what would you have of me?"

"Everything that you are or that you possess, if I have need of it."

"Done." And I stepped forward, drawn by her power, and knelt with bowed head. "I live only for you."

"And would you die for me as well?"

"If that is what you desire, then yes, and gladly."

I felt her hand on my shoulder and I trembled, I – before whom armies had faltered – was helpless beneath the hand of a woman no more than half my size. "You shall die for me, Vlad, and soon, but you will serve me even after."

"I will throw myself from these very walls if you desire it, or fall upon my sword."

"Stand up," she commanded, and I did so. "I promise you a far sweeter death than that, and more. It should have been done long ago, but our paths have diverged farther than I had hoped. But tonight your wait will end and tomorrow your new life will begin."

I didn't understand her, of course, but she implied that we would be together thenceforth and that was all that mattered. I bowed my head. "I wait upon your bidding, mistress."

She was close to me suddenly and I looked up, saw her face shining out of the darkness and it seemed to me that everything I ever wanted, everything worth having in life, was reflected somehow in her delicate features. I believe that she was using the glamour for I knelt before her without being told and closed my eyes as she raised her arms and closed with me. There was a brief moment of uneasiness, and then all uncertainty fled as a the familiar ecstasy returned, multiplied many times over, and it was as though I fell into an ocean of emotion and sank beneath its calm surface.

It seemed an eternity that I was suspended thus, but after a time the enfolding waves began to recede. My senses were in conflict, for on the one hand I felt as though I had experienced a terrible loss. All strength seemed to have fled my body. But at the same time I enjoyed an unprecedented sense of fitness and power. The external world came back with a rush and I realized that I half lay, half sat against a rough stone wall. It was still dark but the distant sky was already lightening, threads of sunlight mixed with the cottony clouds. At first I believed myself alone and felt a great disappointment, fearing that I had dozed or fainted and had dreamed it all. But as I struggled to regain my feet, she suddenly reappeared, a dark cloak wrapped around her slender body.

"Are you of sound mind, Vlad?"

It was an odd question and at first I could shape no answer. Still half convinced that I was dreaming, I merely stared at her, noticing without alarm or understanding that she held in one hand a long wooden stake that had been carved with a sharp slightly curved point. She came closer as I hesitated, almost within arm's reach, and repeated her question, and this time there was an urgency in her voice that penetrated the fog in my head.

"Mistress, I don't understand. What would you have of me?"

Her face softened slightly, but she still held the stake at the ready. "You have had a difficult night. Are your thoughts troubled? Do you know who you are and what place this is?"

"I am Vlad, Prince of Wallachia, and this is my keep. I feel some confusion," I admitted, "and am not certain what has passed between us this past night."

"All will be explained." She glanced toward the horizon, which was glowing with blood red light. "But we have little time just now. You must go inside, Vlad, and remain indoors until night falls again. At no time must daylight fall upon you, not even a shaft through a window. Retire to your council chamber and remain there until the sun sets again."

"I will do as you bid, mistress." I started to turn, intending to descend immediately, but she caught hold of my arm with a grip that was surprisingly powerful.

"One moment longer. There is something else you must do today. There is a force of your enemy gathered near Targoviste. You will call your commanders together this morning and bid them assemble their soldiers for an attack. When darkness falls and not a moment before, you will leave the castle to lead them into battle."

I was incapable of arguing with her, but I hesitated. "They outnumber us, mistress, and they are well entrenched. My troops are not the best and they fear the darkness even when there is no enemy lurking within it."

"They will do as you bid them. Are you not their prince?"

"I am."

"And will you not do as I bid?"

The thought of disobedience made me physically ill. "Anything you command shall be done as though it were my own will."

"Then do as I have spoken. Go now, and mind me in all things. And one thing more. Dress in your very finest for the battle, so that none will doubt who leads your men."

I nodded and turned away but hesitated once more. "And you, my mistress? Shall I see you again?"

She laughed and it sent a thrill through me, a thrill of terrifying joy. "You shall see me tomorrow night, my prince. That is my promise to you."

Letter from Lucy Westenra to Mina Murray, dated 4 September 1875

The dreams I spoke of last time continue, dear Mina, and I can only attribute them to your absence. They are terrible, dark things and sometimes in the night I wake convinced that something cruel and evil hovers just beyond the closed window and that if I rose and threw open the sash it would rush in upon me and gobble me up and I would be lost forever in the infinite darkness of its belly.

Even when I elude the dreams, I have difficulty sleeping, move restlessly from one side of the bed to another. Arthur is a dear and I do everything I can to keep him from worrying, but Jack insists that it is more than a fancy of the mind and that my rest is disturbed by an infirmity of the body. He even brought another doctor to see me, a German or Dutchman or something like that, except that I remember very little about his visit, which seems no more real than some of my recent dreams.

I don't mean to spoil your happiness, dear Mina, now that you are united with your Jonathan at last. I just hope that you won't forget your friend Lucy and that you will come visit me as soon as Jonathan is well enough to travel.

The Journal of Abraham Van Helsing

September 7

Miss Westenra has worsened and her condition is grave. Even the news that her friend Mina has returned to England and hopes to come hither from London as soon as her new husband's condition allows has aroused little enthusiasm, although I have been told they are closer than most sisters. My most recent examination has led me to suspect...but I must set things down in the proper order.

I returned to Hillingham at mid-morning this day, accompanied as before by young Jack, who has now explained his own previous romantic interest in our patient. Despite her obvious beauty, this inclination surprises me as I had thought Jack forever wed to his work, or that at least if he should stray onto the path to matrimony, it would be for a partner whose mental horizons were rather more elevated. For all the child's beauty and innocence, hers is a shallow and inconsequential intellect.

In any case, we found the patient pale nearly unto her own death, and after administering a narcotic to ensure her quiescence, Jack and I transfused from Holmwood's body enough blood to restore some of her color. This sufficed to reassure Mrs. Westenra, who looked in briefly before returning to her own sickbed.

I have insisted to Jack that he attend to Miss Westenra personally and not rely on others to accomplish the task. As yet I have not communicated to him my suspicions regarding the two odd puncture wounds which we discerned on her throat and which show no signs of healing, but in view of her condition otherwise I have little hope that their presence there is coincidental. Unfortunately, if I were to give voice to what I have reluctantly come to believe, even Jack might at this juncture think me one step away from those over whom he has charge.

I must think on this. There is more at risk here than is apparent, more perhaps even than the life of this unfortunate child.

The Diary of Lucy Westenra

September 9

It has been weeks since I last wrote here, although much of that time seems to have passed in a dream. So much has happened, Mother's illness and my own, the formal announcement of my betrothal to Arthur, the flattering but sad offers of marriage from Jack and Quincey, Mina's loss and recovery of Jonathan, her departure to marry and nurse him, my sleepwalking episodes...all deserve lengthy entries here. All this will have to wait, however, as I feel my strength ebbing rapidly despite Jack's assurances that I am on the mend.

I must, however, write of my dreams – nightmares -.in hope that by reducing them to words rather than half remembered images I can dissipate some of their unsettling power. I dread the fall of night even though the cool breezes bring considerable relief from the unseasonably humid days. Horrid shapes inhabit my sleeping hours, great satanic figures fluttering in the night, bringing perverted images of those I love. I have seen Arthur, Jack, Quincey, even Dr. Van Helsing behaving in a manner quite unlike their actual selves, performing carnal acts which I cannot bring myself to describe, and have felt lustful urges for each of them that carry over into my waking hours. Even more disquieting, I feel the same desire for dear Mina, and have experienced moments of actual jealousy imagining her lying in bed with Jonathan, her husband.

Perhaps this is all a product of my lingering illness, a fever of the mind which will pass as the last flames gutter out. But as I watch the sun dip low toward the horizon outside the windows of my room, I feel a sudden wave of anxiety, a sense that I stand on the lip of a great precipice toward which I am slowly being pulled by an unseen force. Pray God that my friends have the strength to hold me back.

September 10

Last night I had the most horrible dream of all. I tried to speak of it to Mother, but even in her days of good health, she was always discomfited by talk, no matter how circumspect, that fringed upon carnal matters. If I spoke frankly of what troubled me, I fear the shock alone would be the final blow to her ailing heart. Almost I thought to address myelf to one of the maidservants, perhaps Elsie, who seems a good sort who would keep a confidence, but even as I approached her, I knew I could not bear to utter the words to another, any other, and so I sent her upon some hastily contrived errand to cover my confusion and retreated to my room and to this account.

There was a man in the dream, or at least I think him a man. Rather he was a huge shadow in the shape of a man with eyes that glowed like embers. Never did he speak but remained at a distance, watching me as I stood in the great room below where but recently Arthur asked me to be his wife and I accepted. There were a great number of people about the room, and I sensed that I should know them, though none specifically seemed familiar. I was the center of their attention, and not surprisingly so since I stood completely unclothed among them. Although I felt a natural horror at being thus exposed, I could make no move to escape the room, nor could I so much as raise a hand to cover myself.

Mina was there as well, standing just beyond my reach, and her eyes were as bright as that dark stranger's as they ranged about the assembled company. Finally she lifted one arm and extended her hand to me.

"Come with me, Lucy. I'll take care of you."

And in her words I found the strength to raise an answering hand, and our fingers touched. She was as cold as ice and I felt the heat of my body rushing out through our joined flesh, but still my feet refused to answer my mind and I could not flee into her arms. And then the shadow was there at my side as well and he took my other hand into his great paw, and again there was a shock such as one might expect falling through the ice into a frozen pool of water.

His eyes stared past me at Mina, and she returned the look with a depth of hatred I know my dear Mina could never feel. Then they were pulling at my arms somehow, though neither seemed to move. I didn't feel any pain, of course, since it was just a dream, but my arms kept stretching farther and farther apart and I heard a tearing sound and knew that I would be ripped in twain if they continued. And then the shadow relinquished his grip and I flew into dear Mina's arms and they closed about me. She held me tightly and all the terror should have gone away, but for some reason it only intensified.

And then someone stepped out of the crowd of onlookers and I recognized him. It was dear Arthur, and he approached almost to within my reach. But when I made to go to him, Mina's arms closed even more tightly around me from behind, and one of her hands was at my bosom and the other trailed down between my legs, and her fingers sank into my flesh with bruising force. Frightened, I wanted to call out to Arthur to rescue me, to take me away from all of this unseemly conflict, but as Mina pressed her body even more tightly around mine my will seemed to lose substance. I felt her lips running across my shoulder and nuzzling the side of my neck, and then a sharp sting of pain so intense it was pleasurable, and I became unnaturally calm even when I realized that I was bleeding, bleeding both from my throat and from between my legs, and it was not my monthly flow either but the result of some horrible, unseen wound Mina had inflicted upon me. Even then I could not summon the will to struggle against her, and Arthur slowly faded back into the crowd.

Once again the shadow was close in front of me, and I still could not see his features for my eyes seemed to slide away whenever I looked to recognize him. But another part of his body was all too visible, his male organ resembling that illustration I once noticed in one of Jack's books, but impossibly huge. I was terrified of him and sought to retreat even further into the shelter of Mina's body, but he...thrust himself upon me and...I find this difficult to write even in this most secret of places. I must rest a little.

Later.

I will finish this before my resolve flees entirely. The shadowy figure closed upon me and that part of him of which I have already written pierced my own flesh, but not in the manner of a man with a woman, but as a spear driven in below my ribs and up through my body into the heart itself. Almost then I felt pain, even in the midst of dream, and Mina's arms fell away and I was falling as well and then at last the terrible nightmare came to an end.

But horrid as all this may be, I have not told the worst. Because it was not that rude impalement that so revolted me that I wakened with bile burning against my palate. Rather it was that this violent assault seemed a release, and it was in fact Mina's attempt to shelter me with her own body that made me feel unclean. Has my mind become so poisoned with this mysterious ailment which afflicts me that I can no longer distinguish friend from foe? Have I somehow fallen prey to the kind of sickness of the mind that condemns men and women alike to Jack's madhouse?

I wish that Mina would come, so that I could throw myself into her arms and know that there I am loved and cherished. But I fear she may not arrive in good time.

Letter from Elsie Goodall to her Aunt Agatha Wandsley, dated September 10, 1875

Is there any further word on the posting you mentioned in your letter of August 14? I don't mean to sound ungrateful as Mrs. Westenra has been most kind during my stay here, but the dear lady is on her deathbed, they say, and the daughter is suffering an illness of the mind as well as the body. The aristocratic blood runs thin, don't it? She's a flutter head on her best days, and a bit of a tart besides, if you ask me, though I imagine she's as good as she should be.

To be completely truthful, Auntie, there's something wrong hereabouts. There's much comings and goings in the night, these doctors and jilted suitors and suchlike. Dr. Seward even sat up in the young miss's room all night once, which isn't at all proper if you ask me, no matter that he is a physician. She's troubled by wicked bad dreams, they say, and the doctor must be at hand to deal with them. It may be the truth; Lord knows, she's been known to walk right out of the house without waking, though I've never seen her do such myself. And this very day she approached me, and it was as clear as could be that she forgot what she was about at the very moment of speaking on it, and made up something useless for me to do just to save herself the embarrassment.

I've had some odds dreams myself of late as well. Just last night I imagined that some beastly shape was flapping its filthy wings outside the window of the room I share with Amelia. I must've been half awake, because I came to myself standing with my nose pressed up against the pane, though there weren't nothing outside to be seen. And later that same night I thought I heard Miss Lucy speaking to someone and another voice answering back, Mina Murray it was I imagined, though I suppose she's Mina Harker now, as they say the two of them got married since she left here. But she's tending to her sick husband down in Exeter or London or some such, and no one knows when or if she'll next pay a visit to Hillingham.

So if you do hear something further about that position, write me immediately, will you, as I don't think there's any future for me here.

Your Faithful Niece,

Elsie

The Journal of Abraham Van Helsing

September 10

It is as I had feared, though I still may not speak of it openly. This morning we discovered Miss Westenra weaker than ever, all of the fresh blood we had introduced drawn off during the night. I almost forewent the infusion of morphia, as the young lady was so weakened that fainting seemed her normal state. But I took the necessary precautions and Jack prepared himself for the transfer of blood without my even having to speak to the necessity.

It left him weak and shaken, of course, but he seemed improved in spirits when Lucy regained consciousness and behaved in a cheerful, even animated manner, although she is still very weak. Alas, I believe her to be in even greater danger than is obvious and have stressed the importance of having someone alert in her presence at all times, particularly during the hours of darkness. I have also requested certain materials which should arrive shortly, and which I hope might keep at bay the evil force which is preying upon the child. I have still not revealed my suspicions to the others. They might well think me mad. Sometimes I think that myself.

September 14

Have been too busy these past few days to make entries here, and tonight I am almost too weak to do so. It is my own aged blood which runs through Miss Lucy's veins this day, and I can only hope that it retains enough vigor to see her through the ordeal to come.

And ordeal it will be, there is no mistaking that now. It is only the ultimate outcome that remains in question.

The fatal blow was struck by a loving hand, but the consequences are no less dire. I had fashioned a forbidding wreath of garlic flowers to stave off the powers of darkness that so beset the child placed in my charge. The odor was strong but beneficial, and I had hoped that by so doing, I might achieve for her a respite sufficient to allow her body to throw off the effects of those vile vapors which have invaded it.

Such was not to be the case.

Even now, after the passage of several hours, the bitter irony stings my eyes and causes my hands to tremble with more than the infirmity of my age. Mrs. Westenra, in one of her increasingly rare moments of strength, visited her daughter's room while the maid assigned to keep watch had fallen asleep. Still, all would have been well had she not misunderstood the situation. Rather, she removed the garlic and threw open the windows to dissipate what she thought might be its baleful influence, misapprehending the situation to her daughter's detriment.

Freed of restraint, the evil force that plagues Miss Lucy was allowed ingress and, I fear, may have pushed my patient beyond the point of recovery. I will not abandon the fight even now, but I fear for the worse and must discover the means to undo the evil even if it succeeds in running its apparent course.

September 16

To the untrained eye, Miss Lucy continues to improve, although how much of that is real and how much merely a seeming I am unable to determine. There is an inner illness that does not lend itself to my medicines, which cannot be driven out by good intentions and rest alone. It needs a more powerful source of healing, which must take root in her soul first if our ministrations are to have any great effect. She has moments of lucidity and others in which she seems another person entirely, a wanton creature who makes vile suggestions, interspersed with long periods in which she lies feverishly abed and refuses to respond to anyone.

Still, my hopes have been raised by the lack of further untoward incident. Precautions have been taken to prevent a recurrence of the sad circumstances of Mrs. Westenra's intervention and the house seems otherwise secure.

September 17

Recovery continues to a point. During the daylight, Miss Lucy is much improved, even dresses and walks about the house and, within certain prescribed limits and always with someone in attendance, has ventured out into the garden briefly. To other eyes she seems greatly restored, perhaps even in the final stages of complete recovery. But my eye is more discerning and my spirit troubled.

Miss Lucy continues to dread the night, and there is a physiological change in her condition during the hours of darkness that is ominous. Her body cools unnaturally once the sun is gone, her heart beats at a much slower pace than is natural or healthy, and her pallor returns, though not so dramatically as in times past. She cannot remember her dreams, she says, but by all reports she tosses uneasily and even mumbles unintelligibly, and on those occasions when I have inquired about the details of these, she has spoken words to which the evasiveness of her eyes gives the lie.

Still, if we persevere, the battle may yet be won. At least I have noble allies in the struggle to come.

The Journal of Vlad Tepes

September 18

I have failed again, and caused evil where I intended only good. For these past many nights I have sought entrance to Hillingham. This cursed inability to enter a home without invitation is one restraint which Enheduanna has never suffered, but unhappily I remain bound. She has always held that it was a superstition, that it was my own mind which barred me, but I believe it is some unsuspected natural law which applies only to those who are transformed by her unnatural power. She who has never died is not affected, but those of us who have returned from beyond the pale are not so fortunate.

The past several nights I have spent attempting to lure Lucy Westenra outside, but I have been thwarted consistently. Someone there is within those walls who either through chance or knowledge has stumbled upon just those wards most efficacious in rebuffing me. I had hoped to subvert Enheduanna's influence and draw her victim out to where I could quickly ensure that she dies free of the taint that presently besets her. On several occasions I have lured her as far as the window of her room, but in each instance, she was either returned to her bed by the presence of a companion, or prevented from taking that final step by the effluvia of that abhorred blossom with which she is lately adorned. Well meaning though these ministrations may be, they threaten to doom her to an unending hell.

Two nights past I conceived a plan which I hoped would overcome these obstacles. I have observed the cycle of watchers for some time and know which of them have minds most amenable to the influence of the glamour. The one called Elsie was most likely to serve this past evening and while I have been able to compel her obedience in simple tasks from a distance, my grasp of this power is so tentative that she often retreats from my interference into a false sleep from which it is difficult to waken her, and in that state she cannot serve me by issuing the necessary invitation to enter. What would be a simple matter for my opponent remains for me a difficult and uncertain prospect. Still, I conceived of a way this situation might be turned to my purpose, and I did not intend to overlook whatever tool might present itself.

I therefore traveled to London where the Zoological Gardens provided a possible solution to my difficulties. The wolves imprisoned there are a tame lot who have lost so much of their instinctive congruity with the natural world that it was only with some difficulty that I communicated to them in the old way and superimposed my requirements over their own. But one among their number was admirably suited for my purposes, a large and basically healthy specimen, although the tone of his muscles was such that the tasks I intended for him would sorely test his stamina.

To that purpose, I caused the animal, called Berserker by the keeper who accosted me during my visit, to escape his confinement and travel under cover of darkness north from London by the most direct route to Whitby. As expected, Elsie was in charge of her young mistress and it was a matter of only a few moments to send her deep into a sleep from which it would take the greatest shaking of the earth or thundering of the heavens to waken her. Under my influence, she descended to the pantry and added laudanum to the brandy which I hoped would thereby incapacitate Dr. Seward and any others who might be present within the household, as I have observed that they gather nightly in almost ritual fashion to fortify themselves in this manner. Accomplishing this without discovery, Elsie returned to her charge and sank into a stuporous slumber. Had it been possible for me to enter unbidden, I could have disposed of the issue in that moment and turned my attention to other matters, but I must perforce wait for the arrival of my lupine friend.

Vulnerable as the windows of her room might be to mortal man, they effectively barred me and concentrated the effects of the wretched blossom strung about Miss Westenra's neck. Enheduanna had been with her three nights past, secretly visiting from her supposed exile to London, but even she must have been repelled by the fragrance because I had not sensed her presence since that time. Were the poor girl beset by a lesser danger, she might well have been wrung free of the imprisoning grasp of our kind, but Enheduanna is an ageless creature and the depth of her experience, the tenacity of her evil spirit, would triumph eventually. I hoped that with my intercession the balance might swing close enough that chance and determination would win through, but even though the war might still be in question, there was little doubt about the ultimate conclusion of the present battle.

Berserker was as biddable as I could have wished, and upon my command he shattered the glass and let in the cleansing night air. Having accomplished my purpose, I set him free, fully expecting him to seek the liberation of the woods to the northwest, but immediately I read in his mind the intention to return to his earlier confinement. Years of captivity had leeched the freedom from his soul, and I felt a profound pity for the ruination of his spirit.

My plan was to exert the influence of the glamour once the pervading effluvia of garlic was sufficiently diminished, but I had failed to perceive that there had been a change within. Mrs. Westenra had entered unbeknownst to me, managed to rouse the maid and send her away, intending to watch over her daughter in the girl's place. With the shattering of the window, she had risen up from the bed, must have stared briefly into Berserker's face, and perhaps even caught a glimpse of me in mid-transformation. For whatever reason, she gave a silent cry and collapsed, and I felt her life's energy dissipate in that instant.

Lucy herself stirred and twice made as though to rise when I called to her, but on each occasion she sank back against the pillows, and although I was able to touch the fabric of her dreams, I was unable to compel her obedience. Indeed, I realized at last I was simply causing unnecessary pain and was certainly though inadvertently responsible for the death of Mrs. Westenra, who was, insofar as I am aware, totally blameless. Frustrated, I raged against the night, but silently, and fled the site of my ill conceived effort in great anguish.

Enheduanna's Journal

September 18

My enemy is my ally, at least this night.

Jonathan and I are ensconced in Mr. Hawkins house in Exeter while he makes his recovery. This suits my purposes, so I have used the glamour to exacerbate his illness somewhat, sufficient to keep him weak of body and unfocused of mind. His inattention provides me the liberty to pursue certain activities of my own. Hawkins, alas, has become a liability. Vlad has no doubt guessed that he was my unwitting agent in ascertaining his plans against me and although it's unlikely the barrister could provide any useful information to do me hurt, I think it best that I dispose of the possibility of such an eventuality. Hawkins' death will also bolster Jonathan's prospects, which cannot help but work to my benefit.

Van Helsing and the others have caused me no little distress with their fumbling defense of Lucy. Twice I have journeyed to Whitby under cover of darkness only to discover myself barred from her presence by their primitive though effective precautions. A clove of garlic is tolerable, but they have filled her rooms with garlands of that ill smelling root, and it sickens me even at a distance. Last night I had planned to use Renfield as my agent, direct him to break into the house, breach the windows and let in the night air, and myself, to finish what I had begun some days before. Lucy has served one purpose fully and I no longer require her living presence to simplify my activities now that Jonathan is my husband, but she could serve me in another fashion once she has made the transition that will follow her death.

Renfield proved intractable, however. Although I was able to ensure his escape, his mind remained too unfocused for proper control. He seemed to confuse me with another, and conflicting purposes warred within the remnants of his reason. It is clear that he has in some form seen to my business, but no worthwhile intelligence could be read from his mind, which was so distorted with madness that I withdrew in considerable confusion. When I set him free, he fled not over the outer wall as I had intended, but rather penetrated deeper into the institution, where he set upon Seward himself, wounding the man before being subdued. I fear that Renfield can no longer be considered anything but a liability, though I will reserve my judgment for a time.

With no clear plan to overcome my difficulty, I returned to Hillingham to consider my alternatives. Imagine my surprise to discover the window already broached, Vlad's recent presence still lingering in the still night air. I felt, and suppressed, a great rage at the thought that he had pre-empted me, presumably rendering Lucy beyond hope of resurrection. But when I entered the room, I found her deep in the sleep of exhaustion, unharmed and closer to redemption than I had imagined possible. Across her unconscious form lay the body of her mother, lifeless and cool, her expression distorted into one of unspeakable horror. I could not imagine what might have happened until I had roused Lucy somewhat.

Her mind was befuddled with shock, which was also to my liking as I intended that she should remember my visit, if at all, as nothing more than a dream. She had poor recollection of the events of the night, her mind dominated by a nightmare image of some beast of the darkness which had invaded her bedroom and killed her mother. Her grief was a powerful emotion that tore at the grip of my will and when I attempted to soothe her into obedience by caressing her body she flinched away sharply, an action which I found so infuriating that I lunged for her and drank so deeply that she sank into a sleep from which not even I could waken her.

The rest of the house was silent. The maids had all

succumbed to the contents of a drugged decanter which lay overturned in the study, except one who slept in her own room in a trance that could only have been imposed by another like myself. It was Vlad doubtless, although his purpose in this instance remains unclear. Seward and the others were absent for the first time in several days, as I had planned and encouraged by stealing into their sleeping thoughts as they lay by turns within Hillingham, causing each to judge the crisis less immediate than was truly the case.

When I left her, Lucy was at death's door. To have pressed any further would have robbed her of all further utility to me. She should perish before another nightfall now, and then in due course dear Lucy and I shall be reunited once more, although the hand of condescension will no longer be hers to offer.

She will survive the change with her mind intact, I believe. Although I have been surprised more than once in the past, I have witnessed risings enough to have some sense of likelihood of success. The deeper the moral conscience, and the greater the intellect, the less likely is it that the spirit will survive the resurrection undamaged. Simple minds like Lucy's rebound more quickly, perhaps because they have fallen a lesser distance. They are sometimes deficient in small ways, but most have proven useful to me.

I had feared that Vlad would wake with his mind gone, for he was ever a deep thinker and brilliant in those subjects to which he applied his formidable intelligence. But he was always without a moral compass, even before I helped him discard these repressive trappings. Within moments of his wakening, his mind was in balance, though perhaps slightly muddled. Even as I sent him to hide from the daylight, I was pleased to see that he was already following my instructions carefully.

The change in his nature could not be concealed for long. It would be decades before he could venture out in the daylight, and even then only for brief moments lest his skin begin to blister and break wherever the light touched it. It would also require practice before he could mimic the consumption of human foods, and he would never draw any sustenance from them. Many other peasant tales about my get are without foundation, but enough are true to make his continued existence among the truly living an impossibility, at least alone during the early years of his new life. On the other hand, it would not do for him to simply disappear into the night. He was widely recognized, though rarely cordially, and it would be inconvenient to deal with such a hue and cry. I had faced such difficulties in the past, and knew how to forestall them.

Vlad led his men as I had bidden him, even though he and perhaps many of those who followed knew that it was a death trap, that they had little chance of success and a great likelihood of disaster. I cared not in the slightest about the outcome. I reached the field of battle long beforehand and searched among the defenders until I found one who would serve my purposes, marking him and keeping track of his movements.

The battle began just after midnight, so tentative at first that I mistook the sounds for just some further roistering among the restive Turks. But it didn't die down and then it grew louder and more general and I realized that the alarm had been raised. When the tide of battle finally reached me, I bided my time, slipping through the shadows. The man I had marked was most cooperative. He was a coward and held back until the fighting was general, then smeared the blood of a comrade on his head and lay down in a thicket, playing dead. I joined him there and the pretense quickly became reality.

It was not difficult to find Vlad. His attack had been well designed but the odds were too heavily against him. The Turks waited until the numbers of their enemy had declined, then moved out from their positions and began to wreak havoc among those who remained. Many broke and fled, but Vlad would not. I cursed the impetuous spirit that held him there, even though it was that same aspect of his personality which had first drawn my interest. If his back was broken or his heart pierced, even his quickened vitality might not be enough to save him. I watched for my opportunity, but it seemed that it might never offer itself, as he was so closely besieged that I could not approach unobserved.

Suddenly he was unhorsed and the fighters scattered, each intent upon his own opponent or opponents. I moved then, arrived as one of the Turks drove his blade through Vlad's shoulder, then fell away with his breast laid open by Vlad's sword. I dispatched one of the two remaining fighters while Vlad cut down the other. He would have turned back toward his beleaguered fellows, but I caught his arm and whispered to him to be silent and follow me. With only the slightest hint of hesitation he did so, and I led him back to the thicket.

"Remove your clothing," I ordered. I stripped the dead man while he complied, examining the body for any scars or other features which might be unique to him. I noticed then that he was missing the middle finger from his left hand, which was distressing but not unduly so. Vlad donned the Turk's clothing and then we both dressed the corpse in his discarded finery. They were a good fit; I had chosen well.

"What purpose does all this serve?" asked Vlad, although I think even then he was beginning to understand my plan.

"Hand me your sword." It required only a few blows to render the man's face unrecognizable. I added a few thrusts to the body for good measure. Satisfied, I then took the mangled hand off at the wrist. "Take that with us and discard it once we are well away from here."

Vlad complied silently, as he must by now have apprehended my purpose. "Come swiftly. We must find a safe haven for you before dawn breaks."

And so we left that place of conflict, and behind us lay Vlad Tepes, Prince of Wallachia. My new companion resembled him in every way, but he was as one newly born, embarking on a new life about which he knew as yet no more than a babe perceives about his own future. Everything was going as I had planned and I felt confident. It was a misplaced confidence, as it turned out, for Vlad held more surprises for me than I could ever have guessed, though it would be some considerable time before I realized that.

Excerpt from Letter of Benjamin Daily to his son Edward, dated September 19, 1875

Dr. Seward's pet lunatic got out of his cell again last night. Maybe this time the man will have enough sense to put him in stricter confinement. If you ask me, he's been a bit daft about this Renfield right from the start, giving him liberties denied to the other loonies, spending hours without suitable safeguards trying to understand the man's mania. As if there was any understanding loonies in the first place.

Anyway he cut the doctor real good this time, he did, a right deep slash on the arm that bled all over the new carpeting. Painful too, I suppose, though Doc Seward made out as how it was just a scratch. Trying to protect Renfield again, he is, and no doubt of that. Why, the man's escaped four times this past month that we know of, and once he was caught trying to sneak back in, mind you. If you ask me, he's been out and about more often than we know. Doesn't set my mind at rest knowing loonies can come and go as they will with no one to naysay them. Makes the world seem a lot less safe a place, if you know what I mean.

From the *Exeter Telegraph*, September 19, 1875

John Hawkins of this community was taken from us yesterday evening. Fifty four years of age but reportedly robust and in good spirits and health until quite recently, he had complained for the past several days of a general malaise but adamantly refused medical treatment. His wife Mary was disturbed to discover that he had not yet come to bed although it was nearly dawn and, rising to investigate, found him lifeless in a chair in his study. Dr. John Watson of Baker Street was called forthwith and pronounced Hawkins dead of a probable coronary ailment. A houseguest, one Jonathan Harker, a long time employee of Mr. Hawkins, is himself recovering from a prolonged, debilitating illness contracted during a visit to the continent, but Dr. Watson has determined that there is no connection and no fear of contagion. Funeral arrangements have yet to be announced.

From a Report Filed by Robert Snelling with his employer, Harris & Sons, Carters, September 20, 1875.

We had proceeded to Carfax Abbey as per our instructions for the purpose of taking into charge a number of boxes as were to be transported to three different addresses as listed in our instructions. Our route took us past the madhouse that appends to the property in question and we was accosted by one of the inmates, first verbally from a window overlooking the road, then physically as we was returning from the Abbey toward the Great Road in order to complete the job as was explained to us.

At that point the same lunatic as had abused us verbally when we arrived burst out of the grounds and attacked us, first pummeling Ted - that's Ted Smollett, who was assisting me in this regard - and then turning on me once Ted had fallen to the ground. I was struck upon one cheek but it was not so much the force of the blow as the ferocity of my attacker's demeanor that overwhelmed me. He continued to shout imprecations about his master, whoever that might be, alternately accusing us of stealing this individual's property or of being in league with him for some evil purpose which he never alluded to directly.

In any case, three men from the madhouse overcame him shortly thereafter and a Dr. Seward, director of that place as I understand it, arrived as we were picking ourselves up. Ted in particular was feeling pretty rancorous about the entire incident, but the doctor was a proper gentleman and treated us well, apologizing for the lapse on the part of his staff and after we were sure that the loonie was being properly attended to he made every effort to set the situation right by us.

We then proceeded to make the deliveries as per our instructions and returned here directly thereafter.

Enheduanna's Journal

September 19

Hawkins is disposed of, sooner than I had intended. His heart was unexpectedly weak and gave way prematurely. He is no great loss, however, and perhaps it is best this way. Jonathan and I left immediately following the funeral and returned to help in clearing up the estate, a task for which the widow is both intellectually and emotionally unfit. Jonathan assures me it will be a matter of only a few days work to set matters on the proper course and that we will then return to Whitby, ostensibly to visit Lucy.

But I have other purposes there which cannot be delayed. Lucy has lingered long enough. I will hence tonight and finish it if she has not already breathed her last.

The Notebooks of Abraham Van Helsing

September 21, 1875

If I am delinquent in writing here this past week, it is only because the events which I must chronicle are so universally unpleasant that I shrink from the task. Lord Godalming dead, his son Arthur returned to Whitby only because we correctly feared the worst for dear Lucy, and my most fearful suspicions were confirmed by her final moments. If such they truly are. There was quite remarkable deformation of the teeth and even some alteration of the jaw line, her pupils were contracted but the coloring there had turned unnaturally, almost brilliantly red. These physical signs disappeared toward the end, and she passed on in as close to peace as one so affected could possibly manage, although her restful aspect is a foul lie.

Lucy had seemed much better after the infusion of Quincey's blood into her veins. The poor girl should have been bursting with the transfusions from four healthy men, but she was so pale this morning, her breathing so uneven and faint, I knew that she could not last out the day. She showed courage to the last, but now it is those who have loved her in life who must be brave enough to serve her in death. Jack already believes, although he does not know that he does. Arthur is so wrapped in grief that he is as biddable as a child, and so determined to find some evil cause to blame that he will be amenable once the sharpest pains have subsided. And Quincey, well, Quincey I think will remain skeptical until the last, but he will go along with us for dear Lucy's sake and because he has an exaggerated and quite appealing love for the idea of a holy quest, a romanticism I find quite surprising in this rough frontiersman. But perhaps it is simply that my impression of his countrymen is mistaken rather than that he has somehow risen above their simple perceptions of the world. I should like to visit there, but a voyage of such length is beyond my capacity at this age.

In any case, I believe we shall form a united front against the evil that still menaces Lucy, even though her natural life has fled, perhaps even more gravely now because of that fact. Only time will tell if we have among us sufficient mettle for the task.

The Journal of Vlad Tepes

September 21

She has bested me again, claiming the soul I had hoped to steal from her. After the misguided attempt that cost the life of Mrs. Westenra, I was resigned to this eventuality. She will rise again, of course, and I will have to deal with her. But later. Delaying for such relative trifles only plays into the hands of my enemy. She is reportedly in London with her husband, Harker, who has somehow escaped the fate I had set for him. As yet I cannot determine whether he has resources beyond those I sensed, or whether others of her creatures intervened on his behalf. Another question for another time.

I must find her and soon, even if it means risking all prematurely. I must never lose sight of the fact that she has lived so many lifetimes that the world can hold few surprises for her, and that no plans I might devise are likely to find her completely unprepared. More than once she avowed that I was unique in her experience. That was why she hesitated to destroy me as she had all of the other mortals upon whom she preyed. At times she told me she would make me her equal one day, but I knew even then that she lied, and eventually made my own plans. I know now that I can never be her equal, but perhaps I might be her doom, and that will suit me well enough.

Enheduanna's Journal

September 22

Even though I believe myself more than capable of handling Vlad, it is always pleasant when fate turns the wheel in my direction. Jonathan and I were out today, seeing to a matter of business, having hired a carriage to spare his still weakened legs from the necessity of prolonged exertion. We were stopped at a crossroads briefly, when he caught hold of my arm and pointed across the boulevard to a cloaked figure standing in the shadow of a tree.

"It is the man himself!" he told me, and to my immense surprise he was absolutely correct. Vlad stood quietly, heavily cloaked and with a broad rimmed hat that marked him as a foreigner, surreptitiously watching a young woman who bore some passing similarity to me, and I suspect from this that he has come to London in an attempt to search me out. I had not thought he could yet tolerate the daylight so readily, but it has been more than a century since last our paths crossed, and it should not surprise me that he would change as I have changed with the passage of time.

The traffic began to move again at that moment, and when I was next able to glance in that direction, Vlad was gone. But I have no doubt that he lurks somewhere nearby, that he is determined to confront me, and that I will only be free of his attention when I destroy him utterly. Almost I admire his tenacity, and certainly I welcome the hint of challenge as respite from the boredom of centuries. A part of me regrets the necessity of destroying him, because of all my get, Vlad was always the ablest and most interesting companion, just as now he is my ablest and most interesting opponent.

I must not give in to sentiment and underestimate the risk. Vlad has cast himself as my nemesis and he is a relentless and dangerous enemy. It is time to position all my pieces on the playing board and move toward the endgame.

The Notebooks of Abraham Van Helsing

September 22

The new Lord Godalming has returned to Ring to deal with the estate of his late father and Quincey has gone along to provide what comfort he may. I have secured from the former his permission to examine Miss Lucy's papers, as the Westenra family, being now extinct, has willed its possessions into his keeping. I hope to discover hidden in these pages some hint of the source of the evil that has so plagued this house in recent days. As much as I would like to believe there will be no sequel to what we have recently experienced, I know in my heart that we have only taken the first few steps upon what might be a long and uncertain journey.

Jack wanders about in a daze and is presently of no use, but he has a stout heart and I am confident that he will be ready when he is needed. The loss has affected him in some ways more deeply than the others, for he has always felt a degree of sympathy for his patients so deep that he grapples with their ailments as though with a physical foe. For my part, I feel a great weariness, as though the advanced years whose ravages I attempt to deny have finally had their way with me. But if this is to be my last great battle, then let it also be my last great victory.

September 24

The discovery of a diary hidden among Miss Lucy's petticoats is a most hopeful sign that illumination may be possible. Though she appears to have made infrequent entries, they must be of more use than the papers through which I have already traveled with weary eyes. Mrs. Westenra's diary indicates that she was troubled by similar though less powerful dreams than those which afflicted her daughter, and she confesses to swings of mood that made her fear for her own reason. In particular, she alternately loved Miss Lucy's friend Mina like a daughter and suspected her of some invidious harm, although she herself admits that the young woman was ever a good friend to Lucy and by all reports is an artless innocent.

Mrs. Westenra had even grown cold toward Jack, confessed fears that the proximity of his asylum had somehow exposed her to some contagion of the mind, and she was gladdened immensely when Lucy refused his offer of marriage in favor of Holmwood, now the new Lord Godalming.

Perhaps Lucy's own words will add clarity to this still murky picture. I will read them this evening.

September 25

The necessity of intruding upon thoughts meant to be private and secret distresses me, but I steeled myself to the task and have now read through Miss Lucy's words three times. They add little to my understanding of the situation, however, and I despair that any explanation can be found unless chance favors us in some fashion.

Lucy had grown very dependent upon her friend Mina, who seems from this account blameless and unworthy of the sometime suspicions of Mrs. Westenra, who may have planted poisonous seeds in her daughter's mind as well, judging by the most recent entries. There is an intensity of emotional attachment that I find disturbing, but if Miss Lucy's intentions were unnatural, neither young woman seems to have acted upon those impulses except in thought, and Mina herself may well be entirely ignorant of the nature of her friend's affection.

In any case, I will shortly dispatch to Mrs. Harker a request for an audience that I might inquire about certain incidents which may be relevant to the subject of our investigation. Certainly it is Miss Mina who had the most direct experience with Lucy's sleepwalking and she might in retrospect hold a vital clue to the solution of this mystery. I know now the nature of the evil that befell the young lady, though it is such that I will not yet inscribe the words even here lest I be judged mad by some chance reader. The source must be found and destroyed lest it spread even further, and Lucy herself must be spared the inevitable fate waiting for her if the hands of her friends do not place her at true rest.

Enheduanna's Journal

September 26

The game has taken a new turn. I received a communication today from one Abraham Van Helsing, a Dutch physician of good reputation, who was apparently largely responsible for Lucy's surprisingly prolonged life. I had caught glimpses of the man during my visits, but he had seemed innocuous and I had not even thought to secure information about him from Lucy. I am annoyed at my own carelessness in this regard, as I should long since have realized that appearances may deceive, that the most unprepossessing of masks might conceal the most startling features.

Even more disturbing was the intelligence he brought me. Lucy - sweet little Lucy with the childish mind I had thought so shallow that I could plumb its every depth with a casual glance - Lucy had kept a secret even from me. There was a second diary, in which she recorded thoughts she could not share with others, and Van Helsing has examined these words and repeated them in summary fashion to me.

It appears that they hold no damning content, although Van Helsing conveyed without accusation his suspicion that hidden meaning lay locked therein, and that I might hold the key. The glamour was of little use for he is one of those rarities who are only moderately susceptible, but I am determined to contrive another meeting, during which I shall attempt to wipe away anything in his mind which might implicate me. After only briefly touching his thoughts I sensed a ready intelligence there, a threat even, and I have since considered delivering a more final blow. But strength is often best turned by a gentle hand, and this Van Helsing might prove an able knight if he can be employed against my enemy.

To this end I have surrendered into his keeping the papers which I have prepared, my false "Mina" diary, a typed transcription of Jonathan's adventures in Vlad's castle, edited slightly to provide the impression I wish to convey. It required few changes, actually, and even if Jonathan were to read the transcription free of my compulsion, it is not likely he would notice any large divergence from the original account.

After Van Helsing took his leave, all began to fall into place. Lucy's defenders are dispersed at the moment but can be readily recalled if there arises sufficient reason. They would be hot to destroy the source of so much woe, and if it can be arranged that they believe Vlad responsible, they will lend themselves to my hand almost without the need for shaping.

The Notebooks of Abraham Van Helsing

September 26

I have just finished an exhausting journey through foul weather to return from my visit, but it was worth all that I have endured to meet Miss Mina, who is now Mrs. Harker, for I found her to be an admirable and plucky young woman who was deeply affected by the terrible end of her so dear friend. Her eyes never wavered though I believe they must have overflowed with tears once I was gone and she had the privacy to express her grief.

My faint suspicions about her relationship to her friend now seem to me a stain upon my own character as I am certain she is too fine a soul to have lapsed so grievously, and her devotion to her husband (who was absent on a brief business trip) is so evident that there can be no doubt of her true nature. She has perhaps unwittingly provided the key to the mystery, for she has mentioned a passing encounter with a recently arrived foreign gentleman who seemed distinctly taken with Lucy. The coincidence of his arrival and her decline is certainly suggestive and must be looked into more fully.

That pleasantness ended, I must be about more dreadful deeds this evening. Jack will arrive shortly and I fear that tonight will see him tested as he has never been tested before. There are disturbing accounts in the local papers and I can only surmise that it is as I had expected, Miss Lucy is not peaceful in her grave but has risen as a great menace to herself and others. I am an old man, numbering six dozen years, and cannot conquer such great evil unassisted. Jack is my best hope of an ally, but even he will only be convinced if I may place before his eyes proof so definite that it will overcome the restraints of what he has long believed to be true. He will be shocked, no doubt, but I am confident that he has enough strength of character to see things through to their unfortunate conclusion.

The course we must follow is evident to me, no matter how unpleasant. We must visit her grave, poor girl.

The Notebooks of Abraham Van Helsing

September 27

It is as I suspected. Jack refuses to credit what we have seen this evening, at least with the surface of his mind, but the seed is planted deep and in his inner self I think he has already accepted the truth. It will take somewhat longer for the shell to follow.

Her grave was empty, of course, but that might have been the work of grave robbers and I did not expect Jack to be so easily convinced. Our timing was most excellent, in that the thing which had once been a lovely young girl returned even as we stood without the tomb, and our presence there disturbed its purpose such that it abandoned unharmed the small child it had stolen moments earlier. Alas, although Jack clearly caught sight of her form as she returned to the churchyard, it was at a great distance and with the added filter of his own incredulity, he was able to dismiss the night's events as mysterious, even sinister, but was not sufficiently convinced to become wholly allied with me for the ordeal yet to come.

After we have broken our fast, I will endeavor to bring him back during the light of day, in the hope that finding her once again restored to her grave, with her form unnaturally enlivened, he will accept the unpleasant truth for what it is.

Later. Jack is torn between doubt and conviction, but I think it now only a matter of time until he is fully enlisted in our great cause. Lucy was back in her grave, her flesh cold but unspoiled to all outward appearance. Indeed, she seemed almost to glow with life, although I knew it to be one stolen from the blood of her victims. There is no lingering uncertainty in my own mind and I have sufficiently convinced Jack that there is something amiss that he has added his request to my own that Lord Godalming and Quincey Morris return as soon as may be possible, as I believe that it would be best if he who was to have wed the poor lady were present at the end, particularly lest he subsequently hear rumor of the awful duty which has fallen to us to perform and think ill of us through misunderstanding.

If they arrive in time, we may this very evening allay Jack's fears, although I am in sympathy already with the great distress this must cause them all. It will be difficult for them to see Miss Lucy for what she presently is; their eyes will forever be inclined to recognize only the lovely lady to whom they were all one time suitors. I must convince them that they owe her an even greater service now.

Still later. They arrived in sufficient time, for Jack and I were just making ready to leave for the churchyard as their carriage drew up and we engaged it to convey us to the grounds. We concealed ourselves in a pleasant grove until the caretaker had secured the gates and quitted the area, then proceeded directly to Miss Lucy's tomb. There in due course they all saw her animate once again, though none could believe that she truly lived.

Lord Godalming she tried to seduce openly, making sensual suggestions and tearing the cloth from her breasts and thrusting them forward in an intensely lewd manner, failing which she made similar offers to the rest saving only myself, perhaps because resolution showed so clearly in my features. This lasciviousness was so at odds with their recollections of the poor lady that all were immediately convinced of - if not the full content of my explanation - at least sufficient that they deferred to my judgment. At the last I thought Godalming would fail, as he hesitated long with the mallet upraised, and his eyes flickered with indecision, but at last the arm fell and after that first blow it was as if he had set open a floodgate as he bent to the task with almost Herculean vigor despite the writhing and floundering of the tormented creature lying under the stake.

After the deed was done, Quincey ushered him outside while Jack and I severed the head and did those other things which were necessary to ensure that she would rest peacefully hereafter. They are all gone to their rooms now, although I doubt sleep will come easily to any in the house this evening, despite the nearness of dawn. It is a horrible task to which we have set our hands, and more horror to follow if we are to track down the monster responsible and deal with him in similar fashion.

Enheduanna's Journal

September 28

My subtle hints to Van Helsing have borne fruit. He is now convinced that Vlad was the agent of Lucy's doom. We are departing tomorrow for Whitby. A letter has come from the good doctor advising us that it would be unwise to stay at Hillingham as Vlad, "the Count" as Van Helsing refers to him, has already obtained invitation and thus access to that house. Is it so? I think it unlikely or he would have moved more forcefully to destroy Lucy before she could change. The good doctor's misapprehension is of no concern, however. Van Helsing also implies that they have together performed some noxious task concerning her which I suspect has cost me a pawn. As careful as I have been over the centuries, I have not always chosen wisely and some of my get have displayed uncertain judgment and have fallen prey to mortal men. I should have waited until I could watch over Lucy closely, for I fear she has betrayed herself in some careless fashion and paid the inevitable price. It is unfortunate, perhaps, although she would likely have been as poor a tool even after resurrection as she proved to be while on this side of her grave. In any case, there is naught I can do at this late date if my suspicions are correct.

Dr. Seward has thoughtfully penned a brief invitation for Jonathan and I to use a room in his house, which adjoins the asylum. This is a very great convenience. Those unhappy walls will become the fortress from which I direct my diminutive army in the battle to come.

Vlad continues to be much in my thoughts. That night when we slipped away from the field of battle, leaving the dead Turk in his place, he was as uncertain of himself as I have ever seen him. I watched carefully during those first few days, because sometimes the transition is too great a strain on a fractured mind and it becomes unhinged. Madness follows, as the blood thirst seems at first impossible to assuage, and there remains no room for conscious thought or reason, only the urge to kill and drink and feel those spent lives coursing through one's own veins. Those so flawed I destroy quickly, for their impulsive nature will not be governed even by me, and they pose too great a risk. Some few others are biddable but their intellect does not survive intact. They are little more than animals, usually bereft of speech although they seem to understand it well enough. They follow instruction readily, but lack even the slightest initiative. Those too I dispatch, for they are of no use to me.

I was reasonably confident that Vlad would not fall prey to either danger, for his will was as strong as any I had ever met. I feared however that his too rigid mind might not be flexible enough to adapt. He was confused at first and asked many questions, but his step was firm and his reason seemed unaffected. When I warned him that we, or at least he, must seek shelter during the hours of daylight, he accepted my words without argument and, unlike most, did not immediately put this restriction to the test. He slept that first day in a shallow cave while I slipped into a nearby hamlet. I had no need to hunt – the dead and wounded were strewn about the countryside – but I required a carriage to take us away from the area. Horses will tolerate me within reason but will not allow me to ride them. I have pretended a great fear of their kind on more than one occasion in the past, and Lucy was ever after me to stop being foolish and go riding with her. A carriage would serve my purpose and it had the additional advantage that Vlad could take refuge behind its curtains if I chose to continue our journey after dawn.

The search took longer than I had hoped. It would not do to have the alarm raised before we had time to quit the area, so it was necessary to wait for the proper moment. Finally, I saw a white haired man put a slip of a girl aboard a rather old but well maintained carriage, commending her to the care of an equally elderly retainer who seemed ready to fall from his seat whenever he raised the whip. I followed them as they made their way down a narrow path that led either to the next village or, depending on their choice at a fork in the road, to a small, well maintained structure, built like a fortress but probably home to some religious order. I was able to intercept them and dropped onto the carriage from an overhanging branch. The driver was so startled that he might have dropped lifeless from shock, but I gave him no opportunity to do so. I dispatched him so quickly that the girl must never have noticed a change in the pace of the coach.

A bit further on, I turned from the road, sheltering behind a thick copse of trees. The girl emerged cautiously, calling what I assumed was the elderly retainer's name. I made a quick end of her as well, and concealed both bodies in a particularly dense thicket, then settled back to wait for the night. When the sky finally darkened, I brought the carriage back to the road. With the retainer's heavy coat to disguise my sex, I boldly drove directly through the village without hindrance and returned to where I had left Vlad. He was sitting expectantly at the mouth of the cave, waiting to be commanded, but when I called him to me I could see by his restless demeanor that the thirst had come upon him as I knew it must. I had considered keeping the girl alive for him, but the chance of her raising some alarm had dissuaded me.

We took the southwest road, Vlad holding the reins while I sat beside him. I knew that he must be bursting with questions, but he remained silent, and I took a perverse pleasure in mimicking him, even though I had intended to explain all before the night was over. At last I took pity on him as the bitter smell of freshly spilled blood touched the air. It affected him sharply, I could see, so I bade him turn the carriage from the road. The sparkle of a campfire was our guide, around which we found three soldiers who had fled the war, two of them bearing fresh wounds. We waited until two slept, then crept upon the third who kept watch fitfully, dozing and rousing. Vlad took him silently and efficiently, and I found my own bloodlust aroused by the enthusiasm with which he essayed his first feeding. I had intended to leave the wounded men to their sleep, but the need had grown suddenly too great.

I had meant to strike silently, but something alerted one of the sleeping men. He roused and must have seen something of my true nature in the dancing light from the small fire. With a shout, he reached for a dirk that lay beside him, but his questing fingers never touched it. His cry wakened the last man, who took to his heels. Cursing my ill luck, I rose to give chase, but he was struck down before he had taken a dozen steps. Vlad had given him such a blow as must have broken his neck instantly, for he flew backward and fell motionless without making a sound.

I knew at that moment that I had chosen well.

September 29

We have arrived and are settled in our new quarters. Crude by the standards I have grown to appreciate of late, the building is old and was only meant to house unmarried men and even those on a purely temporary basis. Seward's own quarters are somewhat more sumptuous, but the furnishing are unimaginative and thread worn and there is considerable disarray except at his desk, which is much as I would have expected from such a tediously methodical man.

I am less content with the situation than I had originally hoped. We were forced to travel by night to arrive and I have already gone longer than usual without slaking the great hunger that still dominates my life. Indeed, dusk was already heavy in the air outside when we finally arrived at the asylum and adjoining household, and in a weak moment I found my gaze fixed on Seward's throat. Jonathan sensed something unusual in my manner and I quickly covered the lapse with a pretended faint. Although there was no indication that anyone noticed anything untoward, I am distressed by my carelessness, my weakness rather, and wonder if the strain of this encounter is working some unanticipated damage to my nerves.

As expected, Van Helsing has gathered together the remaining three members of my small army, and I will find an opportunity this evening to privately approach each in turn and use the most gentle touch of the glamour to help fix them to my purpose. Godalming and the American are still hesitating, one for his grief, the other because even now he has not completely accepted the evidence of his senses. Lucy shall be the focus, their all too human desire for revenge on her destroyer the hemp that binds them. Even now that she has escaped beyond my reach, Lucy shall continue to be of use to me. As will they all.

September 30

It is done. They have each and every one resolved to stay and see things through. Without assistance they are hardly a match for Vlad, of course, but they shall be my foot soldiers, maneuvered by a general whose existence they will never even suspect. Vlad will not be fooled, and his squeamishness about expending these transient lives will hamper his efforts while I will be free to do as I wish.

The first priority must be to attack his refuge. I had hoped to gain intelligence of his movements at Carfax from Renfield, but he has apparently been most troublesome of late and is confined and guarded in such a fashion that even I would have difficulty approaching him without risking discovery.

On a whim, I expressed to Seward a desire to meet this Renfield about whom he had talked so seriously over yesterday's supper and he indulged me shortly afterward, although I was unable to find a plausible means to arrange for a private interview. Renfield recognized me with some flawed facet of his distorted mind, although I have carefully concealed my true appearance during our previous meetings. The peculiarity of his speech was obvious to me but it escaped the notice of my companions and was dismissed as just another aspect of his madness.

Even such fleeting contact told me much. Vlad's touch is unmistakable, strong enough to indicate that on at least one occasion Renfield must have penetrated into the interior of Carfax or encountered Vlad in person, though I was unable to draw that memory forth under the scrutiny of our companions. The condition of Renfield's mind has greatly deteriorated and even given the opportunity to question him in my own way, I am not certain whether I could extract the information I seek, nor gauge how reliable it might be. The risk may not justify the potential gain. I will think on it further before I act.

Jonathan has just called me to dinner, a waste of time but a duty I cannot presently dispense with without raising questions I prefer not to answer. This subterfuge does not normally irritate me quite so much, but I am impatient to move more directly toward the conflict to come.

Later. It seems I am not the only impatient one. The servants were just clearing away the last of the dishes and we were preparing to retire to the study when I heard the ever so faint flutter of leathern wings. I pretended restlessness and crossed to the windows, pulled aside the curtain to expose the gardens. To my surprise, it was the American whose keen eyes first discerned the furtive shape hovering just above the entrance to the topiary. He excused himself immediately, but I didn't suspect his purpose until the sound of gunfire shattered the night's stillness.

Vlad was gone a moment later; having laid down the glove there was no purpose to be served by remaining. Nor would he wish to risk causing any unnecessary distress to those around me. The bullets would do him no harm even if one struck true to his heart but our kind instinctively respond to any direct threat with a rush of rage that might overwhelm even his fastidious nature. I have long since learned to control that anger but I suspect that Vlad's old habits remain strong beneath the veneer of his new existence, and the thundering impatience that I knew in him even before I made him what he now is must survive in some fashion.

Afterward we reassembled over brandy and Van Helsing expressed the opinion, correct as it happened, that it was in fact the Count himself who had appeared thus transformed. He went on to reassure us that we were safe so long as none from this house invited him within these walls.

"Nor should you extend a welcome to any other not known to you personally," he admonished us, "for the vampire is a master of disguise and might appear in some form which would not elicit suspicion. Beware of tradesmen in particular, and guard your words well as even the implication of welcome may be sufficient to his purposes." Seward and Holmwood both flinched as the good doctor named our kind, which he had not done before in my presence. Jonathan merely nodded, his eyes lost in some remote world or time barred to the rest of us, while Morris, the American, held his face so immobile it might almost have been carved of stone.

They were inclined to accept me as a full member of their company, but as the conversation proceeded I reminded myself that there were certain advantages to be obtained by deferring to the male impulse to believe himself competent and women fragile. It was a simple matter to turn the conversation as I wished and to elicit from Van Helsing the suggestion that I remain behind while they visited Carfax Abbey, safe as it were under the covers of my bed.

They were hardly out of earshot before I too was off on my own business. There are few streetwalkers in Whitby, but I knew the areas they frequented and fortune smiled on me. I brought one to earth in a darkened alley and concealed her body in a pile of refuse that appeared to have accumulated over a considerable period of time. I made certain she would not rise and doubt her remains will be discovered soon unless a concerted effort is made to search the area, and it is unlikely that anyone will care enough to raise any alarm about her disappearance. Her purse contained a few coins and her undergarments needed washing; I doubt she made more than the barest of livings in her sad profession. Sometimes I feel that I grant a small mercy by choosing ones such as this, freeing them from such a miserable existence.

Dull though her life must have seemed, her blood was rich and full of energy. I felt completely restored as I returned to Seward's house and prepared for the return of my diminutive army.

As I waited to hear the outcome of their expedition, I gave thought once again to the past. At what point did Vlad begin to diverge from the path I had expected him to follow? Those whom I have chosen to serve me always begin as my devoted servants, and he had seemed no different. Most require a century or more before they begin to crave independence. They begin with petty rebellions, pretending to have forgotten the tasks I assigned them or making some flimsy excuse, a game to see if I will accept their willfulness and pretend to believe their explanations. In my earliest years, I sought to temper their natures, either by reason or by force. The former only led to more open rebellion, and the latter to sullen resentment and secret disobedience. It was easier and safer to avoid this elaborate dance and simply dispose of a servant whose loyalty could no longer be assumed. Training a replacement was tedious and time consuming but less irritating. And time, after all, is something I have in great supply.

Thinking back now, I suppose Vlad never quite fit into the pattern. During the first few days, he deferred to me because of my greater experience, but he never truly acknowledged my authority over him by word or deed. While he lived, he had been my slave but paradoxically with death had come a loosening of those bonds. He would not openly challenge my authority, and his contradictory opinions were always offered as suggestions, but his self confidence and guarded thoughts were unprecedented. I knew before the tenth day had passed that Vlad was unlike any I had met before, that his grandeur had increased rather than diminished by his transformation. I think even then I was aware that he could be a danger at some point, if never my equal, but the novelty of the situation fascinated me and I stayed my hand.

No, that is not the whole story. I have lived most of my life in a tangle of lies and illusions, but I have always tried to be honest with myself. While he was still among the living, Vlad had seemed to me a particularly well formed puppet, a man shaped bauble of unusual beauty that I had coveted and then taken. Now he was much more to that, and I was drawn to him as a man, even though he was no longer simply that, an attraction that I had never felt before. It was exhilarating at times, but also disturbing, confusing, and occasionally frightening. I often felt that I must strike him down immediately, because anything unknown and unpredictable could also be a threat to me, my secret, even my existence. At other times, I thought he might be a key, a way of gaining access to a world of experience from which I had always been barred. As a child, I had tried to play the same teasing games as the other girls my age, but I was the daughter of a king, which was enough in itself to make the young men wary. They would be polite to me and pretend that they were attracted, but their lies were obvious. Had I truly cared, I might have taken offense, but I neither understood the rules of our play nor took any particular pleasure from it. Doubtless they felt greatly relieved when I dropped the pretense and avoided them. But Vlad had wakened something in me, though I did not know it at first.

I had planned that we would sojourn for a while in the city of Mostar in what was then Herzegovina, but the Ottomans were tightening their grip and it was not as easy to move across the countryside at night. We were stopped more than once by suspicious patrols whom I pacified only by means of the glamour. Then as now, caution dominated my planning and I turned us northward, back into Hungary. We passed through lands whose names are now lost,

Carinthia and Styria, before finding temporary refuge in Vienna, a city I had last visited more than a generation earlier. It had changed greatly, hinting at its present stature.

It was there that we heard that Charles the Bold had been killed in battle. I had met the Burgundian once and admired him somewhat, but after all, mortal lives pass so quickly that it could only matter to a few that his death had come prematurely. We had moved on to Moravia by the time Castile and Aragon reunited to begin the campaign that would eventually drive the Ottomans out of their last strongholds in Granada along the Spanish coast. I did not enjoy living in the lands they had ruled, but their constant warfare had provided a very convenient source of blood and I would later regret their passing, although the powers that replaced them soon proved equally sanguine.

Vlad quietly but obviously chafed at the need to conceal himself during the day. He likened it to his childhood imprisonment and took no comfort when I told him he would learn to tolerate the sun with the passage of years. I had taken as a thrall an elderly merchant and we were living in his manor house. His servants believed that their master was paying me to be his mistress, and they laughed and told stories when they thought I couldn't hear them, and sometimes when they must have known that I heard them all too well. Their misconceptions were useful so I allowed them their haughty airs and ill concealed contempt. None of the servants were allowed into my private chambers, and I considered quartering Vlad there during the day, but the chances of discovery were too great. He voiced no resentment when I banished him to the root cellar of an abandoned cottage, and even declared himself well pleased when I was able to secure enough of his native earth that he could rest in it. I have never understood this peculiar desire on the part of my get, but one and all they have insisted upon it. The soil of my homeland is dry and harsh and I certainly would not wish to rest upon it any more than I wish to rest under it.

As with everything to which he devoted his mind, Vlad had become a superior hunter. He copied my cautious planning and careful execution, and he killed only when necessary to slake the inevitable blood thirst, which he now had nearly completely under control. Even as he supped, he maintained his calm demeanor. I tested his obedience from time to time, and he always deferred to my command with no trace of resentment, although sometimes he was clearly amused. I became even more intrigued with his nature. As my thrall, he had been artistic in his cruelty, slaughtering thousands over a misunderstanding, without differentiating between men and women, soldiers and civilians, adults and children. Even family pets had ended their lives spitted alongside their masters and mistresses.

That great cruelty of his youth seemed to have vanished along with his previous life. He felt no sympathy for his victims, but neither did he take joy in their suffering. When necessary, he ended lives to satisfy his own needs, but he no longer killed for sport or in anger. Except once. I will stop now and try to remember everything that happened that night, and then inscribe it here.

Later

I cannot recall the exact year, but it must have been early in the 1480s. My wealthy thrall had been confined to his bed following a series of increasingly debilitating attacks and I was forced to consider the necessity of moving on. Even if he survived as a bedridden invalid, his influence over his own household would be much diminished. His wife had died without bearing any children who lived past infancy, but he had an older brother whose two children began visiting, supposedly solicitous of their uncle's health, though I saw them examining the furnishings and estimating the old man's wealth and what they might expect from his estate. My presence they ignored entirely. To acknowledge me would be to admit to a scandal. Many men of their uncle's position kept one or more mistresses, whether their wives were among the living or not, but so long as everyone pretended not to notice, the proprieties were maintained.

That would not prevent them from escorting me off the property the very day they had the authority to do so, of course.

Their contempt was not bothersome. I had lived long enough by then to have played many parts, from haughty aristocrat to filthy mendicant. Were my true nature ever to be discovered, I would be hunted to my death. I never had any misapprehensions about the antipathy toward me that would arise in such a situation. Over the course of centuries, I had revealed something of my nature to a handful of mortals not in thrall to me, usually inadvertently, in a moment of carelessness, occasionally as an experiment. Even as a child I had been more puzzled than chagrined when I confronted disapproval or dislike, and my reaction had long since settled into indifference. I was neither pleased by praise nor hurt by condemnation, and truthfully I probably felt as much contempt and loathing for these treasure seeking parasites, who had never so much as spoken to my thrall during all the months since I had first come to him, as they felt for me.

Vlad, as it happened, still retained his aristocratic disdain, and more to the point, he remained my admirer even more now that he had become like me. He chanced to overhear their conversation one evening and took offense. Later that same night, brother and sister met their end. Vlad waylaid their carriage, killed the driver outright, then incapacitated the two passengers and dragged them into the forest. It was two days before they were found, the brother impaled on a rounded stake so that none of his vitals were pierced. He was naked, bound and gagged, with his tongue torn out for good measure. Although he still breathed when they cut him down, he was dead only moments afterward. The sister, I think her name was Irina, was discovered at dusk the same day, buried in a pile of manure so that only her head was exposed. Her tongue had also been removed and her mouth filled with the foul stuff. The heat of decay had cut her torment short.

There was nothing to connect their deaths to me, but it was time to move on. We took only a small fraction of my thrall's ready wealth, so little that it would not be missed now that those most interested were no longer alive.

I considered heading west but the people of Bavaria at the time were cheerless and hostile to outsiders. Although I believed myself schooled enough to pass among them with minimal comment, it had become time for Vlad to learn to comport himself among mortals other than during the hunt. There were literally scores of communities that had declared themselves sovereign, although the powers to both east and west were poised to gobble them up. We found a fresh haven in Silesia, a farming community, posing as man and wife, using some of the stolen gold in our hoard to purchase a small home. It would not do to appear too wealthy, for that would invite constant interest in our business, so we let it be known that we had a moderate allowance from one of my mother's sisters and that we were looking for a quiet location while my husband finished recovering from a long illness that made him particularly sensitive to sunlight. With his head covered and wearing gloves, which were fortunately in fashion, Vlad could even appear during the day for short periods of time.

The only drawback was that the village was rather isolated and we were forced to range further than I preferred in order to find prey. It would not do to cull from our neighbors, who would naturally suspect the coincidence if our arrival was followed by a series of attacks and disappearances. Vlad wished to make an exception for the local butcher, who cheated us quite flagrantly at times, but I forbade that retaliation, promising that he might have his revenge but only when we decided to quit the village. Since we purchased his wares only for show and disposed of them at the first opportunity, it was just as well that he thought of us as gullible fools. Sometime later Vlad was cheated of his revenge when the man choked to death on a fragment of bone.

We remained there for several years, during which time Vlad continued to be my devoted servant, although his old personality grew more and more dominant. He never questioned my decisions, but began to suggest alternatives more forcefully and sometimes asked me to explain my choices. This was not unexpected. Those of my get who survive the first few nights invariably follow the same pattern, cringing admiration, and later respectful deference with the recovery of their self confidence. Then begins their decline. The power they hold over mortals affects their judgment. Some begin to take chances despite my warnings, become careless or even reckless, endangering the secret of our existence. Those I destroy quickly and without warning, because once they have set their foot on that path, they are lost to me. Vlad was never reckless. Others of my get have proven to have better control of their nature. They observe the cautions I take and mirror them, acknowledging my superior experience and judgment. For a time. Sooner or later they all begin to believe that they have seen my faults and know better than I what needs to be done. A few have openly defied me in some small matter, to see how far I can be tested. Only three of my companions have remained loyal for more than two centuries, but eventually even these turned against me. I still remember them fondly despite their betrayal. Vlad alone began to rebel before the first century was over, and he was the only one against whom I stayed my hand even when I knew that he no longer felt bound by my will. He is therefore the only one to have survived long enough to defy me more than once, and the fact that he threatens me now is as much the result of my failure to act as his success at evading me when I finally did.

But there is no time for useless regrets. I must forge a weapon from the poor metal of my companions.

The Notebooks of Abraham Van Helsing

October 1

Were we not engaged in a battle against evil personified, I might find myself sharing friend Jack's obsession with his patient, Renfield. Yesterday the several of us accompanied Jack during an interview and Renfield impressed us all not only with his present rationality but with his keen intelligence and wide ranging knowledge. His manners could not be faulted and his demeanor was reasoned and under control, although once he realized that Jack would not be immediately responsive to his entreaties for release, he gave way to a great despair that was almost painful to observe. Truly this is a soul in great torment, a living hell, and once we have dealt with the greater evil whose destruction we have vowed, I am determined to offer Jack whatever services I might provide to help him in this case.

Appearances aside, the man's mind is clearly gravely unsettled. He ascribes several of his ills, and his present terror, to some mysterious presence whom he refers to alternately as his master or his mistress. This confusion is not uncommon among madmen, says Jack, who dismisses it as an artifact of his illness. Perhaps he is right, but still I must wonder if this is stretching the limits of coincidence too far, if instead he has somehow contrived to sense the wrongness that afflicts this community.

There is a great evil here. I feel it in the air, at night always and often during the day as well. And I think the decay of age has finally crept upon me at last, because my thoughts do not come with their usual crispness and clarity. It is as though spiders had crept into my mind during the hours of darkness, spinning their great webs over my memories and weighing them down. Perhaps if I slept better, this might remedy itself. I must ask Jack to give me something to help calm my thoughts at night.

Enheduanna's Journal

October 1

He has moved quickly, as I expected. Patience was never one of his virtues. There were times when his grandiose plans seemed so impetuous that I feared that his judgment was impaired after all, but then I realized that he always drew back if not convinced that he would be successful. I was rarely forced to openly forbid him to act as he wished, and sometimes allowed myself to be talked into taking chances beyond any I would have accepted normally. Vlad was an exhilarating companion, and the world always took on an extra degree of depth and color when he was present. I miss those moments, those thrills of almost fear, and his ability to stir emotions which I had never felt previously was almost certainly what saved him, what stayed my hand when I finally realized that we would soon be unable to abide each other's company. As my enemy, he has since afforded me similar stimulation, but never as intense, or as constant.

And now I must rely on second hand reports as well. Jonathan was reluctant to talk about their experiences last night, but it requires little effort to put him under the influence of the glamour now. He provided the detailed account which I required, including the intelligence that twenty and one of Vlad's coffins have been dispersed already, though twenty and nine remain. Had I not surreptitiously planted in their minds an unnatural caution, they might have acted precipitously yester evening and destroyed those that lay at hand, thereby alerting Vlad to the immediacy of the threat. As it is, he might well believe his presence in Carfax still unconfirmed, or more likely misapprehend my willingness to act.

I cannot believe he would delude himself that I fear him, or that I would hesitate to strike in my own defense. Dominant though I was through those years during which he was my companion, his was an active intelligence that observed and analyzed even when he was outwardly subservient. I never believed that this sally might deal a critical blow, but it will discomfort him once our intrusion has been revealed at the proper moment and, hopefully, throw him off balance.

I must gather all the strength this body can absorb. Henceforth I will pretend to a mild illness, or perhaps simply a fatigue born of the weight of this very stressful time. I will sleep away as many of the daylight hours as I can manage without attracting Seward or Van Helsing's unwanted attention and thus dissipate less of my strength holding at bay the ravages of the day. As devoted as these men are to the welfare of little Mina, they are no match for Vlad without my assistance and ultimately it will be his strength against my own that resolves the issue. I am determined not to fail through lack of preparation; indeed, I am determined not to fail for any reason.

The Journal of Vlad Tepes

October 1

They have moved against me though, unaccountably, their hands were stayed for the moment. I heard them even before they entered the Abbey and retreated into the shadows to observe and perhaps learn their purpose. Five was their number, Harker and Seward and Van Helsing and two others, one of whom I took to be Lord Godalming. The last had an odd way of speaking which I could not identify though it was the language of this England, and I take him to be Van Helsing, the Dutchman.

They took obvious interest in the boxes which remained and I feared that they had discerned their purpose and would destroy them. Harker and perhaps Goldalming faintly sensed my presence, I think, and Harker might even have seen me fleetingly, although I retreated into the deeper shadows as soon as I felt the touch of his eyes. His senses are peculiarly attuned to me though he may have dismissed his uneasiness as simply enlivened nerves.

Concerned lest they destroy my property on the instant, I summoned the vermin that dwell in large number in the cellars and walls of the abbey and drew them forth in such manner as I hoped would repel these unwelcome invaders. At first I thought my tactic had succeeded, but at least one among their number was foresightful enough to have brought a number of dogs which, after initially refusing to act, were provoked to attack and scatter the host that I had assembled.

Even then I could have joined the fray myself and overcome them, for they were ill prepared otherwise. But to do so would have necessarily caused great harm to these men, who are at worse her puppets. If I had any doubts that they had unwittingly fallen under the influence of my nemesis, Van Helsing's casual reference to our conflict in the terms associated with chess would have dispelled them. Enheduanna was ever one to indulge in such metaphors, characterizing those whose lives she ruined as playing pieces set upon a board whose outline only she clearly saw. I am more determined than ever that she shall continue no longer.

But even now, I find myself drawn to her. How much of this is genuine and now much a reaction to my early thralldom, I shall never know. My own get have always been dependent upon me, but it was ever a fawning, entreating dependence rather than true affection, except perhaps for old Josef, who continues as a true and faithful servant almost as though no change had occurred. Hyrkana and the others bow to my greater power, and at times have attempted to flatter me with their attention, but their words were hollow and their bodies playacting. Yes, only Josef, my loyal servant, has ever demonstrated anything approaching genuine respect and fondness, and even that is undoubtedly only a matter of old and ingrained habits learned before I brought him over. Duty is so deeply rooted in him that it survived even the loss of life.

But at the time I truly loved, or at least believed that I loved her. The longing in my breast during those long years before we were reunited was a smoldering fire that tortured me by day or night, particularly by night. It burst into flame when she finally chose to have me join her completely, or as completely as she has ever allowed another to become a part of her life. I lived only to please my mistress during those early years, and while she sometimes took my cleverness amiss, it was meant to enhance my stature in her eyes, not to challenge her authority.

I looked to her for the answer to every question that arose, and sometimes sought for new questions to ask. She taught me caution by word and by deed, for she was always careful even of me. I think at times she regretted her decision to bring me over, for I was never one to be easily governed, not even by my own will. The unhappy circumstances of my youth had deprived me of the usual bonds of fellowship. There existed between Enheduanna and me something much more intense than that, at least on my side, and I think it touched her as well.

Perhaps against her will, perhaps without even realizing it, she allowed me to glimpse her soul. Beneath that ever calm exterior, I could sense the raging fires of her hatred, an emotion which even now I doubt she acknowledges. After centuries alone, she has come to fear the company of any who know her for what she really is. She has mastered the art of masking herself, her entire personality, wearing characters the way mortals wear clothing, modifying her personality through an act of conscious planning, discarding the facade when it has become too worn, or simply when she has grown tired of it. While she insisted always that she was indifferent to those among whom she remained so well hidden, I began to suspect that she had in a sense turned the glamour on herself. Even as a child, she had been recognized by her playmates as somehow different, and not just because of her noble blood. She laughed when she told me how they shied away from her, but it was a humorless laugh and I sensed a wound that had not healed even with the passage of centuries.

It was only after she had told me stories of her earlier companions, those she had made and later unmade, that I began to understand her vulnerability. She desperately wished to be other than alone, but at the same time, she was driven by the desire to punish those who had spurned her so long ago, punish them over and over again. When those she made began to display signs of independence, she invariably destroyed them, making excuses to herself, insisting that eventually they would have challenged her and that she was only acting to protect her own existence. I suppose that the prudent course would have been to conceal my growing self confidence, as I suspect had many of her previous companions, but my spirits were too high, my pride too great to allow me to act other than as I always had. And perhaps in some fashion I desired even then an end to my own pain, at her hand or that of another. That end will come to me soon now, whether I succeed or fail. Nothing can alter me from that course.

I still remember her reaction the first time that I openly questioned her judgment. We were on our way to Buda. Moldavia had just fallen to the Turks and refugees filled the roads. The confusion suited our needs well. Bandits and deserting soldiers killed so many travelers that a few more deaths at our hands would not be noticed. We had accumulated a considerable quantity of gold and some precious gems, much of which we cached along with Enheduanna's most recent journals. She had many similar hiding places for this chronicle of her life, an endeavor I never understood as she refused to allow me to read a single word from them. I often wondered if, her spoken words to the contrary, she knew herself to be as mortal as any other, and hoped to leave behind this written record of her existence, which might survive the death of her body.

Although we could take advantage of the prevalent chaos for the moment, eventually we would have to make more permanent arrangements to secure ourselves against chance mishaps. Enheduanna believed that the Ottoman Empire would continue to expand to the west and north, but I had reservations, and thought that the span of their power had already begun to collapse under its own weight. Their officers did not enjoy the respect of the men under their command, which was troublesome, nor did they fear them, which was disastrous. I had fought the Turk long enough and recently enough to understand something of their culture, and these latest advances seemed to me the last flailing of a mortally wounded creature. Already the Habsburgs in Hungary and Safavids in Persia seemed more confident in their ability to turn the tide. Although the Persians soon faltered and proved me wrong on their account, the Habsburgs flourished as I expected, and the Portuguese drove their own blade in through the Turkish underbelly. Where in all this chaos would we find safe haven?

"We shall make our way to Adrianople," Enheduanna announced one evening. "The center of the world moves east and we shall follow it."

"As you wish, mistress, but would it not be safer to stay where we are until we see how matters unfold somewhat? The land between here and the Byzantine is greatly unsettled."

Her expression told me that I had startled her, as in fact I had intended. It was the first time I had questioned her judgment in even this modest fashion.

"I tire of the rustic life, Vlad. Two strangers, a wealthy woman and her servant," she paused them to make sure that I heard and understood my role, "will not face the scrutiny in such a metropolis as they will in a smaller community. People come and go in Adrianople in their countless numbers every day, and some die and some disappear and often their passing is as unremarkable as their arrival. We will have no difficulty finding a place for ourselves."

It had been a gentle test on my part, and she had noticed, so I merely nodded, acknowledging her authority. When she remained as she was, watching me, I knew our roles had altered, that I was about to be judged. "What would you have me do in preparation, mistress?"

Although my words were deferential, I remained curious about her reaction and something in my stance, or perhaps the set of my eyes, betrayed me. She closed the distance between us quickly and silently, moving with that sudden silken grace which she conceals when mortal eyes are watching. I could feel the radiance of her power as she stood close before me. My own blood ran cool in my veins then as now, but hers was more volatile, its heat sometimes rising to match the intensity of her mood. It burned like a fever now and I tensed, realizing that she had seen more than I had planned to reveal. She placed one hand on my arm, squeezing it with what appeared to be gentle affection, but I could feel the strength in her hand and knew she could kill me without great difficulty at that moment if she so willed it. I was strong then, stronger than I had been as a man, but she drew the iron from my muscles and it was all I could do not to flinch.

"Do you still love me, Vlad?"

"Of course, mistress, as I always shall." I spoke the truth. It is true now, even though I have decided that she must be destroyed, as all of our kind must be destroyed, even I. We are an abomination, a mistake, and the immortality which we possess is an illusion, for surely we are damned and in Hell itself even though we walk among the living. But I loved her then and I love her now.

She was so close that I might have breathed the same air as she if my lungs had still worked in that fashion, as hers did and still do. "I believe you mean what you say, Vlad, but you are wrong. One day you, like all the others, will betray me. Do not hasten that day, for I shall miss you more than most."

"I would not displease you, mistress."

"No, but you will." This last was almost a whisper as she turned away.

We passed from Buda to Temesvar, to Vidin and Nish, skirting my native Wallachia but never crossing onto its soil. We were attacked by a band of thieves on the road to Sofia, who thought to take us unawares in the darkness. Eight of them lay dead within moments, and we both fed over well. Then Philippopolis, where we visited another cache and withdrew both specie and jewels, and finally Adrianople, which would be our home for almost forty years. It was there that we watched one century end and another begin, and it was there that I finally slipped my leash. It had been loose around my throat for some time, for she indulged me more than any before or, presumably, since. Mercy was never a part of her nature, but I believe that I touched something that she had always concealed, even from herself. Her resolve faltered and the stage was set for my escape.

And now I must reward her by bringing about her destruction.

The Notebooks of Abraham Van Helsing

October 1

I secured from Jack today permission for a brief interview with Renfield. He was much altered from yesterday, having turned his attention inward, his despair such a palpable thing that I left the interview chamber saddened and recovered my equanimity only with considerable effort. Renfield seemed resigned not only to his confinement but to some larger and imminent disaster which he would not describe. I almost cut the conversation short but a chance reference to Mina excited him somewhat and he spent no few minutes describing to me his utter devotion to the young lady, entirely disproportionate to his limited knowledge of her, although I was of course in complete sympathy with his feelings, for she is indeed a person of rare nobility, no matter how humble her origins.

He soon retreated into his inner misery, however, and the only other noteworthy feature of the interview was his continued confusion of "master" and "mistress". When I confronted him on this very point he insisted that he had never done so, that it was always his master to whom he referred, but in the midst of his protestations he occasionally mixed the terms again, apparently entirely unawares.

His is a bizarre but fascinating failing of the intellect.

I napped during the afternoon and woke with a single thought at the forefront of my mind. A question, in fact. How had the Count obtained access to Hillingham, as he must have done in order to repeatedly attack Miss Lucy? A servant perhaps? Or Lucy herself in some unguarded moment? The latter seems the most likely explanation. It is of no consequence now, I suppose, but for some reason I was unable to put the uncertainty out of my mind for some considerable time and mentioned it over supper. No one offered any solution, and it appeared as well that none but I considered it a point of any concern at this late date.

Mina has just asked that I join her for a moment as she has recollected something which is not recorded in her diary.

Later. I am glad that I expressed my puzzlement as we dined, because it stimulated a long buried memory. Mina has confided in me that at least one of Miss Lucy's sleepwalking episodes went unrecorded, that on a single occasion she found that her friend had quitted the house entirely and wandered out into the grounds. Mina searched in the darkness for some considerable time before discovering Miss Lucy unclothed and prostrate in the churchyard that adjoins the property. Fearing scandal, Mina told no one of the incident at the time and was so disturbed by its bizarre nature that she failed even to record it in her most private diary.

"Did anything about Miss Lucy's appearance or behavior give you reason to believe that something extraordinary or untoward took place upon this occasion?" I inquired.

"Her night time excursions were always extraordinary, Doctor, but I believe in this instance she seemed quite weak and lacking in will. I ascribed this at the time to her confusion upon waking in a strange place as well as the unsettling coolness of the evening, but there may have been another cause."

"And by neither word nor action did she indicate any awareness afterward of remembering this unusual event?"

"None, sir. Indeed, I thought to tell her of it the following morning, but I feared to embarrass or even frighten her, and simply redoubled my efforts to watch over her sleeping hours and prevent any recurrence."

"Perhaps that was best," I reassured her. "The child is beyond all hurt now, but such a revelation could have brought her great distress at the time."

It seems clear to me that Lucy was the unwitting agent of her own destruction. Her mind was seduced by the Count and her body became subject to his will perhaps on that very evening. It would have been a matter of little effort to extract an invitation under those circumstances, and the walls of Hillingham would never afterwards have prevented his entry.

I am determined to see this evil ended before it preys on more innocent souls.

Enheduanna's Journal

October 2

Over confidence destroyed my father millennia ago when he thought to defeat a better prepared enemy, and today it almost brought down his daughter's plans as well. After the others returned without incident from their expedition to Carfax Abbey, I concluded that Vlad was biding his time, that with the passage of years he had finally learned some restraint and was willing to wait for conditions to be more favorable to his efforts. At the same time, I believed myself safe from any direct attack, and the recent kill had filled my veins with a surfeit of fresh energy, in which condition I often find myself unduly optimistic. But blood calls to blood and the old lust remains strong. It would normally be at least ten days before I fed again, but I wanted to draw even more strength into my body. I will not underestimate Vlad, even when he appears to be mine for the plucking. Pleading an aching head, I retired as darkness fell and escaped through the window, intending to proceed directly to the fishing village and find a fresh victim.

Vlad must have been watching the house, waiting for me to venture out, although from some considerable distance as I never felt even the slightest hint of his presence until I was standing over the supine form of a drunken fisherman who had collapsed conveniently in the bottom of his boat. I was not intending to kill this evening, just draw enough to sharpen my senses, and my attention was so fully directed toward that purpose that I allowed myself to be taken by surprise.

"You look well, my lady."

I turned to find Vlad standing almost within reach, wrapped still in his great cloak, his grossly Slavic features more sharply delineated than I remembered, though I judged him to be not much older in appearance than when we first met. "It has been a long time since last we talked, Vlad."

"Long and long. You know why I am here."

"I know what you intend. Surely you don't believe that you have become my equal already. When I spared your life in Trieste..."

"Spared my life? You had long since taken my life. You took from me all that was human and more." His voice had risen, but now it dropped. "But I was a miserable human when you found me, and perhaps the loss was not as great as it might have been. Nor could you be other than true to your own nature, however unnatural."

"I could have put an end to you, then, had I wished it. You understand my meaning. I might have destroyed you as I should have done when you first challenged me, but I chose not to."

"For purposes of your own. Perhaps it amused you to have a rival. Existence has been a burden for you at times, has it not, as it has for me?"

"At times, yes." He spoke truth, but not the entirety of it. "That doesn't mean I would willingly relinquish it any more than would you."

"It's part of our curse, yes, that we cling to that which we at the same time abhor."

I laughed in genuine amusement. "When not only the people whom I had known but even the country that spawned me vanished from the face of the earth and yet I continued, I too felt cursed. For years I railed against the cruel fate that had transformed me into a creature who was forever alone, who only felt truly alive during the hours of darkness, and who must forever look at the sun as unfriendly and foreign. But as the years rolled past in their endless numbers, I came to an accommodation with the world, and as I grew to accept and understand my true nature, the world itself became more tolerant and I was better able to face the day. As a child, a few hours spent outside brought tiny blisters which only faded with the fall of night. My body learned to tolerate it, and the outward signs grew less troublesome. You too have learned to abide the sun, have you not?"

"In moderation," he admitted. "It draws away my strength and muddles my thoughts, but I am no longer confined to the shadows."

"So why this animosity? Surely I have done you a great service in so prolonging your existence that you can live to see entire nations rise and fall. Your old enemies are all dust now, and their children as well. Not even a mother can give her child as much life as I have given you."

"It was a gift unasked, a curse undeserved despite my great weight of sin. But I no longer resent your act, for I know the power of the bloodlust. At the same time, I cannot allow you to continue as you have done in the past. Perhaps if you had grown in wisdom as I have..."

"Wisdom? Is that the name you give to weakness, Vlad Tepes?"

"I've grown rough skin since last we jousted, Enheduanna. Your thorns cannot prick me. I am armored against your bladed tongue, and it was not the sharpness of your wit that drew my blood."

It was spoken offhandedly, but the condescension implicit in that single sentence infuriated me so greatly that I stepped toward him with my true face revealed and struck with the full force of the glamour.

For a moment, my strength seemed to surprise him and he retreated before me, right to the stern of the small fishing craft where he staggered briefly while seeking to free himself from the glamour. This was not how I had pictured our final encounter, but the moment was at hand, or at least so I thought, and I was ready to see it through to its conclusion. But then he visibly recovered and cast off the grip of the glamour as none has ever done to me before, and a moment later took hold of me, catching both my wrists and pulling me close, his own fangs prominent now as he also showed his true face, lowering toward my throat.

I can only believe that it was the novelty of the situation that robbed my body of its strength, my mind of its usual clarity. For brief seconds, he was my master and I swayed toward him, ready to surrender. But the weakness passed and I thrust my will against his, grappled mind to mind as well as body to body, felt the grip of his hands falter just long enough to wrench myself free.

"You were never strong enough to stand against me, Vlad. You never will be. I have the advantage of centuries and while time otherwise has little significance to our kind, it places you always at a disadvantage. Every strength you find within yourself is one I learned years before. We might be set upon the same path but I will forever be a dozen, a hundred steps ahead of you."

"Perhaps I have quickened my pace, or found a shorter route."

"It's not in your nature, Vlad. Your eyes are always focused straight ahead, unblinking, oblivious to alternatives."

"It may be that I have changed since our last encounter."

I laughed, genuinely amused. "You're incapable of such change, Vlad. It's your greatest strength as well as your most telling weakness."

"All things change, Enheduanna, and all things end. Even you."

"Perhaps, but not at this time, and not at your hand." And so saying I assaulted him again with the full force of the glamour, drawing upon the power as never before. He reeled back, one arm raised as though to shield his eyes, but I forced my will beyond that feeble barrier, reaching for the very core of his being, knowing that once I held it within my grasp, I could turn him to my purposes, though my control would hold only so long as I devoted all my strength to that single endeavor.

It might have ended there, but he was stronger than I expected, or perhaps I was overconfident and inattentive. Once more I felt his mind escape my grasp. A great wind rose, buffeting us about, and I was distracted for only a moment, but long enough that he broke my grip a second time, and resisted my efforts to reassert control. Although he was physically my superior, I had not thought he could hope to stand against the full force of my will, and I still believed I could wear him down in time. He raised his arms as though to grapple with me, but thought better of it, nodded ambiguously in my direction, then eluded my grasp and faded away into the shadows so quickly that I confess he earned my admiration.

I thought to pursue but the manner and ease of his escape were so unexpected that I was left frozen in consternation. Never before had he shown such resistance to the glamour; it had taken more than a thousand years for me to first learn its use, and Vlad, a comparative stripling, was already capable of escaping my most robust assault. I was so bemused that I left without touching the moribund sailor, who had remained completely unaware of the terrible battle taking place over his prostrate body.

I returned to Seward's house in a fury so intense that I raged from room to room, howling silently inside with an intensity of emotion that rivaled that of even the most crazed of those incarcerated nearby, my anger spreading like a stain to disturb their sleep and bring the night staff from their wardrooms with clubs to hammer them back to something resembling silence.

In the rooms assigned to us, Jonathan lay in the stupor into which I had driven him before leaving through the window above our narrow bed. His vulnerability fueled my anger and I came close to risking all that I had striven to build here, my teeth a hair's width from the pulsing vein in his throat. The desire was so intense that long forgotten pain ripped through my body and I cried out, heedless of the possibility this might attract the attention of those others who slept unsuspecting around me. It would not do to have Van Helsing see me in such a state; the man's facilities are dimming along with his vitality, but his mind remains quick and is enriched by a lifetime spent searching for knowledge. He might not believe, might not want to believe, but the seed would be planted and even if he had been more vulnerable to the glamour it would have been difficult if not impossible to suppress that knowledge without destroying him utterly.

With great effort I tore myself away and swept aimlessly back and forth from window to door. The call of the blood was too strong to be denied, however, and at last I slipped out into the darkened passageway, more in control now but still determined to slake my thirst. I passed those doors behind which slept the others of our company, Van Helsing, Holmwood, Morris, and then past Seward's own chambers and down the stairway to the foyer which linked the smaller house to the asylum. A wardsman was on duty there, but he was nodding at his post and it was a simple matter to slip past, ease the door open, and venture into the heart of madness.

They had quieted, at least to the level that was considered normal there. One or two moaned continuously while another called out sporadic imprecations and yet another sobbed softly and inconsolably in the grip of a grief whose source he no longer even recalled. Two warders were on duty here as well, but they had retreated to their station on the mezzanine and were amusing themselves with a game of cards, trying as best they could to ignore the unfortunates surrounding them.

I could have taken any of them, but they were for the most part a sorry lot, infirm in body as well as in mind, and I sought richer blood, something that would restore my vigor and soothe the anger that threatened to utterly destroy my composure. And one spirit stood out like a candle flickering in the darkness, drawing me as irresistibly as if I had been a moth. Renfield, quiet in his cell, but awake, alert, aware of my presence through the use of senses he did not consciously recognize or employ.

A special guard had been laid on to watch his door, but it required only the slightest effort to send the man into a deep sleep from which he would eventually waken disoriented and unrested. I could feel Renfield's awareness even before I let my body alter so that I could slip between the bars and confront him directly.

"Master," he said softly, and bowed his head.

Prepared as he was to see me in the shape of my enemy, Renfield's eyes betrayed his confusion as I approached. I had no patience for such matters at that moment and pressed forward, catching hold of his shoulders and forcing him to his knees before me. Mad blood tasted just as sweet as sane, and Renfield was filled with life, his own and that of the creatures he had consumed in some convoluted imitation of the power he sensed in my touch. It was lucky for him that he remained so robust, because I was sated before we reached the point of no return, although even then I knew he'd never be free of my control now and that his death would be at my hands. He had become my thrall more completely even than my husband.

I returned to Jonathan's side a short while later, waked him long enough to discover what had passed among the others during the day. Their council of war was industrious but doomed to fail unless I interceded on their behalf; Vlad was far too wary to fall victim to their simple plans.

I must involve myself more directly, though without betraying myself.

The Journal of Vlad Tepes

October 3

It is almost dawn and I must rest even though I doubt that I can ever truly be at rest again. I have nearly killed an innocent soul this evening despite my vow never to do so again, and I have caused grievous hurt to a poor madman who lacks the wit to understand his part in a struggle not of his own making that has swallowed him up almost as an afterthought.

I had hoped to gain some intelligence of what was happening in Seward's house, where my enemy has taken up lodging and where she no doubt twists her companions to her purposes. There was no reason to believe that she suspected my suborning of Renfield, and despite his untrustworthiness, I had hoped that he would provide me with at least rudimentary knowledge of her activities. At worst, I would enter the establishment through his cell and explore on my own, prepare for the final assault which I feel will be pressed upon me quickly now. We have tested each other and she is as strong as I feared, but perhaps does not yet realize how far I have come since our last encounter.

Renfield was always an unreliable source, but through his eyes I have seen the physical layout of the asylum and the habits of the attendants. Although he had been moved from his original cell, only a few moments were required to identify the barred window behind which he was presently confined, a barrier which presented no obstacle since I had already received his freely given invitation. I had meant only to look into his mind and discover what chance intelligence might have come his way, but immediately upon regaining my human form, I found myself under attack. Unarmed as he was, Renfield presented no threat to me, but the body reacts instinctively and I responded to the futile assault with unthinking savagery. It was as though a normal human had struck a child's toy of straw and cotton. Renfield was thrown the length of the narrow cell with such force that I heard the snap of his back breaking as he was brought up short against the far wall.

I moved quickly to his side, though there was nothing to be done for the poor soul. I sought the reason for his foolish action and found it. There was a poisonous serpent implanted in his mind, her doing, a knot of thought and emotion that had compelled him to attack me. She was aware of my subversion of her creature and had turned him into a weapon against me.

Maddened even further by his pain, Renfield was battering his face against the floor with such force that his features were already bathed in blood. I reached forward, hoping to bring him some peace, but the commotion had roused the attendants and already I heard the sound of a key in the lock. I could not chance discovery at that moment, not there and under those circumstances, so I quitted the cell immediately, descending into the adjoining courtyard.

My fury had only partially abated, however, and I moved to the opposite side of the building, searching for the window behind which I believed my enemy to be sheltering. It was a foolish impulse that drove me to the offensive, but an impulse that almost succeeded because of its very desperation. I surprised Enheduanna as she sat beside the bed upon which the unfortunate Harker lay in a stupor too deep to be entirely natural. She stood up as I entered through the window, and I believe I saw a momentary alarm in her face, though it was quickly masked.

I closed with her immediately, forcing her up against the far wall, carefully avoiding the trap of her bottomless eyes. I knew I must engage her now, while she was unprepared, and end it quickly, before she could gather the power of the glamour and repel me once again. Even so, she very nearly wrenched herself free at the outset, for she is indeed far more powerful than she appears, but in this contest at least I enjoyed enough of an advantage that she could not break my grip. We stood like lovers embracing one another, straining for advantage. The close quarters made it impossible for either of us to deliver a killing blow, although she sank her fangs deep into my breast. I marked this as desperation, for she could not hope to quench my life thusly, but that was not her intention. Instead she was drawing forth the source of my strength, which must eventually turn the tide of battle in her favor. Realizing her purpose, I shifted my weight so that she leaned backward awkwardly, and when she tried to adjust, I was able to break her hold. She was wearing her true face and it was twisted in rage as I lifted her from her feet and swung her about. She writhed in my grasp and moved her hands to my wrists, squeezing with such intense force that I knew I could not hold her long. In desperation, I threw her back onto the bed where she fell across the supine body of her husband. What might have happened next I will never know, for fate intervened.

The door to the room burst open at that moment, revealing Van Helsing and Seward, both wearing nightdress and staring in befuddlement. I considered pressing the battle despite their arrival, but some of my fury had ebbed along with the life's blood Enheduanna had stolen from me and I thought better of it. I would like to say that I was concerned lest I take innocent lives, but in truth, it was fear of failure rather than concern for her unwitting dupes that motivated me. The bloodlust had possessed me as much as it had Enheduanna, and no living being was safe in my presence. When she turned her face from them, letting it settle back into the guise of Mina Harker, I knew the battle must be halted for now. I fled the room in confusion and frustration, pursued only by her scream of frustrated rage. I felt a similar scream rise in my own breast, but it did not pass my lips.

Jack Seward's Journal

October 3

Last night was such a parade of nightmares, I don't truly know where to begin to record them. First, let me set down here if nowhere else my admission that I have lost much of my faith in the rational world. When Van Helsing first hinted at the cause of our present terror, I thought the man senile, and even after the distressing events in dear Lucy's mausoleum I wondered if perhaps we were suffering from a shared madness. But now I realize that it is the world that has gone mad, not my companions and myself, and that it is necessary that we act to restore as much as we can of an orderly state of existence.

Of the Count's vampiric nature, there can be no further doubt. I saw his face clearly before he escaped through the open window of the Harkers' bedchamber. The features were animal...no, more bestial than mere animals. They were those of a fiend from the deepest recesses of the Hell I had once thought only a metaphor. If such things as Count Dracula can roam free in this life, I cannot doubt that even more ghastly inhabitants dwell in the one that comes after.

We arrived barely in time as it chanced, drawn by the sound of a struggle. Jonathan was deep in a trance brought upon him by the intruder, and Mina was within heartbeats of the end of her young life. Her scream of terror chilled us all even as the foul creature fled our presence.

He is also, I can only assume, responsible for the death of Renfield, the madman, attacked in his cell a few moments earlier. The man's back was broken and his face beaten brutally against the rough floor. After we were certain Mina was safe, Van Helsing operated on the poor wretch but even his skills prolonged the man's life for only a few hours. And so the list of Dracula's sins grows longer.

The double attack has unsettled us all, particularly Mina, who presently avoids even her husband's company, hiding herself in the rooms I have loaned them. I think Van Helsing was sorely troubled by his inability to save Renfield, and he has openly expressed fear that our resources are inadequate to forever thwart the Count. At the same time, I feel that this near disaster has had its positive side, as it has proven Dracula not beyond the capacity of misjudging a situation, and has alerted us to the immediacy of his menace. We will not again be caught so unawares, nor will we remain content to take a passive, defensive posture.

The morning has been spent making plans. Today we will take the attack to our enemy. I trust in the rightness of our cause to see us through against any adversity.

Enheduanna's Journal

October 3

My pride was almost my undoing yester eve, but Vlad's arrogance will certainly be his before much longer. With Jonathan in a sleep from which only I could wake him, I was completing my transcription of Dr. Seward's recordings, the originals of which I will contrive to destroy accidentally in the near future. The few details I expunged from these records are not of major consequence, but I have learned to be cautious even in the smallest of things.

Vlad caught me by surprise, as it had not occurred to me that he might have access to Dr. Seward's quarters, but of course he had visited Renfield already and the buildings are actually one though they seem separate. I must remember that Vlad is no casual enemy, and that mistakes such as this can be costly.

As I suspected, he is physically my equal, perhaps even my superior, and when fully aroused he is almost impervious to the glamour. He was strong enough to restrain me despite my best efforts, but in so doing placed himself in a position where he could not immediately deal me a deathblow. Fortunately I was able to inflict a small wound through which I drained enough of his strength to worry him. Rather than continue a possibly fruitless struggle to escape, I pressed closer, supped on Vlad's own blood, too thin for my tastes, perhaps diluted by his predilection to prey only on simple beasts. His hand closed upon the side of my neck as he attempted to wrench me away, and his nails left slight scratches, but I was able to deflect his efforts to deal me a fatal hurt.

Whether or not I could have stolen sufficient of his strength to overcome him before he defeated me is a question which will not now be answered. Seward and Van Helsing intervened and Vlad fled before them, pursued only by my cry of anger. Had either of these men looked closely in my direction, that might have been the end of the charade, as I have no doubt they would have recognized the truth in my distorted features for my true face had emerged during the struggle. But the shadows served me well, and before they had turned away from the window through which Vlad had made his escape, I was once again the dull, timid Mina Harker whom they were sworn to protect.

Vlad will no doubt mark this as a minor defeat; his ego will not allow him to admit that he might have been bested in a contest of his own design, and on the surface, my escape was narrow indeed. I have once again underestimated my adversary. But there is an advantage here for me that neither of us might have anticipated. It is as yet a dull blade, but one I might still hone into a killing device. Having once again supped on Vlad's undead blood, I hold a part of him within me for a time, and if I concentrate with my own eyes closed against the world, I can almost see through his.

The sensation is disconcerting and at first I suspected it was an illusion, as this has not occurred when previously I killed those of my making. But I sequestered myself from the rest of the company, pleading a distressing headache and a desire to remain quiet, and I was able to focus the visions to a greater degree of clarity. There was a shared spirit between the two of us for a time, and despite our present differences, I believe that we are still more alike than Vlad would admit. The images are obscured and indistinct, and I cannot maintain the contact for long, but should I so choose, I can briefly steal into my enemy's mind and touch his senses.

This can only work to my advantage.

When Van Helsing and the others broke in upon us, a fresh gambit occurred to me, one that I hope will whip my entourage into even greater efforts. I feigned a mild fainting spell, to which Van Helsing responded with his usual cloying devotion. It took only a mild application of the glamour to convince him that the scratches on my throat were in fact evidence that Vlad had tasted my blood, for he was predisposed to believe exactly that. I will wear a scarf henceforth to cover these shameful marks, although the small hurt will have vanished by morning.

In the event that he presses another attack, this subterfuge will provide an explanation if any of my companions notice a transformation of my features, which alteration is sometimes ungovernable in the heat of the moment. In fact, Jonathan commented upon my extreme paleness as Van Helsing was ministering to my injuries, and I noticed Seward staring at my mouth anxiously. Whether it was simply his fear that I had become a thing like their enemy, or some lagging suggestion of my true face, I cannot be certain.

I playacted for them, perhaps with somewhat more melodrama than was required, but I thought a touch of hysteria might add to their general confusion and smooth over any small error I might make. When I suggested the possibility of taking my own life rather than becoming one of the Undead, these supposedly stalwart gentleman burst into tears. As if women were such fragile flowers that a harsh touch on a petal could wither them to the root! I could tell them, if I had a mind to, of women stronger than most men, women who sent armies to their doom, cut the living hearts from their enemies, and who proved themselves second to none in acts of cruelty, brutality, and slaughter. I make no apologies for the bloody acts I have performed, but I have always conducted myself dispassionately, never inflicting cruelty for its own sake. If they knew my true nature, they would call me monster, but I have known far greater monsters and they were each and every one a mortal.

If it had been necessary, I would have used the glamour to color their memories of the night's events, but they have cast a kind of glamour over their own minds which makes my efforts almost superfluous. The human propensity to willfully substitute illusion for reality is a mystery to me, but also a convenience.

The Journal of Vlad Tepes

October 3

The sun will be up shortly but I shall not rest until I set my thoughts in order. After abandoning my attack in the face of overwhelming odds, I found it difficult to think clearly, for I was so consumed with rage that the animal within me had supplanted what is left of the man I once was. Fearing that Enheduanna would take advantage of my confusion to destroy me, I avoided Carfax and came instead to my refuge in the untended churchyard where I have concealed this journal. There is no question but that she knows that the abbey is one of my lairs, and it puzzles me that she has not acted to deprive me of this haven. In any case, I shall use it no further but instead rely on those locations to which I have dispersed the majority of my boxes. If the need arises, I could abandon them all, but to do so would deprive me of their restorative powers and make it impossible for me to continue this campaign with any confidence of success.

Although I failed a second time, it was on this occasion not unmitigated. At the back of my mind a terrible thought has been lurking, the possibility that Enheduanna has traveled so far ahead of me that I could have no real expectation of besting her. Tonight has proven otherwise. In sheer physical strength, I am her superior. She has come to rely too exclusively upon the power of the glamour, and when I engaged her before she could gather its power, she discovered that it was not a reliably effective weapon against me. For the first time I knew that she was uncertain of herself. I sensed as well an unhealthy intensity in her rage and an undercurrent of an even deeper uncertainty. In times past, she would never have allowed herself to display such deep anger, however acutely she felt it. Perhaps in the depths of her mind she fears me more than she consciously realizes, or perhaps even her mind cannot support such an unnatural existence indefinitely.

These idle speculations are interesting, but I cannot trust them. More than once she has chided me for my overconfidence. She admonished me for my rash acts in Ragusa and Prague and during our sojourn in Salonica after we were forced to leave Naples. That at least was due to the indiscretion of one of her thralls, a woman whose steadfastness I had questioned from the outset, rather than my lack of discipline. I pretended humility on each occasion, but never really learned it until we strove against one another in Trieste and she nearly destroyed me. The scars of that education remain unhealed within my mind and soul. I do not intend to repeat that error.

Any further assault on her lodgings must be ruled out. She and her allies are alert to my presence and intentions, and are aware of my ability to enter their quarters. They will guard against me, their own ingenuity subtly guided by her silent commands. The battleground must be elsewhere, but how to lure her to it? I must avenge myself and the countless victims she has claimed during her unnaturally prolonged life. If I fail, I fear that there is no other intelligence upon this earth with the wit, power, and knowledge to defeat her. It is no boast to acknowledge that fact.

I must rest. My mind is in disarray, troubled by images from tonight's conflict, which recalled to me that terrible day which I survived only at her mercy. I must set down an account of what transpired in Trieste, memories of which have chased each other around inside my head for more than two hundred years. Until now, I have never allowed myself to remember them too clearly, but I think that I must understand what happened between us fully and explicitly, so that the outcome this time may be different.

Jack Seward's Journal

October 3

Jonathan's investigations have returned excellent results. We learned quickly of the boxes delivered to Mile End, Bermondsey, and Walworth, and were already aware of those in Carfax Abbey, but these sites accounted for only the greater part of those we knew to have been brought to England. Driven by his fears for poor Mina, Harker pursued the matter further and from one Samuel Bloxam he has identified houses in Purfleet and Piccadilly. By my count, all but one of Dracula's refuges have now been located, although the absence of the final box is perplexing and disturbing. It is my hope that either Bloxam or the cartage company miscounted and that the one outstanding will be found when we render the others useless to the Count. Alternatively, it is possible that the missing one was destroyed or damaged during the shipwreck, or experienced some other mishap.

We will split into two parties after dealing with Carfax, Quincey and Arthur rejoining us at Piccadilly, where the greatest number of boxes are stored, perhaps awaiting further dissemination throughout London. Harker was determined to remain behind to protect Miss Mina, but she appeared quite upset at that prospect and insisted that he would be of far greater service to her in our company than at her side.

The unfortunate consequence of Van Helsing's attempt to drive the evil from her body has convinced us all more than ever before of the danger she faces. That we all face.

Later

It is done, but the creature himself has eluded us. Carfax Abbey was cleansed without incident. Arthur and Quincey then set out for 197 Chicksand Street while the rest of us proceeded to Jamaica Lane. There was no sign of the Count, although we found his boxes as well as a considerable amount of coin, at each of our stops. The five of us were reunited at Piccadilly where, by our final tally, we finished our tasks with one box still outstanding.

We were considering our next step when the object of our minor crusade appeared in person. I was, I must admit, frozen as if turned to stone when he entered. Only Jonathan, perhaps still enraged by the attack on his wife, found the will to move, springing toward the monster with a long bladed knife. The Count eluded him handily, but as the rest of us stirred to life, he abruptly flung himself through a window, landing uninjured in the courtyard below. He taunted us briefly, shouting enigmatically about his quest for revenge. His rage slurred his words and he shouted at Arthur something that sounded like "Your girl was mine to save not destroy" although each of the others heard the phrase slightly differently. He then disappeared into the shadows leaving us no opportunity to descend and pursue.

I feel we have handed him a defeat, but I am troubled by the missing box. Somewhere I fear the Count still retains one safe resting place, and we have no clues as to its whereabouts.

Enheduanna's Journal

October 4 Early Morning

Van Helsing and the others have decided that they should render Vlad's hideaways unusable. I had originally hoped to play this game longer, but after finding myself nearly helpless in his grasp yester evening, I have to concede that their pre-emptive plans should not be discouraged. There is little chance that they will be able to surprise and destroy Vlad as they hope. They will, however, strike a blow to his self confidence and significantly hamper his mobility. And with any luck, that old fool Van Helsing will provoke Vlad into striking him down as I nearly did myself a short time ago.

In order to explain my anger at Van Helsing, I must record last night's history while it is still fresh in my memory. After my companions had reassured themselves that Vlad was no longer on the premises, they returned to report to me that for no discernible reason he had destroyed all our original journals. The truth, of course, is that it was I who had burned them, although not before securing my edited and altered copies in Seward's safe. I had planned to blame myself for leaving them too close to the hearth fire, but when the new Lord Godalming named the intruder as the culprit, I was only too glad to substitute a more satisfactory explanation.

Van Helsing took great pains to secure my quarters against further intrusion. These religious icons he has scattered about bother me not at all, nor will they bar Vlad from entry unless Van Helsing or another true believer is present to grasp them. I suffered his efforts quietly, while raging inwardly with the thirst. The struggle earlier in the evening, the brief taste of Vlad's blood, had waked as great a need as I had ever experienced. He was hardly out of the room and the door secured, before I hastily cast the sleeping glamour over Jonathan and escaped through the window.

My already short temper was not soothed quickly. There were still people moving about the streets, but always in groups, nary a solitary stroller to be found. The whores were all either engaged or sheltering from the unseasonably chill night air. My frustration and hunger grew steadily until I found a night watchman pissing in an alley, and he died with his hands still clinging to his manhood. I slaked my thirst, then carried his body to the riverfront and threw him in. There is a strong current here and he may reach the sea before anyone notices his torn body. It was not as careful a disposal as I might have wished, but my temper was short and there was, after all, no way that the man's death could be traced back to me. If word of it reached my companions, they may ascribe it to Vlad if they so choose.

I returned to the Sanatorium feeling much refreshed, but I was careless while entering and wakened Jonathan, answering his unasked question with the hastily contrived excuse that I had heard something in the corridor. I knew that the others of our company were taking turns guarding the door, and their presence would explain the imaginary cause of my wakefulness. He sprang out of bed to investigate and found a tired but alert Quincey Morris sitting in an armchair carried there from one of the other rooms.

With the fresh blood pouring through my veins, I felt stronger and more confident than ever, and the tickling sensation of clairvoyance that I had experienced earlier in the evening came back full force. I lay back in bed, eyes tightly closed, and let my spirit follow the call of the blood, of Vlad's blood which I had drunk, and slowly but certainly I traced the tenuous link to its source. To my great surprise, Vlad's mind was in great turmoil and his thoughts stank of defeat. I held the contact, strengthening it, making it a part of me so that I could be certain of re-establishing it at will. For what remained of that night, I spied upon his thoughts intermittently, finding them little changed. As the hours passed, I learned to separate his emotions and the input of his senses from his conscious mind and, while not seeing them clearly, I learned enough about his plans to formulate a response. He carries the seeds of his own defeat within himself, as he always has. I have described him to the others as "the saddest case of all", and they believe I have sympathy for his tormented soul rather than contempt for his congenital weakness.

But I promised myself I would describe my unpleasant

experience with Van Helsing. The dotard caught me by surprise. I had not anticipated his latest attempt to be helpful until he touched a holy wafer to my forehead. It was an agony beyond any which I have previously experienced, and I nearly struck the man dead on the spot. Had the sun not come up, I am certain that my features would have changed to such a great degree that no continuation of my masquerade would have been possible. Never before have I been so affected in this way.

My first thought was that in Van Helsing there lived a faith stronger than any I had met before, but now I think otherwise. Vlad's blood courses through my veins and I think it is that which has made me susceptible to this hurt. Hours later, the pain still interferes with my thoughts, and I fear it will be many days before the disfigurement fades, for even my recuperative powers have their limits. I have never understood why the symbols of this upstart religion sometimes cause discomfort to my get. I have pretended piety in various places of worship with no bad result other than boredom, and can only conclude that it is the belief in the mind of the wielder that imbues them with such power. Clearly Van Helsing's faith runs deep, and Vlad's blood has made me vulnerable, at least for a time, to the power of his beliefs.

When this is all over, if Vlad does not take this elderly quack's life, I will bleed him slowly and watch the knowledge of his terrible misjudgment take root in his mind.

Jack Seward's Journal

October 4

I have only a few moments to write today. Mina insists that she knows Vlad has decided to flee the country by sea. This seems to me unlikely, and I fear that her "visions" are illusions at best or perhaps carefully fashioned lies designed by Dracula to mislead us, but we have no better hint of his present location. We have all of us spent the day on the waterfront, seeking news of him, but without result.

Renfield's broken body was interred today. I can only console myself by remembering that his life was a constant torture designed by his own mind, and that at least now he is at peace.

I have not spoken of my new fear to the others, but I cannot believe that Van Helsing at least is unaware of the recent deterioration in Mina. Her moods change suddenly and she spends an unhealthy amount of time closeted in her room, with the curtains drawn over the windows so that she huddles in the half light. She says that she is devoting all of her energies to invading the thoughts of our adversary, but I cannot believe that this is so. The terrible liberty which he has taken upon her body must necessarily affect her mind as well. His taint has not yet corrupted her soul, but it stirs her mind and plays havoc with her demeanor. I am convinced that she will continue to decline with the passage of time as Vlad's influence festers in her breast, and that only through his destruction may we save her from the same fate that took dear Lucy from us.

The others are equally committed, I am sure, particularly Jonathan, but his health is still not what it once was. He sleeps inordinately long and there is often an unhealthy pallor in his face when he wakens. Arthur vows to see matters through, but he is more committed to the Count's defeat than to Mina's salvation, and often sinks into apathetic fits during which he thinks only of Lucy. Quincey is also steadfast but he is unreadable to me. I think the devoted admiration which he once displayed only for Lucy has been transferred to Mina, although I would never dream of accusing either of them of improper conduct.

I do not confess this in the presence of the others, but I have come to believe that our chances of defeating the Count are slim. At best we may force him to withdraw, and that would leave us with one of our own dead, Lucy, and another perhaps mortally wounded. The change in Mina just in the short time since her return with Jonathan has been profound, and even should we persevere and ultimately triumph, I fear her quiet innocence may be gone forever. At worst, we may all meet a sad fate in one fashion or another. I have quietly taken steps to ensure continuity at the asylum in the event of my sudden death, and my solicitor has drawn up a new will at my direction.

Nights are the worst. I have trouble sleeping and wake feeling unrested. The weight of responsibility hangs heavy on all of us, because if we should fail, there is no limit to what further evil the Count might advance in the future. We do not speak of it, but the fact that his victims become his allies is an unsettling one, because that means that anyone could be suborned to his will. That he has not recruited others to his cause in this fashion is something of a mystery, and we are all aware that it might be a respite rather than a mercy.

The Journal of Vlad Tepes

October 4

I have put off for as long as I could updating this account not because I have lacked opportunity but because my unbeating heart is sick with the knowledge that I have been defeated, and so easily. I force myself to the task now in the thin hope that if fate conspires against me, then perhaps it will allow this record to survive and fall into the hands of some power capable of completing the task at which I failed. Enheduanna has chosen her allies well in this battle, for they have somehow ferreted out all of the locations in which I had secreted my boxes of earth, and have rendered each of them inaccessible to me. The unfortunate accident by which one was damaged has rebounded to my benefit, for I rescued it from the wainwright's shop today. If all had been destroyed, my powers would have dulled quickly. As it is, I must leave these shores at the first opportunity.

I must consider my present campaign a complete loss and accept that I should not have allowed myself to be maneuvered into this position. I am bereft of my Szgany or even the children of the night, while she has a small but devoted group of soldiers dedicated to her banner. Most of my ready monies were lost along with my other property this day, and I have few material resources left at my disposal. It appears my only recourse is to concede yet another defeat to my foe and withdraw from the field, to prepare for a fresh battle on another day, perhaps under a friendlier sky. I may surprise her in this, for she has never known me to shrink from a battle unless no other choice remained, but I have learned some of her caution, and the imperative that drives me against her overwhelms my natural inclinations in the matter.

To this purpose, I have with some difficulty purchased passage on the *Czarina Catherine*, scheduled to depart for Varna and other ports along the Danube at tomorrow's dawn. I have tried unsuccessfully to persuade her captain to delay the departure until later in the day, but my control over the glamour is tentative, particularly in the daylight, and I only managed to stoke his predisposition to ready anger. Fortunately, I believe I can raise enough fog on the morrow to give him pause while I dispatch messages to Josef and others by faster means to arrange for my arrival. A swifter ship leaves today, but the *Czarina* carries several bullocks upon whom I may safely feed, while the other caters to passengers only.

Only one ember of luck continues to burn in my favor. During my most recent slumber, I experienced what I can only describe as dream visions, such as have not invaded my mind since Enheduanna drained my life's blood generations ago. There was no underlying narrative quality; they were rather a series of separate images, the faces of my enemies, short bursts of speech. She herself appeared nowhere in this array, and I now believe that by partaking of my blood, she has somehow managed to preserve a part of me within herself, a part of me which shares her experiences. There may be an advantage for me here, or an even greater danger if, as I suspect, she can see into my mind even more deeply than I into hers. I must assume that I have no secrets which she does not know. This is truly a game of chess, for none of the pieces can ever be hidden.

Log of the *Czarina Catherine*

October 5

Departure delayed due to heavy and persistent fog which rose up before sunrise and continues unabated at this hour. Weather otherwise favorable, though chill.

Jonathan Harker's Journal

October 5

We found him! We have identified the ship upon which Dracula seeks to escape us. The man's name was not revealed, but the description of the large wooden box which he caused to be loaded confirms his identity beyond a reasonable doubt. Finally we have a chance to bring this all to an end, even though the vessel had left port before we could reach it.

The ship in question makes various stops prior to arriving at Varna, the port to which the box was consigned. We have determined that a quick crossing and an overland route would be much quicker, an alternative which our enemy either overlooked in his haste, or ruled out for reasons unknown to us. In either case, we have until the 17th of this month to prepare ourselves for what I trust will be our final meeting with the monster.

Mina has retreated into herself again today and has insisted that she be removed from our councils of war henceforth. She fears that the Count may compel her to betray our plans through some arcane means. It grieves me to keep anything from dear Mina, particularly when her very life hangs in the balance. I think it is only my love for her which sustains life in my body, for I continue in poor health, sleeping well beyond the coming of daylight and often needing to be physically roused even then. Jack and Van Helsing insist that there is nothing physically wrong with me and suggest that an improvement in my state of mind would have a wider beneficial effect, but I feel as though heavy curtains had been drawn across my eyes through which only the light of my Mina can penetrate unaltered. If she should perish through our failure to bring an end to this loathsome beast who walks like a man, I have no doubt that I will soon rejoin her, for she has become not the greatest thing in my life, but life itself.

Enheduanna's Journal

October 5

He dares! I was resting this morning in my room when I felt Vlad's impertinent footsteps in my mind. It seems that the advantage I thought gained by taking his blood has its obverse side. Once again, Vlad has taken me by surprise. The powers which I mastered only after centuries come to him much more easily, perhaps because that portion of my blood which flows in his veins has brought him something more of myself than I had thought. Deeply now do I regret the night when I resisted the urge to destroy him as I had all who came before him, and as I have all who have followed since. I have never loved in the sense that mortals do. The casual manner in which they accept such emotional turmoil has always been a mystery to me, although perhaps if I faced such a brief period on this Earth as do they, I might also grasp for every intense experience possible. No, it was not love I felt for Vlad, never that. But I would be false to myself if I did not confess to a great affection. I have regretted the loss of others of my get, whether they succumbed to their own misjudgment and were destroyed by another hand, or whether they betrayed their growing independence of spirit so that I was forced to end them myself. Some were useful, some amusing, and some few were perhaps drawn to me even without the glamour or the call of the blood.

Vlad was the only one whose respect for me was based on something other than fear or slavish servitude. He began to think of me as a companion rather than his mistress, acknowledged my superiority in some areas but questioned it in others. With another, I would have acted when he first began to challenge my decisions, but he always did so in a reasonable fashion, and always accepted my final judgment. Even more importantly, his suggestions were invariably well reasoned and sometimes valuable. I came to see him as an advisor rather than a servant, as a person rather than a tool, and even though I believe now that it was the greatest mistake of my life, I still cannot completely regret my decision. The last years we spent together were like no other period in my life. I was content, and looked the other way, and then when it became obvious that I had waited too long, I offered him my blood as I had taken his, just a taste, hoping that it would bind us together in a new unity. That unity has come now, in some small serving, but it is far too late.

With the fall of darkness yester evening, I sensed an alien presence behind my eyes. It was faint and fragmentary, and I doubt it could have done Vlad any great good, but there is no question that to at least a limited degree, this discorporate communication between us runs in both directions. I cannot allow him to spy on our efforts.

To that end, I have directed the others to keep me ignorant of the specifics of our campaign from this point forward. For the moment, I must trust that my pawns are capable of carrying the issue through to its conclusion independent of my direction. I have never previously allowed my welfare to depend on the competence of others and it worries me greatly to do so now. I can see the many flaws and failings of these men, and at times they seem to outweigh their resources. Van Helsing must have been formidable when younger, but age has blurred the edges of his intellect. Seward has an equally alert and inquisitive mind, but he is in awe of Van Helsing and subordinates his own instincts. Godalming is still shaken from the loss of his Lucy and lacks initiative. Harker is a creature of raw emotion and no great thinker, nor is Morris, although of the lot, he is the one I find most interesting. His rough frontier manners and casual manner of speech misled me into believing him rather simple, but I now recognize in him a flexible mind and a depth of courage superior to that of the others.

Nevertheless, I feel less than completely confident that they can overcome Vlad. But how to aid their effort without knowing what they intend? It is an intriguing puzzle, which I would enjoy more if so much did not depend upon its solution.

I have been trying to remember more of his habits. It seems strange that I can recall so little considering that we spent more than a century together, but that is such a small fraction of my days walking the Earth that from my perspective it was no more than a brief encounter. His was a passionate nature during his mortal years, and even while imprisoned as a youth, he managed to father more than one bastard on one or another of the serving girls. As my thrall, his lust was channeled into a vehement but chaste admiration, and once completely my creature, those physical urges vanished completely. Small loss in my judgment. I have never understood how such mingling of sweaty bodies in awkward and even painful encounters could be a source of pleasure.

He was a brave warrior, no doubt, but his talent was in the ordering of others, not personal valor. I cannot understand why he has launched this campaign against me without allies. His previous failed crusade was a lonely one as well. Perhaps he will learn this time, but if so, I am determined that his enlightenment will come too late; one of us must perish utterly and finally. I dare not risk delaying the end any further.

Although I have tried to remember if there was some single event that might have forewarned me of his altered attitude, I cannot bring one to mind. Perhaps it was an incremental change whose individual steps were so subtle that I overlooked them. The earliest I can recall was while we were wintering in the Tyrol. Another convulsion of religious warfare was threatening to tear Europe apart yet again and we had found easy hunting along the edges of the Holy Roman Empire, as it called itself, though it was neither holy nor Roman. We moved among the wounded at dusk, stopping as though to offer succor, but it was we who came away the richer.

I remember that just before we quit one battlefield, Vlad paused and looked back at the testament of mortal savagery. "You would think that they would tire of all this waste," he said quietly. "But each generation needs must learn all the lessons anew."

"You were once a leader of men like these," I answered. "And it never occurred to you to do otherwise. You yourself ordered men to do this to others, and to suffer the same fate themselves. Did you ever consider that question?"

"No, I did not." Vlad laughed then, one of the few times I have ever heard him do so. "And yes, I was a terrible agent of destruction, was I not? I could not begin to count the lives taken and lost at my direction. But these modern soldiers lack any flair, any true sense of the honor of their arms. They fight their battles just as they would till their fields, never thinking beyond the moment, focusing their eyes always on what is directly in front of them, accepting the way things are as the way things should be."

"That is all behind you now."

"Yes it is." He glanced around at the fallen bodies, twisted into grotesque shapes. "And ahead of me and to either side." He laughed unpleasantly. "I don't think I have ever actually looked at the dead before. Not as individuals. They were always the enemy, my enemies or the enemies of my country."

"They are not our concern, or our responsibility. You are no longer one of them."

"Was I ever, I wonder?"

Later

It is time, I think, to put my thoughts in order and set down the day of our parting in Adrianople. I have made misjudgments in my life, of course, but never one as painful and potentially dangerous as I did during those last days we spent together. We had quitted the city some decades earlier, waiting for more than a generation to pass before returning. Most of the intervening years had been spent in Egypt, Alexandria first, then Cairo. Crete had seemed a possible stopping place, but the Turks were enjoying a brief resurgence at the time and the island was sorely beset. Vlad was restless and wanted to push further south into the Ethiope, but I overruled him. I had become accustomed to a certain degree of comfort, and no longer wished to live and hunt in the wilderness. The larger cities had all of the advantages of the wild, and they also had feathered mattresses, warm clothing, and other amenities I had no wish to forego. The food these mortals eat seems tasteless now and I have little use for most of their art and literature, but I have a weakness for music and fine clothing, and would not give them up willingly.

Vlad did not contest my decision, but it chafed him visibly, which was my first warning that something was wrong. In the past, he had reacted to my authority by either accepting decisions meekly or teasing me good naturedly until I ordered him to stop. Never before had I seen him grow sullen and irritable. His mood seemed to pass after a few days, and I decided to consider it an anomaly, since in all other ways he had proven to be the best companion I could have wished for.

We waited until the century was well ended before returning to Adrianople. We arrived in the guise of widow and servant. Vlad posed as a Sufi cultist who abhorred uncovered flesh so that he could wear heavy robes during the hours of daylight, although he had already grown to tolerate the direct touch of the sun for short periods of time. On the day of our arrival, I had second thoughts, for the city had deteriorated markedly during the past few decades. The thoroughfares were more crowded than ever and the soldiers less disciplined, posing as much danger to the citizenry as they did to its enemies. The streets were poorly maintained and littered with offal, beggars young and old beset us every time we ventured out of the small house which I had purchased, and the city officials openly solicited bribes where formerly they had been circumspect.

Although we could have done without servants, it would have raised too many questions. I was very selective, choosing at last an elderly couple whose children had all died and who were living in a tumbledown hovel, having been discharged by their former master and left penniless. They were so grateful that they might well have served us even knowing the truth, but I used the glamour on them in any case, finding their simple minds malleable enough. To my great surprise and pleasure, they both worked diligently if somewhat slowly, and for the most part they were more than adequate. The man was not quite right in the head and spoke very rarely, but he busied himself around the property even when he had no direct instructions. I think the woman suspected something, since we only ate mortal food when we were entertaining, but even without the glamour to restrain her, I think she would have held her tongue. We were, after all, the only thing standing between her and starvation.

We purchased furniture and such other goods as were needed to suit our pleasure or match the face we wished to present to the world. Vlad seemed to have forgotten our disagreement, and I was almost able to dismiss his silent rebellion as a momentary aberration. We had no trouble finding prey on the first night we hunted the city's streets, although we must needs wait until the small hours of the morning even in the foulest neighborhoods. The streets teemed with people even at the most unlikely hour, carousing soldiers, refugees who had been robbed of what funds they had managed to bring with them and slept where they found dry pavement, the corrupt city watch, and those who would kill for a pair of sandals or simply for the joy of it.

Then came Delianides. He was a Greek who had thrown in his lot with the Turks, embracing their religion and mimicking their dress and manner. For all that, he did not enjoy their complete trust, and in a foredoomed effort to circumvent their suspicions, he became their most ardent ferret, a man who saw spies and saboteurs lurking in every shadow, and who never faltered once he had fixed upon an idea. I was posing as a Persian, which is essentially the truth although I have long passed beyond the point where I identify myself with any group of people. I am a people unto myself, after all. Delianides called upon us during the second month of our stay, and I was prepared to entertain another bumptious official with his hand poised to receive gifts. He had not been in our house for more than a few heartbeats before I recognized that he was going to create difficulties for us.

For one thing, the man would not sit still. Though I had invited him to rest on a cushion, he remained standing, moving slowly around the room, examining each piece of art or furniture as though it might be some form of contraband or a diabolic device in disguise. He asked many questions, often impertinent, about my past, my servants, my reasons for coming to Adrianople, the source and extent of my funds, the history of my fictional husband and the circumstances of his death, my plans for the immediate and remote future, my politics, and my religion. At first I answered readily, but I had not given thought to my new character in such great detail and feared that I would be caught in a contradiction. Tentatively I reached out with the glamour, but Delianides was one of those rare individuals who seem to have a natural defense against such tampering. My probing had no result except perhaps to make him more irritable and suspicious than before.

He eventually accepted a small bribe – a larger one would only have fed his suspicions – and left me with polite words which he did not mean. Vlad had hovered on the fringes of our conversation, and I had sensed his smoldering anger so clearly that I was surprised Delianides had not felt it as well.

"That man means us no good."

"He was certainly unpleasant, but if one swatted every fly that buzzed nearby, there would be little time for anything else."

"We have not heard the last of him. You are beautiful and rich, my lady, but his eyes never saw you as a woman. We should not trust a man who has so completely conquered his passions."

"Better that than one who gives passion full reign. Problems with simple solutions usually mask graver matters."

Vlad proved correct in this case. A new street vendor established himself across from our new home the following day. He was unusually healthy and well attired for a mendicant, and seemed indifferent to the volume of his sales.

"We are being watched," Vlad said solemnly.

"Indeed, but there is little enough for them to see during the day."

"And by night?"

"We shall have to ensure that the nights appear equally uneventful."

It was no great task to play our parts. I hired a carriage to take me to the market once a week while Vlad remained in the house to discourage clandestine searches, and to avoid the sun that still irritated his skin. Our servants were questioned several times, often with seeming casualness during supposedly chance encounters, twice by official interrogation. I examined their memories after each and was satisfied that they had said nothing untoward, but the scrutiny continued long after I expected it to end.

"It is that man, Delianides," insisted Vlad. "I felt his enmity the moment he entered the house."

"Perhaps, but he will move on when he finds fresher game." I believed that to be true, but I was beginning to share Vlad's annoyance. We had hunted the previous evening, leaving the house stealthily under the cover of darkness, and although I felt confident we had not been observed, I could not help noticing that the two supposed mendicants huddled nearby wore well made clothing under their tattered cloaks, and that they were so positioned that they could watch both of our gates.

Three months or more passed before we saw Delianides again. As before, he appeared at our gate unannounced, but this time he was not unaccompanied. Two heavyset members of the city guard stood on his flanks, both striving to conceal their boredom. Delianides was a small man and I imagined him as a bowl of fruit standing between two guttering candles. The servant woman ushered them in at my instruction. Vlad was out on a brief errand, one of his rare excursions, so I received them alone.

"Good day to you, gentlemen. How may I be of service to the city guard?" I deliberately did not ask them to seat themselves.

"There have been rumors," Delianides said quietly, his eyes shearing away from mine, skipping around the room, resting briefly on each object added since his first visit, an Etruscan vase, a tapestry from Persia, a pair of hammered gold sconces. "We are, of course, obligated to look into them, no matter how unlikely they may be. For the security of the city, you understand."

"I understand perfectly," I answered promptly, not sure that I did. Was the man after another bribe? A bigger one this time? Somehow I doubted it. He would not turn down the coin, but he was after different game. "Was there a specific rumor that I could help you with?"

"Spies," he said shortly, and stepped away from his companions to examine the tapestry more closely. "Foreign influences creating unrest among the populace."

"You would know that far better than I. I rarely go among the populace, except at the market."

"And your servant?"

"Vlad? He almost never leaves the house, and he is very parsimonious with his words. An aspect of his religious vocation, you understand? He has little to do with worldly things."

"Have you known him long?"

"Many years," I replied, smirking inside. "He has been a good and loyal servant to me."

"He has his own room here in your house?"

"Of course."

"Would you have any objections if I asked my men here to search his belongings? Just to eliminate any possibility of suspicion."

I would have balked them if I could, but no plausible reason came to mind. As far as I knew, neither Vlad nor I retained anything that might be used against us. My current diary was written in a dead language, and Vlad kept no similar document. He slept in a box of his native earth, but kept a straw pallet in his room for appearances.

"Do as you wish."

It took only a moment, for Vlad's room was all but bare. The guardsmen appeared more bored than before, but Delianides seethed with suppressed energy. His unexpressed animosity stirred my own anger.

"Would you like to examine my sleeping chamber as well?"

I expected him to decline, but he surprised me by nodding. "That would be best, my lady. It would help to lay these disturbing rumors to rest."

"They must be disturbing indeed to bring such a high placed official out to search a widow's bed." I meant for him to hear the sarcasm and he did, and for the first time in my experience, ventured a very slight smile.

"I live to serve," he said quietly.

Their search was perfunctory even so. My diary was out in plain sight, but attracted no comment.

"I thank you for your cooperation, my lady. How long do you plan to remain in the city?"

"For as long as it pleases me. My resources are sufficient but not unlimited. I enjoy the excitement of city life, even if I lack the energy to participate in it as much as I might like. But the prices in the market are much higher now than when I last visited, and I am forced to adopt a degree of frugality."

"Then perhaps we will meet again."

"I look forward to that eventuality."

They were no sooner out the door than Vlad emerged from his room, having entered surreptitiously. "I told you that man meant us ill." His face was dark with fury.

"He is a tedious man with little imagination, but you are right, he will do me harm if he can."

"Then perhaps harm should find him beforehand."

I shook my head. "Not yet. He is a man of some importance and questions would rise if he should be found murdered in his bed, questions which might lead to us."

"I can arrange his death so that there will be no hint of our involvement. Thieves might break into his house, or assault him on the street."

"You will hold your hand until I order it!" I snapped, but my anger was a reaction to Delianides, not Vlad. He had violated the privacy of my bed chamber and I found myself resenting it quite deeply, even though it had been I who had made the offer. I know that he would have made the suggestion himself in another moment. Frustrated by the inability of his agents to acquire any genuine intelligence of us, he had moved openly, even brazenly. I think now that Delianides somehow sensed the differences between us, a rare talent I have encountered only once since. Or perhaps he just needed to have a victim, and a reclusive widow suited his purpose.

When I had shown my anger in the past, Vlad has always subsided, perhaps sulking for a short while but never responding in kind. That day marked a turning point in our relationship.

"You have grown overcautious, mistress. Your reluctance to act places us both in grave danger!"

"Mind your tongue, Vlad." My voice was quieter but still firm, demanding compliance. "The role of willful child does not suit you."

"I am no child!" His sudden rage was so great that his features wavered, revealing hints of his true face.

My response was immediate and almost involuntary. I struck out with the glamour, driving a wedge of unbearable pain into his mind. He staggered away but I followed, seized him by the arms, and threw him against the far wall with such force that my new vase fell from its alcove and shattered. "I saw my tenth century pass before your family even had a name, Vlad Tepes! You will always be a child in my presence!"

I had expected him to cringe before my fury, but instead, incredibly, he surged forward, his true face completely revealed now. It was so unexpected that I hesitated, left him free of the glamour, and so unencumbered, he might well have attacked me, although I feel certain that he could have done me no great harm. It was almost put to the test, because he came so close that I could have heard his heart beat, if he had had one to hear. His arms were raised, hands poised like talons ready to rip out my throat, his eyes boiling with anger. But then he began to tremble, and it was almost as though he were shrinking back, lowering his arms, his features settling back into their human form, his anger fading like mist in the morning sunlight.

"Your pardon, mistress. I forgot my place."

I was shaken as well, although I would not let him see it. "Yes, you have displeased me greatly. Take yourself away until I bid you return."

With the very slightest of bows, he retreated to his room, leaving me to deal with the sudden realization that the time had come. Vlad was no longer content to be my creature, and could even become a threat to me. I could no longer trust him and must bring his existence to its inevitable end, and more than ever before in my very long lifetime, I regretted the necessity.

One of the consequences of such a long span as I have enjoyed is a great sense of patience. Mortals rush through life because there is so much that needs to be done in such a short period of time. A mortal man might plant a tree to provide shade for his children, but I plant one to enjoy myself. Hasty actions often have unhappy results, but sometimes the reverse is true. A matter considered too deliberately grows into an even larger problem. So it was with Vlad.

I knew that very day that I had no choice. This particular crisis was over, but another would arise, and another after that. Sooner or later, Vlad would be unable to govern himself. I had little fear of an open attack; Vlad's powers were of scant consequence then. But what he could not accomplish by force he might achieve by stealth. Immortal I may be, but I am not invulnerable, though my body has healed itself in the past of wounds that should have meant my death. But if a sword strikes my head from my body, I will be ended as surely as though I were an ordinary woman. Even I have my limits.

I should have fallen upon him that very night, but I persuaded myself to wait. The servants I held in thrall would be unacceptable as companions, and I had not been alone for a long time. He would have to be replaced, but surely not right away? And I might never find his equal.

Darkness fell. We were not due to hunt for another two days, but I was restless. I entered Vlad's room, expecting to find him consumed with remorse, but he was not there. His great cloak was gone but all else seemed undisturbed. Even then I was not greatly alarmed, for he occasionally walked the city streets at night even when we were not hunting, but I was disappointed and somewhat piqued. I might have ventured forth alone but decided instead to await his return.

It would have been a long wait. I did not see Vlad again for more than a century. He knew enough of my history to understand what his rebellion, however slight, must have signified to me. But he did me one final service that night, before leaving Adrianople for an unknown destination. They found Delianides' torn body the following morning, lying in a filthy alley where, against all reason, he had apparently been trampled to death by horses and savaged by dogs.

The Notebooks of Abraham Van Helsing

October 5

Our plans move forward. I have this day spoken to Jonathan about Mina. He has friends whom he will engage to watch over her while we pursue the fiend to his lair. I have inscribed a list of precautions they must take. Even in his absence, the change in her body will slowly progress. It can be retarded, I believe, but only the destruction of its cause can reverse the foul illness that pollutes her sweet body.

All of our company are in good spirits otherwise. Quincey has procured for us a number of firearms, despite my assurances that they would be ineffective against the one we seek. If all goes well, we shall be waiting at the dock when he arrives in Varna, and we are each and every one of us sworn to prevent Dracula from reaching shore. We are a large enough company that I expect little trouble from local brigands, but I suppose that it does us no harm to be prepared for even that unlikely development.

While I share the elevated spirits of my companions, I have doubts as well. This evil we face has lived far longer than we, and will not be defeated easily.

Enheduanna's Journal

October 6

That meddling fool Van Helsing continues to irk me. He has quietly campaigned among the others to bundle me off to some remote site while he and the others carry on with the battle. Poor Mina is to be cosseted in some rural hideaway while her fearless protectors beard the enemy in his den.

This shall not be. I feel certain that they will fail without my assistance. I must convince them that my peril is greater in their absence no matter how remote I may be removed from matters. Jonathan will bend to my will most easily, as he is most susceptible to the glamour. Godalming seems hardly to see me or the others and often lets his attention wander, and I suspect his intellect has suffered an irreparable wound. Quincey, I think, will be glad of my company, and seems the type to admire an assertive woman. I think I shall be able to turn things my way.

I considered dispensing with Van Helsing. Although they have surrounded me with their imagined guards and wards, their own sleeping quarters remain undefended. It would not present any great difficulty to lure the Professor out into the streets, and end his miserable existence somewhere distant from our quarters. Two matters dissuaded me. They all believe that my glimpses of Vlad's activities can only be brought to the surface of my mind during hypnosis, and Dr. Seward does not share Van Helsing's ability to invoke such a mesmeric trance, although in my case that state is merely feigned. The second matter is that I do not wish to dispose of Van Helsing in haste. He has angered me more than any mortal has for more than a century, and I wish to take adequate time to reward his actions with a suitable death.

So I will suffer the man for a while longer.

The Journal of Vlad Tepes

October 7

We are well away now. I fed before coming aboard, a carter's horse stabled near the docks, and the bullocks are numerous and healthy. The greatest threat of the passage should be tedium, since I must conceal myself from the crew. By remaining below, I shall also deprive Enheduanna of any hint that we have altered course. Before departing, I dispatched letters to Josef in Galatz, Maltz in Trieste, and to the owners of this vessel. Her captain is a surly, insolent fellow, but I believe he will follow the instructions relayed to him. The preparations for my arrival will have been made.

I am still troubled by my defeat, but I have learned something as well. In a simple contest between us two, I have the strength to win through even though she is ever ahead of me in mastering the gifts peculiar to our kind. What I had not anticipated was that she would surround herself with resourceful, though ignorant, allies. It is Van Helsing and these others who have given her the victory, and who may yet prove my undoing.

I retire from the field this day, as I did once before, but our struggle is not over. As she has bent those others to her purpose, so also must I in the future. A victorious army requires good intelligence of the enemy and units capable of independent action. It is a truth I should have retained from my mortal days.

Letter from Quincey Morris to Robert Morris (never mailed)

October 8

Dear Brother, I know that I promised to write you more frequently than I have done, but events have transpired here that have left me little time for personal pursuits, and about which I find it difficult to choose the right words. I was never easy in my speech, as you know, and putting pen to paper is even more difficult.

Suffice it to say that I have good and true companions and that I am engaged in a matter of honor which I shall relate to you in greater detail when we have settled matters and I am free to return. The nature of that struggle is not why I write to you this day.

I have always believed myself an honorable man, and that my occasional lapses have been through bad judgment rather than any innate flaws in my character. Having said that, I must confess to having dishonored our name, in thought if not in deed. I have fallen in love, Robert, with a glorious girl whose purity and nobility are unparalleled in my experience. She comes from humble but respectable antecedents and has comported herself always as a proper young woman should. Why then, you ask, do I feel that I have fallen from grace?

It is simply that she belongs to another, is in fact the wife of a man I number among my friends. My affection for this lady has gone unspoken, but I believe not unnoticed, at least by her, although she has given no overt sign that she recognizes the depths of my feelings. Were circumstances otherwise, I would absent myself from their presence immediately, but to desert them at this hour would be an even greater sin.

They are calling me now. I will finish later.

Enheduanna's Journal

October 9

Although the others are all wrapped up in preparations for our journey, Quincey has been finding excuses to remain in my presence. He is clearly smitten, and through this weakness I shall bind him even more closely to my cause. Although it is no longer felt necessary to post a guard in the corridor, I have sensed him up and about after we have retired and know that he passes the door to our rooms with regularity, often hesitating before moving on. I am tempted to play a game within the game.

Later

It is as I thought. The house had grown silent as midnight approached. Jonathan slumbered under the glamour while I waited, waited so long that I had almost abandoned the effort, was in fact about to slip out through the window in search of prey when I heard footsteps beyond the door to our chamber. They continued past, then stopped, and began to return. I reached for my robe, then thought better of it. When I unlocked and opened the door, I wore only my nightdress.

As I suspected, Quincey stood there, his hands clasped behind his back, his face drawn into an expression of exaggerated misery that almost caused me to burst out laughing. It vanished in an instant, replaced by neutral concern except for his eyes, which always betray the inner soul.

"I hope I didn't disturb you, Miss Mina. I was restless and thought to walk for a while to settle my nerves."

"You could never disturb me, Quincey. I number you among my truest friends."

"You honor me undeservedly." He glanced nervously away as I turned to face him, artfully allowing him a brief glimpse of my bosom.

"Not at all." I softened my voice and reached out with the glamour, gently at first. Some have no resistance to its sly caress, as was the case with Lucy, but others have proven far more resistant, as did Lucy's mother, and there are a few I cannot touch at all. Quincey seemed to me of the latter sort, but when the human heart intervenes, even the strongest spirit can be duped into betraying itself. As I suspected, he flinched back, puzzled at his own reaction. I took a half step toward him and playacted a spell of dizziness, reaching out awkwardly for support. Quincey rushed to my side, his arms catching hold of me.

"Are you all right? Should I call Dr. Van Helsing?" His eyes were wide with alarm, but his voice vibrated with another emotion.

"No, let him rest. It was only a passing faintness. If you would just lend me your arm for a moment longer, I am sure I will regain my strength." He wasn't loathe to do so, and I wrapped the glamour about him again, gently this time so that his hidden mind remained undisturbed. His grip tightened and he drew me slightly closer to him, changing his stance unnecessarily to cover the movement. I could smell the perspiration on his skin, sense the heat radiating from his flesh, hear the beat of his suddenly accelerated heart, feel the way his arms clung to my body, unconsciously possessive, but the last and most important sense was denied me. I could not taste his blood.

Perhaps at another time.

"Do you think we will succeed, Quincey?" I tried to sound frightened and uncertain.

"Most assuredly. With a company such as ours, who could possibly stand against us?"

"So I too would have thought, but I have been in error before, sometimes grievously so."

I felt his arm tighten ever so slightly around my shoulders. "I cannot imagine such a thing, dear Mina. You are a good and thoughtful person."

"Even so, I have made choices in the past which I now regret."

"You should not blame yourself for Lucy's fate. All of us here share that responsibility, and all of us did our best." He was suddenly silent, apparently realizing that a confession of past inadequacy might not be reassuring.

"There are other matters, decisions made too quickly, without considering the other choices available. Sometimes it is difficult to marry heart and mind to the same course." I touched his mind with the glamour, nudging him toward the possibilities I wished to plant there.

"Jonathan still seems troubled by his illness," he said awkwardly.

I gave a short nod. "He is much changed, though it shows only in small ways. It is as though hot metal had pierced his soul and burned out much of the best in him. He is forever lost in his own thoughts and often I cannot reach him. I feel great pity for his condition, and I confess as well that I fear he is no longer the man I thought I loved."

I shivered and then removed myself from his grasp, as though suddenly realizing its impropriety. "You must forget I said that, Quincey. It was unworthy of me and disloyal to Jonathan. I have not rested well and the devil is in me at times and compels me to say things I do not mean."

"Rest easy. I have already forgotten the words, and you should not judge yourself too harshly because of a moment of uncertainty and doubt. Just remember that I am your true friend and always shall be, and that you may call upon me at any time I am needed."

"I shall remember, and thank you, dear Quincey." And I returned to our room, satisfied that I had accomplished all that I had intended.

October 10

Van Helsing and Seward have been hinting again that I should remain behind, and have so far dismissed my arguments to the contrary. Godalming seems to be swaying to their side, although he is often distracted and contradicts himself, and only Jonathan argues against them. Quincey has expressed no opinion and seems preoccupied much of the time, apparently divided within himself. I have sensed him staring at me when he believes me unaware. If the opportunity arises, I must enlist his aid more actively in this matter.

Later

Over supper this evening, I tried to confront Van Helsing about his persistent efforts to set off without me. He proved unusually stubborn, and when I tried to use the glamour, his efforts to change the subject redoubled, as though on some level he sensed my intervention, although there has never been any such indication in the past.

On the other hand, Quincey has clearly become a pawn for my use. He was waiting outside my door again tonight. I emptied the water jug out the window and emerged, supposedly beset by thirst, my nightdress draped in an even more revealing manner than previously. Lucy would have been better at this, I confess, as she was more practiced at coquetry and more impressively endowed as well, but men make fools of themselves so readily that it requires hardly any effort to encourage them.

"Oh, Quincey. I didn't know you were out here."

"I beg your pardon, Mina. I had not meant to startle you."

"There is no harm done. I just need to fetch some fresh water." I held up the jug.

"Please, allow me." He stepped forward and took the vessel from my hands, contriving to let his fingers touch mine. I pretended to notice nothing, but it was glaringly obvious that even such a brief contact had touched him deeply. These mortal men, for all their talk of fiber and muscle, are soft inside like a beetle one might casually squash. They must pleasure their women swiftly before their flesh fails them. Even the most upright falls with time.

"I do not wish to take advantage of you, Quincey. The service you have already rendered on my behalf has placed me deeply in your debt." I allowed my eyes to drop modestly and adjusted my garb awkwardly, so that it revealed more for a moment before it covered all.

"Don't speak of debt, Miss Mina. Your friendship has rewarded me a thousand times over for what small contribution I have made."

Once again I reached out with the glamour, allowing it to flavor his emotions ever so slightly. "Surely what we share is more than simple friendship, Quincey. Those things which we have witnessed have lit flames that will burn so long as we live. I feel that all of us have become bonded together as if forged by a smithy," I tentatively reached out and brushed my fingers against his arm, "although those links are stronger to some than to others."

There was a flash of panic in his eyes and I realized that he was precariously balanced on a fence. I wished to pull him toward me, but risked pushing him over the opposite brink. A little guilt would not cool his ardor, but he must not be allowed to think himself less than honorable. "You are too kind, dear Mina."

I let my hand drop to my side and tried to appear wistful. "Not at all. Under other circumstances, if our paths had merged at a different point, I think we might have been even more to each other than we are now. Yours is a noble spirit, Quincey, and there are facets to your character that I hope to find in Jonathan, if he becomes well again."

"Jonathan is a good man and loves you, Mina. I am sure you will find him fully restored in time."

"It is good to hear you say so." I placed a hand on my breast and sighed. His defenses wavered and I swayed toward him, too precipitously as it happened. Somehow he sensed danger, stepped back and lifted the jug as though just remembering it. "Your water. I'll return with it straightaway." And he was gone before I could utter another word.

It is best not to rush him, I believe. His foot has been set upon the first riser, but if I nudge him too quickly, he will fall back and all will be undone. I must be patient; I have no reason to be otherwise.

October 11

I am inordinately pleased with myself. Today I have successfully turned back the efforts to dissociate me from the ongoing effort. There seems no chance any longer that even Van Helsing will suggest leaving me behind. Oddly enough, it occurred to me to use their perception of my vulnerability as a weapon rather than a disadvantage, and the ploy has worked beyond my expectations.

Simply put, I made each of them swear to me that in the event that it become obvious that I was changed past hope of redemption, that they would kill me themselves rather than see me become a creature of darkness such as Vlad. Predictably, Jonathan was the most difficult, but I persevered and wrung from him the same vow as the others. To keep their word, they have no choice but to hold me close to them, and all talk of abandoning me in some English refuge has ceased. The last major obstacle in my path has fallen. It now remains only to grapple with Vlad himself, and bring this longstanding conflict to a close.

Tomorrow we leave from Charing Cross, a quick voyage across the Channel, then by land to Paris where we will catch the Orient Express. Jonathan has made reservations in Varna – an ugly town if memory serves me but one where I know I shall have little trouble finding suitable prey – and there we shall await Vlad's arrival. Even now I feel moments of regret that this has become necessary, but I can no longer take the risk that he may one day catch me unawares.

October 12

Quincey has become my second shadow of late, seeking out my company even when I haven't tugged on the strings of glamour that I have tied around his heart. Indeed, he is at times a nuisance, keeping me under such close scrutiny that I must be forever on my guard. I slipped away last night to lure a child from its bed, and upon my return I found him hovering outside the window of our room at the inn where we were spending the night. He proved stubbornly resistant to the sleep glamour and remained there faithfully until the first hint of sunlight tinted the horizon, then hastened to his room to avoid discovery. I managed to return to my bed barely in time to anticipate Jonathan's wakening.

Quincey has shown me something about myself that I had not realized, that as much as I feel that I have never really been a part of this mortal species, there are still moments when I envy them the simple but intense pleasures of their emotions. It is a small sacrifice to make for unending life, but it sometimes takes on an exaggerated significance because it is forever denied me. Would Jonathan have loved me had I not employed the glamour almost from our first meeting, finding in him a malleable soul who could be twisted to my purposes? Quincey had already ensorcelled himself without my assistance, and seems genuinely to have fallen in love with his image of me, if not my true self. And as much as it humbles me to admit it, I feel flattered by his attention.

Such will not prevent me from using him as I must, but if it becomes necessary to sacrifice him before the game is over, I will feel the worse for it. And that is a kind of confession, I suppose, that even the company of an admiring mortal is better than none at all. I have been too long without a long term companion, and must remedy the situation when all of this is over. I already tire of Mina Harker and her narrowly circumscribed existence. Perhaps I will run off to the new world with Quincey and there make him one of my own. We shall see.

Jack Seward's Journal

October 13

I confess to a profound dislike of travel by rail. The incessant clatter disturbs both my sleep and my digestion, the class of people one encounters is often undesirable, and the accommodations barely supportable. At home the trains are at least moderately clean, which is not the case here. My companions insist that the berths are more than adequate, but I find them coarse, uncomfortable, and filthy.

There remain almost two full days before we reach Varna, so I must resign myself to the situation. The others all seem to have withdrawn into their own thoughts and we rarely converse beyond what is absolutely necessary. There is at times an odd distance between the Harkers, not in any way hostile but rather as though they had wakened one day to find themselves wed to strangers. Quincey is also acting very uncharacteristically, often finds an excuse to leave when Mina is present, and no longer attends our daily hypnotic sessions. He seems too stout a fellow to be bothered by her close brush with evil incarnate, but perhaps it distresses him unbearably to see her in such a precarious state. He retreats to his compartment and compulsively cleans the Winchesters which he has secured for us.

Godalming and Dr. Van Helsing have taken to playing chess incessantly, with the latter almost always victorious. Arthur seems to have recovered something of his spirits in recent days, and I hope that this healing process will continue. For some time I have been concerned that the tragic death of Lucy, followed by the even greater shock of what he was forced to do in her tomb, had broken his mind as well as his will. He talks infrequently, and when he does, it is always about our purpose, the death of Count Dracula. If he has any plans beyond that point, they are locked into a corner of his mind as we would set aside a book to be read at a later date.

It is difficult to judge the temper of the others. Mina has grown increasingly withdrawn and tight lipped. Jonathan is distracted and still sleeps too much. Van Helsing keeps up a brave front, but I see the worry in his eyes, particularly when he is looking at Mina, and he looks older and more weary almost daily. I sometimes feel that he knows more than he is revealing to us, but if so, I must trust that he has good reasons for his reticence.

For my own part, I am very tired and wish to have this done with, regardless of the outcome. I sometimes feel older than Abraham.

October 14

Tomorrow we will arrive in Varna, our long journey at an end, although perhaps it will only truly be completed when we have struck the head from the monster's body and freed ourselves forever of his shadow. We seem frozen in a tableau here on the train, each hour indistinguishable from the one before. Even the passing landscape seems to repeat itself, as though we traveled in one unending circle.

It occurred to me today that Dracula might have left the ship prematurely and evaded us, but Van Helsing has said that according to legend the Undead cannot cross open water unless protected by a sheath of earth from their native land. Mina's face betrayed her skepticism, even before we examined that possibility critically. It is almost certain that the Count preyed upon the crew of the ship that brought him to us in the first place, so he quite evidently left his resting place from time to time. So in this case at least, the legends appear to be wrong.

The Journal of Vlad Tepes

October 14

There is little to do aboard ship, and I dare not even mix with the crew lest they suspect something. Sailors are a superstitious lot. I have secluded myself in my cabin, feigning illness, and it has only today occurred to me to take up some of the time by bringing this journal up to date. I could relate a detailed description of what has passed since we left England, but matters of interest would fill barely a page. So I will instead set down for the first time the account of my defeat at Enheduanna's hands when we crossed paths in Trieste and I thought to destroy her.

It is difficult for me to describe the change that came over me in the century following our parting, difficult because in order to explain it, I must first understand, and understanding has come only with very difficulty and in hints and whispers rather than broad revelations. Even now it is incomplete. I know only that I can no longer abide either that which I once was or that which I have become since. When I left Adrianople, I felt nothing but contempt for mortal men. They were no more to me than cattle, although sometimes a good deal more irritating. I hunted and killed through necessity, but the joy that I had felt as Enheduanna's thrall had died along with my mortality. I did not hate those whose blood I took.

I traveled back to Egypt first, then down through the Ethiope and into parts of that continent that had no proper name. I took the lives of men when they were available, of strange and sometimes fierce animals when they were not. I carried with me only sufficient of my native soil to restore my full powers as I slept, and I lost track of time as I moved from one savage land to another. At last I turned north again, and in Berbera took my first thrall, the captain of a small trading vessel, who carried me to Aden. There I trekked across the desert, where I eventually crossed the Tigris and the Euphrates. At last I reached Ormuz, and for a time I stayed there, then east again to Baluchistan and Bijapur. More than fifty years had passed since Adrianople, during which time I had kept my own company for the most part, and found myself a most unsatisfactory companion.

I stayed in Mangalore for more than thirty years, learning to tolerate the sun for longer periods. I took a rich, unmarried merchant as my thrall, posing as his adopted son, succeeding him when he died. After a century alone, I had rudimentary use of the glamour and could summon the fog, but in neither skill was I Enheduanna's rival. I colored my hair to feign age, but the time came when I could no longer stay without risking comment. At first I thought to travel east, but in the end, I chose to return to my native soil for the first time in nearly two centuries.

Wallachia was still part of the Ottoman Empire, although the rise of the nation states in western Europe clearly marked the permanent end of its westward expansion and, as it turned out, the beginning of the final collapse. The military frontier between them and the kingdom of Hungary was a dangerous, sometimes chaotic place, which suited my purposes admirably. I found my castle, long deserted, and used much of my accumulated wealth to restore it, convincing some that I was a distant but genuine descendant of my uncle, bribing those who were less easily swayed.

I recruited servants from among the Szgany, the gypsies, many of whom seemed to understand something of my nature. I never chose prey from among them and they have never betrayed me. Grown lonely, I took my first wife then, Hyrkana, and the coarse creature which she became discouraged me greatly. Twice more I experimented before concluding that the curse was even more insidious than I had realized. Even Enheduanna's get were often twisted monsters who had to be destroyed promptly. Only a handful retained any appreciable portion of their previous intelligence and demeanor. My secondhand attempts were even greater failures.

It was then that I first made my vow, swearing never to take another human life unnecessarily and to create no more of my kind. That last word betrayed my uncertainty, but I have killed only perhaps a dozen men since then, and only when necessary to preserve my secret or my liberty, never simply for the sake of their blood. To my mind, most deserved their fate.

I see that I still have not answered the most important question. My new resolve was not a response to the words of some prophet or philosopher, nor did I experience a vision or dream which compelled me to see the error of my ways. Perhaps it was just that, having seen so much death, I had had a surfeit of it. For all the many lifetimes that Enheduanna has walked this Earth, I doubt she has seen at close hand half as many dead as I had in just the few short years of my mortal life. Certainly I am responsible for many times the number she has claimed; entire communities were exterminated at my command.

I had first started to think of my victims as individuals while still in Africa, perhaps because their lives there were so different from any I had known previously. Idle curiosity became genuine interest, and I began spying upon the people through whose lands I passed. It would not be true to say that I felt any compassion for them, nor do I now. The capacity for that emotion, if I ever possessed it at all, was torn from me along with my life. But even in the face of inevitable death, humans aspire to build, to create, to learn, and that drive has earned my respect. Their lives are so short that a premature death seems to me an even greater tragedy, a wasted potential. It is strange that I should finally grow to admire my fellow men only after I was no longer numbered among them.

I still believed, or told myself I believed, that immortality was a gift, that its cost was justified by its benefits. Now I knew the gift for what it was, a horrid curse that separates our kind from all other living beings, which consumes our souls and suggests the possibility of eternal punishment on Earth, let alone after we have left it.

And so it was that in 1734 I decided that it was up to me to remove this scourge from the world, that perhaps in some small measure I could redeem myself and all my misdeeds if I were to wipe out this taint forever. But to do so meant that I would have to find Enheduanna, who must certainly have left Adrianople long before now, and contrive to destroy her. Then and only then could I end my own existence.

Enough. I will finish this on the morrow.

Enheduanna's Journal

October 14

It is amusing to watch these mortal beings fumbling around the edges of my reality, trying to understand something that has moved so far beyond them that they are to me little more than domestic animals, bred for their meat. Potentially dangerous, of course, but only if I grow careless. Today I listened as they discredited the notion that our kind cannot cross running water, which is only a half truth. It has not even occurred to them that Vlad and myself are as superior to our get as they would be to a naked savage. One newly changed would almost certainly perish during an ocean crossing, although a river would be merely unpleasant. Prolonged voyages are, of course, difficult even for me because of the need to feed discretely, but that problem can be overcome as Vlad discovered by traveling with livestock who cannot complain to the crew. With suitable provisions, it is possible that I might one day visit the new world, although at present a trip of that length would necessarily present too many difficulties to make it a viable project unless I suborned an entire crew. But I remember when sailors hesitated to travel beyond the sight of land, and when wind and sail were the only motive force. Not even I can anticipate what new wonders the future will bring.

We are proceeding to Varna where Goldalming has made reservations for us. I am still able to catch glimpses through Vlad's eyes, although the connection has begun to fade as his blood becomes my blood and loses its transcendental properties, and the images which I am able to pluck from his mind are invariably uninformative. He rests constantly in the darkness, and the only hint of his whereabouts is the slow rocking of the vessel in which he is concealed. Trieste has been much in my thoughts lately, and I think in his as well.

Although by design my companions do not confide in me, their intentions are transparent. I must assume that Vlad has learned as much as I know of their plans, and if that is the case, he will be prepared for a confrontation when the ship docks in Varna. I can only hope that Van Helsing and the others have planned wisely, because there is little I can think to do to further our mutual cause at this moment.

October 15

Seward complains constantly about the accommodations at the Odessus, but I have stayed in far worse lodgings. The *Czarina* has yet to arrive and Godalming is exerting every effort to gain intelligence of its present whereabouts. His energy has returned mightily but there is a feverish intensity in his eyes which I have seen before in those driven to the breaking point. Van Helsing and Seward were speaking of it between themselves earlier today, but they changed the subject when I made my presence known. I think he will last out our present endeavor, but bereft of a purpose, I believe the shock and grief may become too much for him. He would be a small loss, I think, but every piece has its place in the game.

The Journal of Vlad Tepes

October 15

More of the same. The crew complains of the incessant fog, but it is none of my doing, and I find that while I can summon the mist, the power to banish it is beyond me. Preparations for my arrival should be well advanced by now. Josef has never failed to do as I have bid him and I am confident that this will be no exception. I fear that this is the last time he will ever serve me, though I hope for the best.

I promised myself that I would finish the account of the sad events in Trieste and so I shall, though it may be the last entry I shall ever record here. I had resolved to destroy Enheduanna and end her line, but in order to do so I must first discover where she laired. More than a century had passed since I had left her and she must have changed her identity at least three times, more likely four. Although I knew a great deal of her habits, most of this was of no use. She preferred cities, or had when last we had spoken, but even if that were still the case, Europe was sprinkled with such places, as well as the north coast of Africa and the Arabian peninsula and beyond.

I had re-established my trading empire and had agents in many parts of Europe and around the rim of the Mediterranean, but there are many wealthy widows in the world. She might also be posing as a married woman, with her husband in thrall, but I considered this less likely. It presented additional difficulties and despite her exhortations to be cautious and thorough, she had grown laggard in some ways. I put it about that I was searching for an old friend who was living incognito, even provided some rough sketches of her face, but a year passed, then another, then five more.

There were numerous mistaken reports, of course, more than I could possibly investigate personally. I visited many cities during those years, Posen and Vilna, Prague and Vienna, Sofia and Istanbul. Each was a disappointment, although some few of those widows lived a style of life so similar that I sometimes wondered if Enheduanna was a truly unique being after all, although in each case I was able to reassure myself to the contrary before moving on.

I found her in 1741, completely by chance. The Austrian army had just been defeated by the Prussians at Mollwitz, dealing the Habsburgs their first great defeat. Although I had lost some property in Silesia during the conflict, I was more than compensated by the profits I made selling supplies, to both sides in fact. I was in Strasbourg, investigating a woman who matched my description and who was, in fact, so near in appearance that she might have been Enheduanna's sister. The resemblance was so close that I had initially wondered if my one time mistress had found the means to subtly alter her face. But when I made an excuse to call on her, I knew immediately that this was to be another disappointment.

There was considerable upheaval throughout Austria, so I took a southerly route home, passing through Venezia and then along the Adriatic coast to Trieste. That city had become quite an active port and although I had no agent there, some of the goods loaded aboard ships in its harbor had been purchased with my gold. I had thought to spend a single night there before striking off overland in a rented carriage, but I chanced to visit the local marketplace and there I felt her presence.

It was faint, too faint to be Enheduanna herself, and I was

nearly frustrated by the crowds before finally tracing the source. An elderly woman stood at a fruit seller's kiosk, haggling spiritlessly, her shawl drawn so close that I could barely make out her features. I passed close behind her and felt a rush of satisfaction. The woman was a thrall; I could feel the alien touch in her mind, though I dared not probe further lest I leave behind some hint of myself.

I followed her with no difficulty. If she had turned abruptly, she would have seen naught but a darker shadow in the close set streets. But she didn't turn. Clutching her purchases tightly against her body, she moved with surprising quickness and obvious purpose, threading her way up and out of the market district. The streets grew wider and brighter as we climbed above the city, and the accursed sun blazed down so intensely from a cloudless sky that I longed to hide myself away. But I would not give up this opportunity and I followed, making no further effort to conceal myself, although I lagged a good distance behind. There were few people about in this part of the city and I had no fear of losing sight of my quarry.

She turned in at the gate of a chateau, a small one but still much grander than I had expected. A servant opened the door for her and she disappeared inside. I think he may have glanced in my direction, but I continued past without turning my head, not stopping until a bend in the road concealed me from his sight.

Even then I knew better than to act precipitously. I returned to the inn and extended my stay, then dispatched letters delegating authority to some of my agents, using the excuse that I had contracted a debilitating illness and would remain in Trieste for several weeks while recuperating. Even alive I had never been a good judge of men, and this failing held true, for they squandered or appropriated much of my wealth in my absence. Something of this I anticipated, but if I had been successful, I would have considered my wealth well spent. A day later I purchased a much more humble house a short distance from my quarry and employed a single servant, who would not live under my roof and who would not therefore need to be enthralled. Then I set about planning the death of my mentor.

She was posing not as a widow this time but as the Lady Marta, niece of a wealthy Russian aristocrat, sent into a prolonged exile after an inappropriate love affair. Three local people served her, an elderly woman and her son, who both lived in the chateau, and a carriage driver and general factotum, who did not. I was able to follow the young man one morning and determine that he was also a thrall, and contrived to have a conversation with the driver, who was not, although he was so protective and uncommunicative about his mistress that I am certain she had used the glamour to shape his feelings.

Lady Marta had arrived in Trieste two years previously, accompanied by an older man, a servant, who had since died of uncertain causes. Although she tended to keep to herself, she received occasional invitations and was deemed an acceptable if rather ordinary social acquaintance. Many of her class had called to pay their respects, but she only rarely invited them to return. There had been something of an air of mystery about her at first, but she had proven herself to be dull company and the gossip had moved on to more productive subject matter.

I ached with the need to confront her, but I knew that to do so unprepared would be the height of foolishness. Also, and I must be honest here if nowhere else, I still felt a great reluctance to act against her. Perhaps this was an artifact of the unnatural relationship between us, for she was in a sense a mother to me and a lover as well. Doubts crept into my mind about the wisdom of my decision. At times I thought that she and I were an abomination which must be wiped from the Earth. But there were other times when I questioned my right to act against her. I have never felt the need to grovel before some patriarchal spirit who rules the universe, but I did feel that there must be some underlying purpose to life, and perhaps a creature as unique as Enheduanna was a part of that purpose. If so, who was I to interfere with the ways of the world? I had seen her perform many bloody deeds, had joined her in performing them, and had taken more than my own share of lives. How could I claim to judge and condemn her?

I faltered, but I recovered my balance and continued. I was a flawed weapon, no doubt, but if I had been fashioned for a purpose, it was the one I saw before me.

The attack must come in the darkness. She would be more powerful then, but so would I, and in the daylight I could not possibly hope to best her. It must also come as a surprise, because even my great ego would not allow me to believe I could overcome her if she was prepared for the contest. If at all possible, she should be separated from her thralls, for they might distract me or interfere in some way.

In the years since I had set off on my own, I had learned the virtue of patience, although the need to act churned in my breast so violently that it was a grave trial for me to simply wait. It was not difficult to watch the chateau surreptitiously, as the lanes nearby were heavily bordered with lush trees and shrubbery. There were several sheltered spots from which I could have played the spy during the daylight hours as well as the night if I was so inclined, and indeed on a few occasions I did so.

There was not much to see. For more than twenty days I kept my vigil. She may have entertained visitors during the daylight hours, but no one but her servants was ever there after darkness fell. The old woman was regular in her habits. She visited the market every third day to purchase fresh fruits and vegetables and occasional small pieces of meat, presumably for herself and her son. On alternate trips she was accompanied by the boy, for on these occasions she purchased more items than she could readily carry herself. She always paid with gold from a small purse, and rarely haggled over prices. Not once did I see her speak to anyone other than in the course of her duties, although her son traded crude remarks with some of the young girls they encountered.

I could not openly attack them without warning Enheduanna of my presence, so I resorted to subterfuge. One of the vendors was a heavy set young man who was often accompanied by a particularly comely lass, whom I took to be his wife, for they were very familiar with one another. She had an independent spirit and teased him mercilessly, and she was perhaps a trifle overly familiar with some of the men who came to their stall. I touched them with the glamour and found both susceptible. My abilities were still limited and I could not control their thoughts or actions, but I could push them onto paths they were already inclined to take.

On their next visit, the thralls came nowhere near my unwitting allies and I was sorely disappointed, but six days later they returned and this time the young man wandered off on his own. I was fully prepared to try my powers on his mind if required, but that proved unnecessary. He approached the stall and with my provocation the young girl engaged in an unusually obvious flirtation. The burly man objected, voices were raised, and blows were exchanged. I had hoped the boy would be incapacitated, but my luck was even better. Four of the city guard appeared and led both combatants off to the magistrate.

The old woman searched fruitlessly for her son, hampered by her unwillingness to ask for help, and eventually started back to the chateau, heavily encumbered by her purchases. I followed at a discrete distance, then watched the house from concealment until darkness fell. At no time did I catch even the briefest glimpse of Enheduanna and, indeed, I had not seen her at all since arriving in Trieste.

Darkness came at last and I felt the strength return to my body. The old woman was still inside and might have to be dealt with, but at least the boy was gone. I might never have such a chance again, and every day I delayed increased the possibility that through mischance I would betray my presence. The prohibition against entering a home uninvited does not apply to those inhabited by our kind, so I circled to the rear of the building, hoping to effect entry through one of the second story windows.

I had no sooner dropped into the cobblestoned courtyard when a voice came from out of the darkness.

"You might at least have come to the front door, Vlad. You know how I hate to receive unannounced guests."

She was standing in a small alcove so dark that even my eyes had difficulty picking out her form. Her voice was familiar, as was her faintly mocking tone. I straightened up from where I crouched. "I apologize for my ill manners, my lady."

"You left me with no word, Vlad. That was unkind of you."

My mind was working furiously. She had anticipated me, but for how long? Was she prepared for this encounter, or might she mistake my purpose or underestimate my determination? "I thought it best to absent myself as discretely as possible."

"Will you come inside? I know you need no invitation here, but I offer it anyway." She stepped out of the shadow and I saw her more clearly. Other than her costume, she was exactly the same as when I had last been in her presence.

I hesitated, fearing a trap. She must have sensed my ambivalence because she laughed. "Come, Vlad. How can you hope to destroy me if you cannot even enter my lair? I assure you there are no traps within, no thralls waiting to leap upon you with sharpened stakes or sever your head with tempered steel. Come, let us talk awhile."

"The time for talk is long past," I said firmly, but I moved forward, toward the door rather than to attack her. With that incredible grace of movement that she never reveals to her mortal companions, she was through the door and beyond my sight almost without having stirred a muscle.

Despite her promise, I entered warily. She seemed totally confident, although I suspect she would act similarly even in the face of inevitable defeat. I followed her to a large room whose appointments were sparse but rich in quality. She had already draped herself over a pile of velvet covered pillows, and when I entered she gestured toward a matching set opposite hers. Between the two stood a table carved from some rich, dark grained wood, and atop that stood a decanter and two thin stemmed goblets, as well as a chess set arrested in the midst of a game. Even from that distance I could tell the decanter contained fresh blood. Its essence tainted the air.

I knew then that my cause was lost. My best chance to defeat her would be to time the confrontation so that I was at the peak of my powers while she was at her weakest. This blood was less than an hour old, and she must already have drunk her fill. The source was obvious. She had sacrificed her thrall, the elderly woman. Which meant that she had anticipated me and was fully prepared.

"How long have you known that I was in Trieste?" I asked.

She laughed. "I knew before you arrived, although I was less certain that you would find me. I have followed your career ever since your return to Transylvania. You should not have assumed that I would not learn that your family castle had been restored by a long lost relative who then took up residence and draw the obvious conclusions. I have even amused myself by planting rumors of my presence at times so that you and your agents would have something to occupy your time.

I felt no emotion, neither anger nor despair, but I was puzzled. "Why then have you spared me so long if you have known from the first that I meant to destroy you?"

"Because it amused me to do so. I envy you in one way, Vlad. You are complete unto yourself, even more so than I. While still a thrall, you were able to act independently, and once you were completely turned, you distanced yourself from me almost from the start. I don't imagine that you have ever felt lonely, either in life or afterward."

"I feel no need to inflict myself upon others, if that's what you mean."

"That's not what I mean," she replied with some heat, then cooled immediately. "But perhaps I am describing shades of color to a blind man. Let us say, then, that it gave me some satisfaction to know that there was another in the world who knew my nature but who would not betray me to mortals, although he might kill me himself if it were within his power."

I saw no point in dissembling. "And I would still do so if I could, but you have won the game, my lady, and I am forfeit."

She was silent for a long moment and then, ever so slightly, she shook her head. "No, not yet. There is no sport in winning when your opponent is unaware of the rules. You will leave this house tonight just as you are now, untouched in mind or body. On the morrow, you will leave Trieste and you will not return for at least one year, is that understood?"

I hesitated. "I understand your terms but not your purpose."

"And perhaps you never shall. Leave it at this. I spare you this one time only. Henceforth we are acknowledged enemies, each committed to the destruction of our opponent. I find the world a more interesting place with you in it, but do not assume that I will be merciful a second time. When next we meet, one of us will cease to be and the game will be over."

It was only later that I began to understand. For all her bravado, Enheduanna remains an uncertain and lonely child, and even the existence of a deadly enemy who knew her true nature was better than to be completely unknown. I left the chateau a short time later, confused and dispirited, but in the days that followed, during a prolonged period of seclusion in Transylvania, I renewed my vow to destroy my dark mistress. For the world's sake, yes, but also for her own, because even though she does not realize it herself, she has become her own greatest victim, condemned to an eternity of loneliness and suffering.

Enheduanna's Journal

October 16

Still waiting. I ventured out of the hotel last evening and found prey at the waterfront, a ragged man whose mind was severely disordered. His blood was thin and sour but it restored me considerably. I threw his body into the sea. I am increasingly impatient and this eternal waiting wears on the others as well.

October 20

No word as yet. The days pass with dreadful slowness, the nights somewhat more pleasantly. I grow increasingly irritable and nervous due to the confinement and uncertainty. Two nights ago I fed again, although it was not necessary, a child I beguiled through his bedroom window. The body will not be found.

Last night was another matter entirely. I slipped out of our window and made my way to the waterfront with no real purpose except amusement. Although the thirst is never completely gone, it does not normally demand satisfaction until ten or more days have passed since a feeding, and I have abstained for a fortnight or longer with no ill effects. After that, my appearance begins to alter and my strength to fail. I was bored, however, and found myself actually missing Lucy Westenra's endless prattle. Although our kind quickly grows far beyond human, we cannot completely forsake our roots, and I sometimes miss the simple human things that are taken for granted by those around me.

There are a handful of taverns not far from the wharves, patronized for the most part by sailors, dock workers, prostitutes, and pickpockets. Their behavior is crude and unseemly but there is a bitter enthusiasm there that appeals to me. I haunted the fringes of the crowd, not joining in but not concealing myself either. My clothing was chosen carefully and with a few adjustments shifted from demure to suggestive, and it took little effort to blend in with the wastrels offering their bodies to whoever held sufficient coin. It was somewhat more difficult to avoid the attentions of the men, although those who persisted were generally dissuaded by a touch of the glamour at the appropriate moment.

In this fashion, I spent more than an hour, even allowed one fine fellow to obtain for me a pint of bitter, which is actually more tasteful than the tepid wines Jonathan favors. He planned no doubt a more intimate encounter, but he succumbed to the drink he had consumed so readily that it took no effort on my part to dissuade him. I left him slumped dreamily over our table and reluctantly decided to return to the Odessus.

A sound from the alley piqued my interest, or perhaps I was still bored, because I investigated what seemed to be the cry of a child. Instead I found a bearded sailor with an oversized wen on the side of his neck crouched over one of the tavern girls, whose clothing had been roughly torn from her body and who lay motionless now, bleeding profusely from the nose. It was in fact the smell of her blood which drew me closer, not any intention to rescue her from whatever fate the sailor intended.

"'Ere, wot's this? Want to join the party, is it then?" I had thought him local, but he was obviously an English sailor. He half rose, but I ignored him, my eyes drawn to the dark smear on the unconscious woman's cheek. The thirst was suddenly upon me and I knew I would not leave this scene until it had been slaked. "Leave us!" I hissed, and sought to touch the edges of his fear. He flinched, but only slightly, either insulated by the ale he'd consumed or simply by a nature so brutish that he was insensitive to my power.

"Nar, I think not." His voice was lower, and he was upright with a fluid grace that surprised me, stepping over the prostrate body and reaching toward my arm. If he was expecting me to retreat, I disappointed him, lunging forward instead. And then it was that the tension of this constant waiting upon Vlad's arrival surged up inside me like a palpable wave of fury and I seized his leading arm and snapped the bone like a twig.

He roared, more from surprise than pain I think, and caught hold of my shoulder with his uninjured arm. He might as well have hoped to control a waterspout. I slipped inside his grasp and struck him on the underside of the chin with all of my strength. There was a sharp crack as his head flew back, a broken jaw if not the neck itself, and he staggered, tripped over the legs of his still motionless victim, and fell silently to the ground. I was just turning toward the latter when I felt an impact that impelled me forward, half turned and saw that my antagonist had not been alone. My right arm had lost all sensation when his companion struck me with the cudgel that was now raised for a second blow, but the sensation came back within seconds and I ripped the weapon from his hands even as it descended.

I think my true face must have emerged at some point because when the moon suddenly emerged from behind its woolen curtain of cloud and bathed us briefly, he recoiled from me with an expression of stunned horror. That he had dared strike me was insupportable and I used his own cudgel to good effect, leaving him slumped and motionless with his brains spilling from his skull. Only then did some of the rage subside. My original adversary was alive, but his neck was broken and he would not survive long. I left both men where they lay. Their condition will no doubt be dismissed as the consequences of some drunken brawl.

I could have spared the woman since she had witnessed nothing which could compromise me. She was an unusually comely lass with fair skin and dark hair, but I knew I would be unable to rest until I had tasted her blood. It seemed a waste as, under other circumstances, I might have made provision for her to rise. Most of my get, even Vlad, remained biddable for some period following their transformation, and she might have provided some amusement during this endless waiting. Alas, quartered as we are in the hostelry, this course of action would be foolhardy at best, so I reluctantly stilled her life in such way that she could not rise, and then used the dead man's cudgel to belabor her face and throat with such savagery that no one will recognize the telltale marks of my presence. Let them think that one or both of the men beat her to death before their quarrel became equally deadly. It least it spared me the effort of disposing of the body.

Jack Seward's Journal

October 21

This enforced inactivity is gnawing at our nerves, and we have taken to avoiding each other's presence except for meals and for the twice daily hypnotic sessions. Mina provides no new information, and at times the trance fails utterly. Our nemesis seems still at sea, but surely he must come to shore within the next three days. There has been no report of foul weather, and the *Czarina* is by all reports a sound ship which should have made good time.

Mina seems more withdrawn than ever, has taken to napping

for much of the day as well as sleeping through the night. Van Helsing fears that she is gradually falling away from us and into the depths of the damned. I noticed as well that she is favoring one arm slightly today although there is no sign of a wound, and when I asked her about it, she responded in a most uncharacteristically curt fashion.

She more than any of us must be conscious of the passage of time, and its import for her if we do not confront the Count soon.

Jonathan Harker's Journal

October 22

Mina seems to grow ever more distant. She barely speaks even when we are alone. During the day, she sleeps so deeply that at times she does not respond even when I jostle her elbow and call to her. Her nights must be even worse, though I confess that my own condition once the darkness has fallen precludes any direct knowledge of her state. For the past several days, I have lost consciousness almost upon the moment that I lie down, and I sleep until dawn as though heavily drugged. I have spoken to Van Helsing and he assures me that there is nothing wrong, that sometimes the mind retreats from the insupportable into a private world of its own that allows no easy intrusion. He believes that I will sleep normally again once the Count has been dispatched. I pray that he is correct.

Only Arthur seems immune to the miasmic ennui that has settled over our party. He is up and about each day, sending communications hither and yon, seeking word of the phantom ship's whereabouts. Even Quincey's calm demeanor shows signs of tension. He prowls the corridors of the Odessus each night and naps fitfully during the day. When awake, he cleans the Winchesters he has procured for us with unnecessary diligence, even though we have not practiced with them for several days now due to the shortage of ammunition.

Jack Seward and Van Helsing huddle together and I confess to feeling some degree of annoyance at being excluded from their deliberations. We urgently need some ray of hope, some sign that the end of our travail approaches. If not, we may be defeated by our own weakness rather than the efforts of our adversary.

Telegraph from S. Mrozek to Lord Godalming, Hotel Odessus, Varna, dated October 23.

No sign of vessel here this date. Freighter arrived this morning reports no sighting en route.

Jack Seward's Journal

October 24

Arthur received a message today which indicates the *Czarina* may be off course. There was no positive identification so this might be a mistake. In either case, there is nothing further we can do until we know more, so our vigil continues.

October 25

Mina was noticeably less enlivened today than yesterday, so much so that I fear for her. Van Helsing clucked his tongue and enjoined the rest of us not to worry unduly, particularly in front of the dear lady, but I know him well enough now to recognize the depth of his own concern. We none of us discuss the disturbing reports Arthur has been receiving, but the continued uncertainty continues to erode our confidence.

Enheduanna's Journal

October 25

Van Helsing still insists upon our twice daily hypnotic sessions, even though I have provided no new information since before we arrived here in Varna. They have progressed from being amusing to boring to irritating, but I can find no good excuse for refusing to participate. If there is anything to be gleaned from my occasional moments of weak contact with Vlad, it is too subtle for me to recognize. I do know that Vlad fed two days past, but the thirst was subdued rather than allayed and it must have been that he slipped ashore briefly to sup at the throat of some draught horse or other such animal, or perhaps a sow. I think he would stoop even that low rather than unnecessarily harvest a living soul.

Frustrated, I tried last night to strengthen the bond between us. Rather than passively wait for his dozing mind to let slip some clue as to his whereabouts or intentions, I attempted to intrude myself more actively, concentrating on manipulating the fingers of one hand. Using what I thought a gentle, undetectable method, I closed out all that surrounded my physical body and willed my consciousness to cross over that link and enter the mind of my enemy.

He is either wilier than I thought, or I was clumsy. I felt his awareness of my presence and I attempted to withdraw, but before I could do so, Vlad sprang his trap. The way back became more tenuous, obscured by shadows that even my eyes could not penetrate. I grew disoriented and detached. Not only did I not know how to return to my body, neither did it seem particularly important that I do so. He had laid his plans well and I might have been fatally wounded had he not been betrayed by his own vanity. The flash of gleeful self satisfaction jarred me and stoked my anger. It was as if lightning poured from that inner sky, illuminating the landscape. I saw the road back to my own body and took it swiftly and triumphantly, leaving Vlad to thunder impotently in my wake.

Nevertheless, I was badly shaken by the encounter and when the sun dawned today, I found its touch distinctly uncomfortable. Much of my strength was squandered in that fruitless and unprecedented encounter. I will plead weakness and rest for most of this day and tonight I must feed.

Tomorrow, hopefully, we will see an end to things. Godalming insists that the vessel must arrive tomorrow no matter how poorly sailed.

Jack Seward's Journal

October 26

Still no sign. I am too overborne by depression to write more.

October 27

Even Arthur seems deflated by events. Has Dracula somehow anticipated us? If so, where is he now?

Enheduanna's Journal

October 27

Although my companions do not share their counsel with me, it is easy to extract what I wish to know from Jonathan in our bedroom each night. Under the compulsion of the glamour, he reveals all, including his dawning suspicion that Quincey's devotion to me is more than mere friendship. Fortunately our present living conditions make any kind of assignation difficult, so he has no cause to fear. Once Vlad has been disposed of, however, the situation will change.

Vlad has, I think now, outwitted us. There is no longer any doubt in my mind that he has somehow persuaded the ship's captain to avoid Varna in favor of some other port. We knew that he had caused a great number of letters to be dispatched before he departed England, and I suspect the gist of some of them was to arrange for alternative escape routes. I spent last evening studying maps of the area and paid the chambermaid to procure copies of the local train schedules. There are two probable and three unlikely choices. Time is of the essence, however, because yester evening I touched Vlad's mind briefly and the motion of the *Czarina* has changed.

I believe she is in port. But where?

October 28

Oh clever Vlad, though not clever enough, I hope. Godalming had a message today indicating that the *Czarina* has made port in Galatz. I thought that his most likely destination, and I am reasonably sure of his route from there forward. The news so discouraged these muddleheads that their rule against my participation in their deliberations was allowed to lapse. I laid out my speculations about Vlad's probable overland journey and almost slipped by advising them of the departure time for the train I knew we must take. Fortunately, I had made a point of my habit of memorizing shipping schedules back in Whitby, and when I made reference to this fact, Jonathan and Quincey both spoke up corroboratively and the minor crisis passed. Nevertheless, I must take up again the false diary of Mina Harker and add to it several entries which will support my version of events if the need arises.

October 29

The train is less swift than I might have wished. It stops at each hamlet through which we pass to take on and discharge passengers and freight, and occasionally livestock as well. The delays fuel my anger, which threatens to emerge despite my efforts to control it. The pointless hypnotic sessions with Van Helsing and the others are an added source of irritation and I am resolved to let them seem as ineffective as they really are unless and until they serve my purpose. Van Helsing will no doubt construe this as further sign of my decline and may be less forthcoming in my presence, but Jonathan will continue as my faithful if unwitting ear in their council.

Tonight I may learn the details of Vlad's plan. When I subverted Herr Leutner and bent him to play my part rather than Vlad's, he named to me certain of his associates who were also involved. One of these is Peter Skinsky, who was employed to secure passage for Vlad's boxes of earth originally, and who logically must be involved in the return of the one surviving. The train will not reach Galatz until the morrow, but I can fly tonight on swifter wings and question him without the restraining influence of my stalwart friends. In their absence, I believe I can be considerably more persuasive.

Later

It is as I had guessed, but it is always rewarding to have one's deductions confirmed. I reached Galatz just before midnight and employed a streetwalker to carry a message to Skinsky, requesting a meeting at a tavern nearby "to discuss matters pertaining to our mutual benefactor, who has recently returned to us". His path would necessarily force him to pass a small cemetery where I hoped to waylay him, but he made my task even easier by choosing to save time by crossing directly through it.

It was a simple matter to extract the information I required.

Vlad came ashore in Galatz, his box and person conveyed by an agent named Hildesheim who appears to have been ignorant of the true nature of his mission. Vlad arrived very weakened, according to Skinsky, and disappeared that first evening to feed, returning only slightly improved, but apparently satisfied that his ruse had succeeded. Skinsky then placed him in the charge of a company of gypsies and knew no further element of the plan. I satisfied myself that he was speaking the entire truth, at least insofar as he knew it, before feeding upon him and leaving him to be found in the morning. There are wild dogs in the area and I have no doubt they will be blamed.

October 30

I made certain suggestions to Godalming this morning which will expedite his search for information. I have also inscribed in the Mina diary the systematic method by which I plotted Vlad's most likely courses of action. Quincey escorted me to our lodgings here while the others pursued their various activities. He seemed ill at ease although the signs were subtle enough that the others do not seem to suspect anything unseemly. He is clearly infatuated with me, even without benefit of the glamour, and I remain sufficiently human to be flattered by his attentions and amused by his obvious discomfort about betraying the trust of his friend Jonathan.

My husband bores me, I confess, and it is possible that I have over applied the glamour to keep him asleep the last several nights. He was never a great wit or deeply perceptive, but of late he seems to have trouble concentrating on the task at hand. When this present situation has been resolved, I will have to consider other arrangements, perhaps a distressing accident. Quincey is a man of some means and is great in spirit, but an alliance with him presents problems as well. Ideally, Seward would be most advantageous as a husband, but I find him nearly as insufferable as that dotard Van Helsing.

Faced with the requirement to act rather than passively wait, Godalming regained some of his former fervor and rushed hither and yon for most of the morning, eventually hiring a steam launch with which some of our party will pursue Vlad up the Sereth while the rest travel cross country. I was not entirely happy with the details of this plan, but was unable to alter their resolve without acting out of character, and the glamour is unreliable when I attempt to cast it about more than one individual at a time.

In any case, I will be free of Jonathan for a while, as he has been chosen to accompany Godalming in the launch. Quincey and Seward will take to horse and follow the land route, with Van Helsing and I following as best we can in a carriage. It was suggested that we travel on horseback, but my aversion to the animals and my inexperience were well known. Truthfully I think Van Helsing was relieved by the knowledge that a carriage would be required.

I can no longer share consciousness even fleetingly with Vlad, and assume that the link has been broken in both directions. His blood was like fire in my veins, but even the fiercest flame eventually dies. Even now I regret somewhat the need to destroy him, for nowhere in the world is there another such whose power rivals my own, and never has been. But he has declared me enemy, and I see no chance of persuading him otherwise, and so it must be.

October 31

I dissuaded Van Helsing from indulging in another fruitless hypnotic session this morning as there seemed nothing to be gained. I have not told him that the link has failed, because this sham may yet prove a useful device to maneuver him for some purpose. I will not abandon it until I have to. We are at Veresti now and the carriage is hired for tomorrow. The prospect of continuing in his company alone is not a pleasant one, but at least the end is in sight.

Jonathan Harker's Journal

October 31

We leave momentarily on the next portion of the chase. I am loathe to leave Mina behind, but she is I suppose as safe in Van Helsing's charge as she could be anywhere. The change in her is barely visible to the others, but I can feel her growing more distant, more enwrapped in her own concerns, her temper more brittle and her concentration more diluted. We must destroy this monster and cleanse her soul and mind.

November 1

We are flying the Roumanian flag now. It smoothes our way when we encounter the occasional local official even though neither Arthur nor I speak more than a handful of words in the native jargon. We have not made as much progress as expected due to the unusually heavy traffic on the river and some problems with the launch's propeller, but the worst of that seems past us now.

I feel a great sense of anticipation. The end of our quest seems almost within our reach. But I confess to apprehension as well. Valiant as are my companions, are we sufficient to bring to an end such a great evil?

Jack Seward's Journal

November 2

We left at first light this morning. I regretted early on that I have not ridden much these past few years, as my muscles have begun to ache unbearably. Were we not on such an important mission, I would be having second thoughts just as it is barely begun. Quincey shows no such discomfort, however, and even though our horses appear to be evenly matched, he is often forced to slow down to my pace. I must accustom myself to this quickly as we do not have the luxury of time sufficient to cater to my lack of stamina.

The Notebooks of Abraham Van Helsing

November 2

Our second day on the road passed quickly. Mina has spent most of this day sleeping in order that she may drive at night. I was reluctant to accept this arrangement, for even if she were her normal true self, this would be an irksome task too coarse for such a fine, delicate woman. And she is not her true self. Her slumber is unnaturally deep and in fact during the afternoon when I stopped to prepare a brief meal, she did not respond to my call, and her flesh was unnaturally cool to the touch. I fear she falls ever deeper under the sway of this undead creature whom we seek.

When she did bestir herself later, I offered cold sandwiches and fruit, but she declined these as well and maintained her fast throughout the remainder of that day, insisting that she would eat after nightfall while driving in order to save time. She does appear somewhat enlivened now that the sun is in decline and her long sleep all day may have refreshed and restored her. At least for the moment.

I persuaded her to allow me to hypnotize her during a brief stop, although she was reluctant to invest the time required. This perhaps contributed to the unsatisfactory results, as she indicated that all she could see was darkness with no hint of the Count's present whereabouts or condition.

We were stopped twice today by petty local officials who inquired as to our business and destination. Fortunately, I speak the local tongue sufficiently well to answer their questions, and the delays were not greatly inconvenient.

Since our hours of consciousness overlap so little now, Mina and I have not exchanged many words during the last two days. I have spent much of the time in introspection and speculation, and as unwelcome as the prospect is, I must consider the possibility that we will fail and that Mina's descent into corruption will be beyond our power to impede. If such is the case, prompt and terrible actions will be required to save her soul from a living hell. Such a duty would be by right that of her husband, but I would spare Jonathan that if I might. He has loved her dearly and long and seems even more devoted to her than was Arthur to his Lucy. Nor is he a particularly strong man, though his heart is noble and his intentions pure.

I have decided therefore that should it prove necessary to free her by those terrible methods which we perforce applied to Miss Lucy, then it shall be by my hand that the deed will be done. Jonathan may ever after hate me for it, and that is a weight I will bear to my grave, but better that he place his animosity on the shoulders of an old man who will shortly be gone himself than live a life always feeling that his hands are stained with the blood of the one he loved best.

Enheduanna's Journal

November 3

At least I am spared Van Helsing's prattling for most of the day. He reluctantly accepted the wisdom of my plan to urge on the horses while he sleeps through the darkness, although we have had to purchase new animals since the first pair were unable to keep up the pace. We stopped briefly last night at a slovenly inn, long enough to bathe and take on the fresh team, then returned to the rough roads that thread their way through this turbulent countryside.

With luck we should reach the Borgo Pass tomorrow. It has been well over two centuries since I last viewed that place, and I return to it with mixed emotions. When I first encountered Vlad, back when he was still a mere human being, though even then of such physical and mental stature that he seemed like a breed apart, this was a wild and perilous landscape and it has changed little since.

Late this evening, I paused to let the horses recover their strength and then used the glamour to ensure that Van Helsing would not waken. This is a largely unsettled area, the soil too uneven and rocky to bear crops, but wherever there is a road, there are people to be found, and it was not an arduous task to locate a small homestead tucked behind a craggy hill. I killed a dog and frightened the penned livestock until the man of the house came out sleepily, cursing under his breath, his eyes lidded with sleep. When I approached him, he gaped disbelievingly, and said not a word before I was close enough to use the glamour and ensure his silence, and then I fed deeply and made certain that he would not rise before dropping his body into a well.

I tried once more to reach Vlad with my mind, but I am more convinced than ever that the bond has been sundered permanently. The end game is near now, the minor pieces cleared from the board, and the final move tantalizingly close.

November 4

We have reached the Borgo Pass, and it is exactly as I remembered it. Time runs differently in this part of the world, or perhaps it doesn't run, simply walks. None survive at this late date of those whose paths crossed mine during my last visit, but still I seemed to attract an inordinate number of unfriendly looks at the tavern where we stopped to eat, from those who shared the road with us or toiled beside it as we passed. This always has been an inward looking, inhospitable region, but the populace seems informed on some hidden level of my superior nature, and they hate and fear it even if they cannot name the cause of their dislike.

I was careless today as well. Van Helsing was driving when we reached the head of the pass, a heavily overgrown area where myriad roads converge and then separate, each disappearing quickly. There were no signs to indicate our path, but I knew the proper one and directed him to take it without hesitation. He is not quite as distracted as I had thought, however, and immediately asked me how I could be so certain when we lacked both map and signpost. I recovered quickly and assured him that Jonathan had described the route in great detail in his letters, and that I remembered quite distinctly which road led into the pass. Although he did not seem entirely satisfied with my explanation, he nevertheless did as I bade, and we were soon rushing forward as rapidly as the declining state of the roads allowed.

Later. Much later.

This evening's events have been sorely puzzling. Vlad's grasp seems to be weakening even without my assistance. For years he has kept his three wives locked within the walls of his castle, unless my spies have been fooled in some fashion. In his absence, that sluggard Josef has served as governor in his place, although he has never been near the equal of his master and may have let them slip between his fingers before this. In any case, he has failed in his duty because we have seen them this night.

Van Helsing feared that our horses had been driven too greatly and that they were in danger of perishing did we not rest them for a few hours. Although I was loathe to waste even a moment, it seemed likely that we could spare the time. So I consented to allow him to build us a small camp with a robust fire.

I sensed them before they made themselves known, the slight excitement of the nerves that we sometimes feel when we are in the presence of others of our kind. At first I thought that Vlad had somehow outwitted us all, that we were taken in ambush, and that I would have to fight him assisted only by the physically weakest of my small army. My face must have betrayed my alarm because Van Helsing tensed and asked what was troubling me.

"I thought I heard something," I temporized.

He was on his feet, searching the shadows with those dim but lively eyes of his and I was rising too when the first of them emerged, just her face visible in the mist. Although I knew all their names, I had no way of telling one from the other, but I guessed that this must be Hyrkana, the oldest of Vlad's wives, come to devil us. But just as I knew her true nature, so too did she recognize the power in me because she called me "sister" and invited me to slay Van Helsing and join them.

My companion misapprehended the situation even though he understood her speech and rushed to my defense, using fire and holy objects to ward them away from us. In his enthusiasm he caused me some minor distress as well, and my temper flared briefly, but I remained in control and allowed him to drive off the others. They slaughtered the horses and fed off them before departing and the smell of fresh blood on the night air was almost too much for me. I found my eyes drawn to Van Helsing's throat and if he had spoken but one ill timed word, I would have ended his life then and there.

He was shaken to the core of his soul, even though he had repelled them successfully, but he quickly regained his self control and sought to reassure me. Within that failing, dying body lies a strong will even now. I find myself regretting that I never met Van Helsing in the vigor of his youth. He must have been an interesting young man.

The Notebooks of Abraham Van Helsing

October 4

This night cannot pass too soon. In our preoccupation with destroying the master, we have been lax in considering his creatures, three of whom might well have destroyed us this past hour. They have left now but certainly will not have forgotten us. I must act tomorrow, alone, to end this peripheral threat.

Even more distressing was the effect of their presence upon Mina. Her eyes were illuminated by an unholy fire and her body seemed filled with an unnatural tension that she could barely suppress. Had these harpies continued their siege of our campsite, I fear the worst might have happened, that Mina might have succumbed to their seductions and left my side, or even have turned upon me, her protector. She sits across the fire from me now, inscribing something in one of the two diaries she maintains, the secret one which she has always concealed from the rest of us. Things might be better if I stole a look into it, because I believe that she records there her most hidden feelings, including those relating to her slow transformation. I dare not, however, because it would be too great a betrayal of the trust she has placed with me.

Jonathan Harker's Journal

October 4

There being no hope that we could repair the launch following our accident, Arthur and I have purchased horses at what would be an exorbitant price even for superior animals, but we have no choice. We have directions and a map of sorts, and sufficient provision for the next three days. The rest of our journey must be overland. If Mina's speculations were correct, we may already be too late. I can only pray that it is otherwise.

The Notebooks of Abraham Van Helsing

November 5

Mina did not waken when the sun rose this morning and I have not attempted to disturb her. Rather I have left her a note exhorting her to remain at our campsite, within the circle of wards which I have placed to protect her, and await my return. The horses are dead, and carrion eaters disposed of even their corpses during the darkness, but I feel almost a return of my youthful energy now that I can see our destination.

It is above and ahead of me now, a great, looming, but decaying castle perched upon what appears to be an impregnable cliff. The road is largely overgrown and is deeply rutted and eroded, but remains passable, at least for a man on foot. I suppose a horseman could also negotiate the surface, but I cannot imagine a carriage successfully progressing past the first small plateau where I have paused to rest and write this passage. It has taken half the morning to get this far, and I must hasten onward in order to complete all before the turn of the day.

Late Afternoon

It is done, and even though I know that I have set free the three souls imprisoned in the undead flesh I left behind me, it feels as though I have taken lives, and the images will haunt what remains of my nights on this earth. I can only hope in that greater life to come that the Lord will see fit to remove those memories from my mind and give me peace.

I reached the castle at noon, seeing naught along the way but a crazed gypsy woman who approached me angrily, calling me alternately master and other names so vile I will not repeat them here. She demanded that I return her daughter and harried me for some time before peering close into my face.

"You are not him," she said at last, with a look of such great defeat that I sought for words to comfort her, but they eluded me and she was gone so quickly it was as though she'd melted away.

Moments later I reached the castle, whose doors were barred. One window had been broken open by a limb fallen from a nearby tree and I managed to climb along the rough bark and slip through. It was dark and drear inside, but there was sufficient light for me to make my way about. Most of the rooms were empty, even of furniture, and by the time I had explored half the castle, I was beginning to despair again, fearing either that I would not find my quarry before nightfall, or that they had quitted the castle altogether and that I was on a pointless quest while Mina lay vulnerable behind me.

Then I found the first of them curled up in a crate in one of the small pantries, and after that the second in a closet, and the third in a box meant to hold wood beside one of the enormous fireplaces scattered throughout the castle. I did what had to be done then, and as the light began to fade once more, I climbed back out through the broken window and started back down.

They have all three gone to their final judgment. May they be judged only by their deeds before they were transformed.

Mina was just beginning to stir when I reached her side, and although I spoke not of what I had done while she slept, I think she must have sensed something of it because she looked at me sharply and then glanced back over her shoulder toward the castle, now invisible in the shadows, and her mouth twisted into a brief, bitter smile.

Jack Seward's Journal

November 5

It is too dark to travel these uncertain roads any further today, but we will be off at first light tomorrow. We have had good news and bad. The bad is that we have not arrived in time to intercept Dracula and those who bear him. The good is that we were sufficiently prompt to have caught sight of a band of half a dozen horsemen accompanying a rough wagon. It was almost at the limit of our vision, but if they camp as we do, we should catch them quite early tomorrow, and if not, if they travel even in this darkness, we may still overtake their slower advance before another night falls.

I am writing by the firelight but it has begun to rain lightly so I will stop for now. With God's help, tomorrow I shall detail the glorious end of our adventure.

Enheduanna's Journal

November 6

It is done, and I feel oddly empty rather than as triumphant as I expected. And it was a near thing.

Van Helsing and I waited most of the day in a small cave facing the main road. He urged me repeatedly to join him at the small fire he nursed at the front of the cave but I preferred the shadowy interior. As the hours passed, I confess I grew increasingly concerned. Vlad may have been shaken by events in England, but this would not prevent him from defending himself vigorously, particularly on his native ground. If my small army was to defeat him, they would need the sunlight on their side.

I was the first to espy the wagon, drawn by a pair of horses and accompanied by half a dozen of Vlad's gypsies. They were clearly aware of the pursuit because their progress was dangerously rapid on such an untrustworthy road. Moments later I saw two horsemen appear, whom I at first assumed were Quincey and Seward, although in fact those two arrived shortly thereafter. It was Jonathan and Godalming who closed with the gypsies first, although the others were not far behind.

Van Helsing tried to restrain me as I began to descend from our perch, but I would have none of it and shook off his grip without looking back. I wanted very much to be present at the end, to see the last light die out in those dark, perceptive eyes. But such was not to be.

The chase continued and the three distinct parties merged. I smelled blood in the air as I ran toward them, saw one of the gypsies fall, though he crawled away. Quincey faltered when he closed with another, but remained on his feet, joining Jonathan, who had leaped onto the wagon and forced the driver to halt his team. I was still high enough on the hillside to see something of what happened after that. Jonathan broke open the box and slashed wildly with a large blade, but he must have missed the heart because Quincey finally joined him, flourishing his Bowie knife, and it was only when his arm fell that the fatal blow was struck.

Even from a distance, I saw the change. One arm rose as if in protest, fell back weakly, and Vlad's head rose partly into view. The heavy shock of hair went first, crumbling to dust, then the body fell in upon itself, disintegrating into an unidentifiable mass within a few heartbeats. Vlad was gone, never to rise again, and even though he had been my enemy for even longer than he had been my ally, the world seems now a less interesting place for his passing.

By the time I reached them, the deed was done. The gypsies had already disappeared, no longer having any reason to be there. Jonathan crouched, staring into the depths of the box as though searching for something he could never find. Godalming also appeared to be suffering from mild shock, had walked off aimlessly, and Seward was in his wake, attempting to comfort him. I suspect that at long last the grief he must have felt over the loss of Lucy was pent up no longer. This senseless concern with the lives of others is a weakness which shall ever make them inferior to me; it is the lever by which I can move their entire world.

Quincey was standing alone and when I called his name, he turned partway toward me, then stumbled and fell to one knee. I saw the dark stain spreading along his side and knew from whence came the tantalizing smell of blood. I called his name and he opened his mouth as though to reply, then fell heavily to the ground, groaning softly. I came to him then and knelt beside him and the call of the blood was so powerful that I knew that I could not resist, although of all those who served me at present, Quincey was the one I most wished to spare.

A quick glance over my shoulder reassured me that Van Helsing was too far behind to interfere or even observe what I planned to do. Quincey was still conscious, still trying to speak.

"Hush now, Quincey," I whispered to him. "It will all be over soon. You have been my faithful servant and your loyalty shall not go unrewarded."

His eyes clouded with confusion and he relaxed slightly as I bent lower over him and then his life's blood was flowing inside me and it was as though hot wine flooded my veins. He was young and strong and his body was unspoiled by excess of drink or other vice. When I was certain that the wound was now mortal, I used a hairpin to prick my finger, then pressed it to his lips.

"Drink of me, fair Quincey. It is the most precious gift I have." His wits were thoroughly muddled by then and he knew me not, and I am uncertain whether or not he accepted enough of my blood to rise again. I was unable to do more because Van Helsing was hard on my heels at that point. I rose to my feet and anxiously called to him, imploring him to save dear Quincey, but of course he could not.

We buried him there in the shade of a copse of twisted trees. Someday I shall return to see if he walks the earth anew.

November 7

Our return trip will be at a much more leisurely pace. I had not given much thought to the future, but now that Vlad is no longer a factor, it is time to make fresh plans. It grows more difficult with each passing year to change identities, even with the glamour to help, so I must needs be more circumspect. It would not do to arrange my own "death" and then encounter an old friend in my new life. Even were I to relocate to the continent, I would not be entirely safe. The world has become a much smaller place these past few years.

I could remain as Mina Murray for some time to come, but that prospect appalls me. Jonathan clings too much, requires support at all times. I think his experiences have permanently drained away much of his youthful strength. He has also become more interested of late in our conjugal relations, and while the glamour allows me to escape these duties by imposing illusions of their consummation, its continued application will inevitably destroy his mind, just as it did that of Mrs. Westenra.

It would be far simpler if Jonathan were to meet with a fatal accident, and I have already promised myself Van Helsing's useless life. Godalming is deteriorating before our eyes, and I have seen the look on Seward's face and know that he believes Arthur's sanity has grown fragile. Once we are back in England, I shall endeavor to provide the impetus to force him over that brink. He will not end up in Seward's madhouse, but his family will almost certainly confine him to escape the shame. With Quincey dead, that leaves only Seward to be dealt with, and then Mina Murray can vanish from the canvas without hindrance.

Once this chapter of my existence has been brought to a close, I shall gather together all of the written materials chronicling these last few months and start a new hoard somewhere here in England similar to those I have concealed on the continent. As many as have been my days, each one remains precious to me, and I find already that parts of my life are beyond my recall, their memory pushed aside by fresh experience. Only by periodically re-reading the notes that I have made for myself am I able to maintain a sense of my own history.

Letter from Jack Seward to Jonathan and Mina Harker, dated December 2.

I regret the necessity to inform you that Arthur is no better. Indeed, he is much worse. At times he believes that everything we experienced was simply a fever dream. It is a comforting illusion, one which I often wish I could share. At other times, he recognizes

Lucy's absence and then recalls that awful scene in her tomb and cries aloud that he has murdered the woman he loves and should be taken in charge for his crime. That brave spirit whom we once knew has gone forever, I fear.

As I suspected, his family will not give him up to my care, although they have agreed that I may continue to visit him whenever I am able. They have altered a suite of rooms for his particular use, and able bodied and discrete servants have been employed to see to it that he does no harm to himself, nor disgrace to his name and title. It is an unsatisfactory solution, but I can offer none better.

I hope things have brightened in your lives at least. For myself, I sometimes think that it is only appropriate that I spend most of my waking hours in a madhouse, because the wider world beyond seems even more forbidding and illogical.

Letter from Sergei Yossarian to Dr. Jack Seward, dated December 2

In response to your latest query, I must inform you that Dr. Van Helsing has still not returned as of this date. If, as you indicated, he took passage November 2 on the *Danube Queen*, he must have changed his plans because I have interviewed the purser of that vessel who informs me that no such name is to be found on his list. Nor have we had any letter from him. His colleagues here have expressed some concern as the doctor is long past the days of youthful dalliances and has never before disappeared without advising us of the terms of his absence.

If you are able to ascertain any knowledge of his present whereabouts, I hope you will be kind enough to forward such intelligence to my attention.

Letter from Alfred Joyner to Leslie Small, dated December 5

Dear Leslie,

The most ghastly thing has happened to me, old chum. I told you in my last letter that my uncle recently purchased a block of derelict buildings near the waterfront, intending to tear them down and erect a new warehouse. I had not expected to be in any way intimately involved with this transaction, but he took exception to my eating his food and sleeping in his house without contributing anything to their upkeep, a stance I cannot in good conscience term completely unreasonable.

In any case, I found myself dragooned into helping with the preliminary inspection of the premises, which consisted mostly of accompanying an engineer through the noisome buildings while he made notations about the condition of the property and I kept my eyes open for anything that might be of value within the debris. It was boring rather than onerous, until we reached the third address.

The stench assaulted our senses the moment we stepped inside. The engineer, a pleasant bloke named Quidley, asserted that something must have crawled inside and died, "probably a stray dog". We began our survey despite the noxious atmosphere, but upon entering one partially enclosed cubicle, we disturbed a veritable cloud of flies. Quidley drew back but I confess to having felt a perverse desire to see the animal's corpse. Would that I had not, for it was the body of a man. The cold weather of late had preserved the body somewhat, and I saw at once that he was of advanced age. His throat was torn out and his eyes were empty sockets.

Quidley gathered himself enough to enter when I described what lay before me. "Probably some derelict came in to get warm, died in his sleep. Rats have been at the body."

I thought and still think otherwise. The clothing was of too fine a cut and too good a state of repair for the man to have been penniless. It occurred to me to search the body for any papers which might have proved his identity, but he had none. The only clue to be found was a pocket watch inscribed with the initials "AVH", which lay beneath the body. We reported the matter to the police, but they evinced no great interest, and seemed to share Quidley's explanation of the man's origin, and demise.

From the London Times, December 14, 1875
Tragedy at Sea

After neighbors of Mr. and Mrs. Jonathan Harker of Bartleby Road reported their unannounced extended absence, Constables William Hartwell and Thomas Canterbury pursued inquiries as to the possible whereabouts of the absent couple. It was determined that they had set out in a small hired boat on the morning of December 9 and had not returned. Mr. Albert Yardley, operator of Yardley's Wharf, reported the missing boat but no action was taken in the matter. On the afternoon of December 11, the vessel was found capsized by Jacob Whitsonby, a local fisherman, and towed to shore. As of this date, neither body has been found but the worst is feared. Friends of the deceased indicated that there were no surviving children.

Note from Edward Palmer to James Chatsworth, dated March 25, 1920.

I have made some small effort to verify several of the minor details of this account on my own. The final document contradicts the postscript in Stoker's manuscript which suggests that the Harkers were still alive in 1882 and had a son, but there is no evidence to support this in the materials I have gathered, and it is quite possibly an afterthought invented to give the novel a happier ending. It may even have been added at an editor's insistence. I did find the original news story about the presumed accidental drowning of Jonathan and Mina Harker, which did in fact take place as the newspaper article indicates. Jonathan's body was washed ashore a few days later but Mina's was presumed taken by the sea.

I am off to Scotland on business which will consume at least a fortnight or two, but I don't imagine that you will have much to tell me before then anyway. If anything of interest turns up which you feel merits my immediate attention, you can reach me through my office in Aberdeen. I will write when I have a certain date for my return, and perhaps we can meet at my club for dinner. Please express my good wishes to Margaret and the children.

Letter from James Chatsworth to Edward Palmer, dated May 25, 1920.

I am sorry to hear that things are going so badly there as the children keep asking when Uncle Ted is coming to visit again, and even Margaret has confessed that she would not take it amiss if you should call upon us. The mystery which you presented me is, as I mentioned in my last letter, an intriguing one, and rather than force you to wait any longer, I shall summarize the results of my investigation here. The full documentation and more detail await your return.

There are, of course, two parts to the puzzle, one here and one abroad. The documents provide a wealth of small detail which we have been able to verify, although the sum of these is not conclusive. You already know of the death of Jonathan and Mina Harker, who died childless and with no living relatives except for her parents, the Murrays, who attended the memorial service but whose further movements are obscure. The Westenra family did in fact reside in Whitby and is now extinct, mother and daughter dying within days of each other, the former of a brain fever, the latter presumably from grief and a delicate constitution.

Arthur Holmwood succeeded his father but died while still young and without issue, never married in fact. There is no record of his engagement to Lucy Westenra, no evidence that they had even met as a matter of fact, but he was of unsound mind for many years, lived in seclusion, and the family has carefully shielded his reputation from the outside world. I was unable to find any record of Quincey Morris, and the manuscripts provide too few clues to trace his supposed history in America.

Doctor Abraham Van Helsing was a physician of note, specializing in disorders of the blood. He made frequent trips to England, although there is no record specifically proving that he was here during the time in question. Van Helsing disappeared while traveling abroad but the details have been lost. A fire at Scotland Yard destroyed the records which might have referred to the discovery of a body in an abandoned warehouse, and there are no newspaper accounts reporting such an incident. Van Helsing was quite frail in his declining years and had occasional periods of absent mindedness. There was indeed a Doctor John Seward who administered a home for the insane. The building still stands, but is no longer used for that purpose. A fire in 1906 destroyed all of the facility's existing records, so I have been unable to verify the existence of a patient named Renfield. Seward himself also disappeared mysteriously.

Carfax Abbey was torn down around the turn of the century and has been replaced by a row of shops. As yet I have been unable to determine who might have handled the rental of the property, so the question of whether or not it was rented by Count Dracula – who is also real by the way – remains open. The accounts of the "bloofer" lady are authentic, but the party responsible was later identified as one Mary Canton, a madwoman, who was apprehended stealing an infant from a tram.

A few other facts have also been confirmed, but I should caution you at this point. Everything which we have verified as true was part of the public record at the time. Stoker, or the presumed unknown original author or compiler of the manuscript, could have ascertained all of this from the newspapers augmented by a few discrete inquiries. I should mention as well that we have found nothing to corroborate that any of the parties involved knew one another, not even Van Helsing and Seward, who practiced in different specialties. The firm which employed Harker no longer exists, so we cannot fix on any connection between them and the Count.

Now as to Dracula himself. As you might expect, it has proven to be much more difficult to gather evidence of his activities. He was certainly alive as late as 1870, although by then he must have been quite elderly. The castle still stands, although it has been vacant now for nearly half a century. The local people shun the place, which has largely fallen into ruin, but it is a remote, backward region where superstition still reigns over reason.

My agent there, Bracken, was told that the Count "went away" more than a generation ago, which presumably means that he died, and that the servants kept the place up for only a few months before they dispersed. Bracken rented a horse and visited the ruins, which he described as being situated in unfriendly terrain, but although he reached the outer wall, he was prevented from investigating the interior by the presence of a goodly number of wolves, which still frequent that part of Europe. By his account, they literally pursued him until he was beyond the Borgo Pass and he was unwilling to make any further attempt to visit the site.

A search of the surviving local records was equally unsatisfactory. There was no reference to the castle's tenant whatsoever and only passing allusions to its existence. The family line is not officially extinct, but only because of laxness in the government's accounting. Bracken made one further discovery, which I shall describe momentarily. First I wish to summarize.

There is nothing in the remarks above that disproves the narrative we are investigating. This is of considerably less significance when we realize that nothing proves it either. The author, Stoker or someone else, may simply have done a remarkably good job of matching his imagination to existing facts. Since all of the principle parties died or disappeared shortly after the events in the story, it would have proven very difficult to ascertain the truth even in 1897, when *Dracula* was apparently written. It is even more so today. If I were planning a similar project, I would have proceeded precisely in that manner, drawing my characters from the recently deceased or missing, particularly from those whose deaths were unusual or mysterious.

That said, Bracken's last discovery is a perplexing one, and it came more by chance than through his industry. He was checking on one last rumor of surviving records in Tibiu where he was set upon the trail of an elderly woman supposed to have been a servant in Dracula's castle. The lead was so promising that he delayed his departure, but he was disappointed when Frau Braulich proved to be of unsound mind. Having proceeded so far, he was loathe to leave empty handed, so he engaged her in conversation and was further disappointed when she indicated that she had not in fact ever been to the castle.

But she knew of it, and insisted that her cousin Josef had lived there all his life. Whether or not this could be the same Josef to whom Dracula referred is an open question, of course, but she also mentioned that her cousin had "died in his master's place". Bracken reported all this, and I initially dismissed it, but you've thoroughly provoked my curiosity so I exerted myself for one final effort. I made inquiries with the shipping line which operated the *Czarina Catherine*, which was lost off the coast of Denmark in December of 1875. The captain had long since died and they were unable to put me in contact with any surviving crew members, but the elderly clerk who answered my letter had worked on the docks in Galatz as a boy and he remembered the ship and its last successful voyage.

He also remembered its only passenger, a tall, dark man with burning eyes who seemed to the young boy almost larger than life. The occasion was particularly memorable because the man was met by a slightly more subdued version of himself, a man so similar in appearance that my informer believes they may have been brothers.

If this was in fact Count Dracula arriving back on the continent, then his "brother" may well have been Josef, the servant, come to meet his master.

The reason all of this stuck so firmly in the man's mind is that the new arrival promptly insisted upon chartering a smaller vessel to carry him to an undisclosed location while the other man took custody of the luggage from the ship, which consisted of a single large, oblong box, and removed it from the dock in a wagon driven and accompanied by a party of rough looking gypsies. That is all the man remembers but, if we assume the rest of the story is indeed a true one, this leads to an interesting possibility.

If Dracula knew, however indistinctly, the plans of his opponents, might he not have employed a ruse? And if it was Josef, his look alike, whom the others pursued by land and eventually killed, then is Dracula himself still alive? And if he is alive, then is he still out there somewhere, planning yet another assault against his one time love and long time enemy? Or has that final battle already ended?

And is that not an even greater mystery than the one we started with?

The End?

Find out more in *Dark Muse*.

www.ingramcontent.com/pod-product-compliance
Lightning Source LLC
Chambersburg PA
CBHW072236170626
46813CB00003B/1258